GREY MATTER

C.S. MCMILLIAN

This book is a work of fiction. Names, characters, businesses, organizations, places, events, and incidents either are the product of the author's imagination or are used fictitiously. Any resemblance to actual persons, living or dead, events, or locales is entirely coincidental.

ISBN-13: 978-0-9912989-3-8
ISBN-10: 0-9912989-3-4

First Edition

Cover art by Angela McMillian

Edited by Charles Gulotta

For Kari

Chapter 1

It had been a busy summer. The heat index hovered around one hundred most of the three months, leaving the citizens of Dallas in a frenzied state of violence. Mr. Hornby, sprawled on the metal table in front of me, was the first specimen added to the fall collection of aching souls to be released. I wrangled him in the parking lot as he planned his next *infant snatching* from yet another new mother exiting Mercy General Hospital.

I sat a few feet away, watching, waiting for my turn with him. His snoring only provoked my vexation as I imagined him salivating, preparing to destroy a newly formed family. I had to distract my thoughts or I would end this prematurely, failing to give him the proper send off before the release. I shuffled my thoughts to my surroundings, beyond the dirty soul in front of me.

My dad's former workspace had been turned into my own private lab where I did battle with the Gamemakers. It really was poetic when I thought about our similar foes. He most likely battled them in this same office, alone, on a constant basis. They snared his mind with pernicious voices. In the end, cancer took him — one of the many tools to finish the job when the Gamemakers are done playing. But his payback was warning me about them in a letter. Dad, I see them: the blurs and glitches, attempting to throw me off track. Don't worry, I have learned the truth. I hoped he could hear me, and was rooting for me.

It was time.

"Good evening," I said, watching him writhe, attempting to loosen the thick leather restraints around his ankles and wrists. "I suppose you're wondering what the hell you're doing here. 'I don't belong here' is probably what's going through your mind. I can assure you, Mr. Hornby, this is exactly where you belong. If I were to allow you to continue, overpopulation of your kind would ensue." He wasn't listening to me. His dark empty eyes were too busy searching for a solution to his predicament.

I shed my navy overalls, revealing my uniform. His bewildered expression quickly changed to intrigue when he turned his attention back my way.

"Ironic isn't it, my uniform? The process has to be official."

His heart rate — displayed on the portable monitor above his head — increased as I prepped the solution and withdrew it into a syringe. Thrashing his head back and forth, he attempted to expel the bandage that was shoved into his mouth. I stared down at him. My expression was that of pity and disgust as I patiently waited for him to finish his tantrum.

The clumsy fool dropped his last victim, injuring the child in his apartment. That's when we were called. A faulty product isn't good for business. More often than not, these scum aren't clever — on purpose I suspect. The Gamemakers inevitably want them caught, to reveal their willingness to inflict terror in the hearts of the innocent, and ultimately bring another player like me into the arena. A game is not fun with only one participant.

"If you're quite done, I would like to complete your release," I said. The anger in his eyes revealed to me that he wasn't ready to accept his fate. He had been wronged somehow, or his parents were to blame. None of his choices were his fault. I've seen it before, a longing pity for oneself in that last moment of vulnerability. "Your restricting suit will soon be shed, and then the discomfort will cease."

I know they're watching, as they do with every release, itching to breed another one onto the vast playing field. When I first began this venture, I had been desperately searching for the presence of the soul, hoping to catch a glimpse of the elusive entity. I wanted to know if what I saw surrounding my dead sister's body that day in the above-ground pool was actually her soul. Since then, I have come to terms with my infatuation; I know that the human soul exists, having caught glimpses of it many times. Now, my mission is much simpler. The battlefield is infinitely huge, the enemies are as many as they desire. I play by trumping the players that they strategically place here to cause mayhem. Of course, they play dirty — at least they think they do — by tossing out seemingly false visions, attempting to distract me. But I know the truth, that the visions are real. It is the reluctance of society to accept these as true that has bound our minds to accept nothing but what we think we know.

The solution traveled along the IV line and into Mr. Hornby's left arm. Moments later the heart monitor's alarm sounded. His struggling ceased, and a calming sigh moved slowly across his face. A brief temperature change in the room without a dark blur brought a smile to my face. They were up to their tricks again, tossing the senses in a hat and pulling out one at random for me to observe.

Though the manner in which they allow the observation is sporadic at best — many times nothing is seen or sensed at all — I stay vigilant, always ready for a new twist in the battle. I have my cameras strategically placed around the room, and I have my journal for notes and reminders. I don't feel the distractions are meant for harm, but rather a smoke screen — an attempt to use my own mind against me.

• • •

I hadn't worked up the nerve, before now, to visit my mother's gravesite. Her passing last year nearly ended me, but I have come to accept her death, along with the passing of my entire family. My dad, sister, and mother's headstones sit uniformly in front of me, displaying the dates of each of their deaths.

I recently purchased the last plot in the line next to my mom. I have the headstone waiting, etched with my name. Like everything in this life, it was only a matter of time. The date of my death would be carved into the stone below my name. I'm not quite ready to cross over. In fact, I'm just getting started in my new, much clearer direction. I feel sure there are others like me out there, but I have yet to find them. If I were the only one, this world would surely be overrun. They wouldn't allow that to happen; they need conflict for the game to continue.

In my hands were three flowers I had picked up at a local florist. The lady who sold them to me hesitated before retrieving them from the back, warning me of their meaning. This was the first time I had ever been questioned before purchasing my mom's favorite flower. Intrigued, I listened to her explanation.

"Begonias mean caution or beware," she said, and then asked to whom I was planning on giving them. When I told her they were for my dead mom, dad, and sister, she flinched, revealing false sentiments stifled behind heavy eyes. She shifted her gaze to the floor and abruptly turned around, fetching the three flowers without further words.

I wanted to laugh, but I held it in, if only to save the

woman from permanent damage to her manageable beliefs. I don't know why people react like their own life has been suddenly shattered by the news of my family's death, as if they feel my sorrow. If they only knew their own story, most would remain inside their personal pits of despair, never to reach out and offer empathy, never grasping the real truth.

I didn't know if my mom knew the meaning of the flower, or if she even cared. But knowing my dad's fight with the voices, the flowers may have been his idea — another subtle warning to accompany his letter.

My initial intention for this visit was to make it a yearly tradition until my time was up. It would help me remember — not that it was easy to forget being surrounded by filth on the streets — why my path was so important, how easily the decent are shadowed by the nonstop chattering teeth of the evil. The blanketing cloud of turmoil and despair is heavy and not easily removed once the corners have been stretched.

After I placed each begonia next to the headstones, I sat in the soft grass and faced my family. I didn't have much to say. I knew this was only the resting place of their once living organic suit. If I were to speak, it would be for my own soul to hear. I had many questions about the next step: why, where, and most importantly, what are the rules? I didn't think that was too much to ask for. Some say this is a test, others say this is a process like a step in making bread. The vagueness only proves their depth of cluelessness. When they find their purpose, they will not offer further explanations.

While leaning back, lost in thought and staring up at a cluster of thick clouds, I heard a woman's soft crying from behind me. I shifted my head around and saw a lone woman kneeling against a tall headstone three rows back. She was wearing an aged black dress, including gloves and a veil, as if she had just stepped out of a portal from the 1800s. Most of the time I keep to myself, and normally I wouldn't interrupt a grieving stranger, but something about this woman was nudging me closer.

I walked silently to the row where she was kneeling, trying to avoid the dry fallen leaves. She hadn't noticed me yet, or if she had, she was ignoring me. I wasn't sure what I was going to say once I approached her, and hoped she would be the first to initiate conversation. I was only five headstones away when I noticed her crying had stopped. A sudden gust of wind ruffled the leaves around my feet and she lifted her head and looked over at me, her dark veil shielding her facial features. I stopped and stood in place, unsure how to proceed. She slowly got to her feet, her tattered black dress resting atop the dead leaves and grass.

"Ma'am," I said softly. Realizing the word exited hoarsely, I cleared my throat and said, "Ma'am, I don't mean to intrude on your privacy —" Before I could finish my sentence, she turned around and took off running in the opposite direction. "Ma'am," I said again, reaching out my arm and briskly walking toward her. "I didn't mean to —" When I reached the headstone where she was kneeling, I stopped and read the writing on the stone: *Peter Headlong 1945-2003*. Bewildered, I looked back up for the woman in black, but she had disappeared. I glanced around the empty graveyard, beyond a gathering of thin pines, but saw nothing. She was gone.

It took a few moments for the information to process. Peter Headlong was the owner of Peter's Grocery, where my dad was manager for most of his career. Now that the old grocery store building was abandoned, it was the location of my lab. Peter and my dad were best friends growing up. His wife had died long before him, according to the headstone next to his own. So who was the mysterious woman in black? I wasn't sure, but I had a good suspicion that the Gamemakers had something to do with it. Entire human forms? These were bold new tactics, enhancing the stakes.

Chapter 2

"Medic 15, I need you to respond to the corner of Burndale Avenue and Park Street. Stand by for more information," the female dispatcher said over the radio in the rig.

"Medic 15 copies dispatch, place us en route," I said, and then attached the mic back onto the metal clip. I flipped on the lights and siren.

"What the hell is this, respond and stand by for more information?" Clyde said from the passenger seat. "Damn dispatchers think we're at their beck and call! Do this, do that, I'd like to go down there and shove this radio —"

"Medic 15," dispatch interrupted. "You're responding to a hot air balloon accident. The latest information from police is that the balloon has come in contact with power lines and is possibly on fire. There are two souls on board... Medic 15, stand by, we're getting more information."

The MDT or, mobile data terminal, beeped, displaying the information from dispatch in orange digital letters on the screen in front of Clyde. We were approaching the intersection of the incident. I peered up into the sky through the windshield — clear, blue, and cloudless.

"Finally some excitement," Clyde said. "Son of a bitch! A hot air balloon on fire, now we're getting somewhere. I'm sure as hell glad it's not another damn gomer tote." A gomer tote was what Clyde preferred to call a nursing home patron. I despised NH calls just as much as the next paramedic, but I didn't share his malice toward the elderly. It isn't their fault they're stuck in a suffering pit of jabbering dementia run by a malfunctioning human waste disposal system. Our prisons as we age learn and improve on new ways to make us suffer.

"Medic 15, police on scene confirmed that flames *are* visible," dispatch said.

"Burn baby burn!" Clyde said, repeatedly punching the roof of the rig.

"Medic 15 copies dispatch, we're approaching Park street," I said, and placed the mic back down. "Clyde, you really are an idiot."

"Come the hell on Tryke, you have to admit, this is pretty cool, man."

"Innocent people burning alive in mid-air? That's cool to you?"

"Whatever, Saint Tryke," Clyde said, sneering.

I was far from a Saint, but I certainly didn't enjoy the suffering of others. Well, not all others. Sure I had my flaws, but I like to think of them as beneficial to my specimens. They have their weapons, and I have mine.

As we turned onto Park Street, it was obvious that the balloon had taken this route — vehicles were pulled over and lined along the curb. Rows of onlookers peered into the sky as if an alien craft were slowly penetrating earth's atmosphere. About a half-mile ahead of us, and twenty feet in the air, was the yellow and red balloon with its now smoldering basket and its passengers wedged between two power lines. The onlookers were definitely getting a free show.

"Whoa, man... this is some serious shit. The power lines are arcing now, look!" Clyde said.

"Yeah," I said calmly. I had a feeling that the outcome wasn't going to be a pleasant one. An innocent person was going to suffer needlessly by having their flesh burned while fighting to stay alive.

We pulled the rig behind the Engine Co. and parked. A small group of firemen were huddled in front of the truck — gear in hand — watching the spectacle helplessly. From the basket of the balloon a female's screeching voice was desperately yelling for help. Under her, a safe distance, were two fire Captains in white helmets failing in their attempts to keep her calm.

"Grab the monitor and bag," I told Clyde. He frowned and marched around the rig to retrieve the gear.

"Hey, Trey," I said to one of the firemen. Trey and I became friendly acquaintances after making many calls together. He knew his stuff as a medic and I could always trust his examination of a patient if they arrived on scene before us.

"Hey, Tryke," he said, shaking my hand. "This is some crazy stuff, huh?"

"Yeah, it is. So what's the plan?"

"According to my captain, the city is in the process of shutting down power to the area. We have two victims, male and a female in the basket. We're not sure about the male's status, he hasn't moved. And the female is too frantic to give us any information, as you can hear for yourself."

"At least it's not on fire anymore," I said.

"Yeah, but for how long? If the city doesn't hurry up, we're going to witness a public burning," Trey said.

He was right; this could turn nasty, and quick. The basket was already frayed and partially charred. I pondered, as I looked up, how the two of them had managed to stay inside. If the basket weren't so tangled and intertwined in the power lines, I would recommend they jump.

Suddenly, a booming sound rocked the air from nearby. We all hunched over, cowering instinctively. It sounded like a transformer had exploded. I turned and looked in the direction of the boom and saw smoke rising fast. From behind me, the female in the basket let out a screeching yell. I turned back around just in time to see the power lines arcing, letting out a brilliant flash, reigniting the basket.

The woman had an anxious look on her face. She was deciding her fate: stay and burn alive, or leap through the flame-engulfed hole in the basket and take her chances with the twisting arcing lines of certain death. The odds were definitely not in her favor. She had few seconds to decide — the flames were licking up the side of the basket where she was hovering.

The two captains below latched their arms together and made a makeshift-landing pad. They began yelling, emboldening her to slip through the burning hole toward them. It was a valiant effort on their part.

"Come on lady, jump," I whispered, "you don't have a choice."

For the first time this shift Clyde was quiet. His face was stuck in a perpetual state of awe. I had a horrible feeling that he wanted to see this go badly. He was what I deemed a tourist medic, wanting to witness any bit of mayhem available, leaning toward the suffering of the victim, innocent or not. His type in this field isn't rare. In fact, I've found that it's quite common. He's just more vocal than most.

The frantic woman's hair caught fire, making the decision for her. She let go of the sides of the basket and slid through the burning hole, toward the tangled arcing lines. For a brief moment I thought she was going to clear the lines, but she instinctively reached out her hand and grasped one for stability. I grimaced, waiting to hear the crackling of flesh, but it never came. After a moment of stunned silence from the crowd, I realized what had happened.

The city had cut off the power just in time.

She plummeted into the makeshift-landing pad that the two captains had formed, nearly knocking them to the ground. They quickly moved her — arms slung over their shoulders — from under the flame-engulfed balloon that had begun raining burning debris.

"The power's out! Put the deck-gun on that balloon!" the captain yelled, dragging the female toward us. The fireman perched on top of the engine, eagerly awaiting his turn to play, directed the powerful stream of water out from the deck-gun toward the basket, quickly smothering the flames. They moved a ladder truck under the now smoldering basket and retrieved the male.

Clyde and I immediately began work on the female. She had second-degree burns on her right hand and legs, and some first degree on her neck. I glanced over at the male as they brought him down the ladder. He didn't appear to be breathing. If he is dead, I thought to myself, it's probably a good thing, considering the extent of charred flesh I could see.

"Damn lady, you're a lucky son of a bitch," Clyde said, while bandaging her hand. "Luckier than the bastard that was with you."

"Really, Clyde?" I said. "Ma'am, ignore him. He has his own issues at the moment."

Lucky for him she was still in shock and didn't acknowledge that he had said anything. I still didn't know the relationship the woman had with the male. For all we knew, it could have been her husband or son.

I reluctantly left Clyde to finish with the female while I made my way over to the male that Mark and another fireman had sprawled on the ground. With the heart monitor in my left hand and the airway bag in the other, I halted in place and turned back around when I saw Mark's grim expression from beside the male patient. As I suspected, the man was beyond saving. It was a horrible thought to be burned alive. Most die from smoke inhalation before the burning of the nerves — that's what I've heard anyhow — but it still leaves one cringing in wonder.

• • •

When we arrived at Mercy General's burn unit, the female in the back finally talked. She explained how she was on her third hot air balloon lesson and that the male was her instructor. Of course, Clyde had to chime in.

"That crispy critter was your instructor? I'd get my money back if I were you," Clyde told her before we entered through the double doors of the unit.

Meet Clyde Parker: crude, angry, and mildly insane. A paramedic who has been on the job less than a year. He hates mostly everyone and curses more than a sailor with Tourettes. He's younger than me by a year, which makes him twenty-five. He's also completely bald, which may be part of the reason he's mad most of the time. I only say this because he's mentioned it during cursing tirades when he has had to remove his hat on a call.

He wears a permanent frown and is insistent that we keep the radio blaring heavy metal. I don't mind most of the time because it drowns out his rants. He regularly pisses me off, but I mostly laugh at his disdain towards others and life. I have my own morbid view of the world and could hardly criticize his.

Clyde is my temporary partner on medic 15, while Dave is off gallivanting on a beach somewhere on his second honeymoon. Dave married my girlfriend Lesley's friend, Angie. He told me that one of his main reasons for marrying her was that she got along with his daughter. I couldn't argue with him when he decided to get married not long after his last divorce, because he seems genuinely happy, much happier than I ever saw him with his ex. That wasn't saying much considering anyone, or even an inanimate object, was a step up from his previous demon-cheating wife. I've always considered Dave resilient when it came to women. He has this conviction that he is going to find his destined mate at all costs. But I wasn't so sure he wasn't just out looking for reasons to sulk, searching for a woman to inflict pain so he could invoke his right to self-pity.

I do feel bad for him though on occasion when I see him having to share his child with his ex. It's hard to imagine having to endure constant contact with the woman who broke my heart until our daughter was old enough to be on her own. I have never understood how Dave missed what I saw the first time I met his ex-wife, Claire. I wanted to warn him back then, but who was I to interfere? At the time I was single, and my involvement with women didn't go further than an encounter in the bedroom. Even now, I am in a constant struggle to understand Lesley, my first romantic relationship.

My life has definitely changed since my involvement with Lesley began. But I can't complain, because I enjoy the companionship. Our views of the world are similar, but not so similar that we don't challenge one another.

Lesley was accepted to medical school and started this fall term. Ecstatic would have been putting it mildly when she got into UT Austin; the fact that her dad was an alumnus just added to the excitement. And of course being somewhat close to yours truly was a plus. The three-hour drive for her to Dallas was a perfect distance. It allowed me time alone, and most importantly, she couldn't sneak up and surprise me during one of my releases.

Her chosen path of study was pathology — the darker side of the specialty, *forensic* pathology — focusing on causes of death. Her ultimate goal is to become a Medical Examiner here in Dallas. I suppose our interests are not too far off from one another, though mine are a bit more twisted. She searches for causes of death and I rid the world of diseased souls. Okay, maybe it's a bit of a stretch, but we all play our parts in this world and we're all interconnected in some way.

She has already become overwhelmed with the schoolwork; I hear about it daily. I try to be the good boyfriend and listen. Thankfully I'm good at being quiet. Besides, I don't think she wants my input. She seems perfectly content to rant to a quiet face, or into a cell phone. I've been more than happy to oblige because it keeps me from screwing things up with my clumsy words.

Over the years, I've made a point of avoiding relationships of any form, especially the romantic kind. Lesley managed to infiltrate my curious side with her witty, dark comments and her natural beauty. I seem to be handling things okay. So far so good, I guess. She was more worried about the long distance relationship than I was. I do find myself missing her, but my side venture has definitely kept me busy between our visits. Anyhow, she didn't have to worry about me and another woman. I wasn't much for browsing, which can lead to stressful situations. I was already on shaky ground with how far Lesley and I have gone in the relationship realm. No sense looking for trouble.

Chapter 3

I moved out of my one-bedroom apartment and into my mom's house. After her death, Lesley and I cleaned and organized for weeks. We had two garage sales, and I even found some stocks and bonds that my dad had stashed away in an account. It wasn't a fortune, but I paid the mortgage off and have since made some additions to the house.

I turned my dad's old makeshift library into a real one, almost suitable for a Victorian mansion. Okay, to be fair, not that extravagant, but a curved stacked bookshelf with a sliding ladder and a fireplace was close enough for me. One-half of the shelves held all of his books, the other my own. But the best part of the room was what you couldn't see. It is the addition I am most proud of, one that sprang from a boyhood dream of mine. I have often thought about, as I'm sure a lot of young boys do, how cool it would be to have a secret passageway that only you knew about — a hideout of all hideouts, a hidden room. And no, it's not for what you might think I would use it for. Peter's abandoned grocery store is still the location of my lab. I had to keep my battle with the Gamemakers separate from my home life; it is critical to my survival.

On one of the bookshelves sat a framed picture of my family at the lake from when my sister was still alive; it's my favorite memory of us all together. The frame, when twisted the correct direction, released a switch that turned the entire bookshelf into a huge door leading to the hidden room. The small but comfy space had a desk and a few flatscreen TVs mounted on the wall with a direct video feed to my lab — an added security measure to my increasingly dangerous lifestyle. The small room was where I did my thinking and planning. It also housed my important documents, including my dad's journal, which sat on the desk beside my own two.

At the beginning of summer, I started a new journal. The pages filled quickly and were now practically bulging, probably due to the heat wave over the summer, if one could actually tell the difference down here in Texas — it was either hot or hot as hell.

Thankfully it was now fall, by far my favorite time of the year, not only because it offered a break from the unrelenting summer sun, but it also meant more rain. And rain was the one thing that could soothe my worries and place me in the optimum position to close my eyes and fall asleep. Insomnia, my old pal and nemesis, hadn't returned since plaguing me last year when I started my venture. I suspected he was waiting for an opportune moment to pounce. Or, maybe he saw that I had finally found a path, a firm direction, and no longer need his expertise in helping me drag things out from my subconscious.

• • •

Halloween was in two days, and as usual the crazies would be out in droves. I had always speculated that the psych wards released their patients on Halloween morning as a joke to humanity. I imagined the staff following closely behind in unmarked white vans, watching their patients inflict mayhem on the sane. They'd allow a few to get captured by police or EMS, and then they'd pick them up later, still wearing their yellow gowns from Mercy General Hospital.

Thankfully, I was off this year and wouldn't have to drag another poorly-dressed vampire or werewolf into the ER. Last year we responded to a wave of the supernatural wannabes. The night ended after a huge battle at a local bar. It was actually quite an amusing call, now that I think back on it, but I didn't think so at the time. One of the vampires, whom I had the privilege of transporting, was actually convinced that the bartender was a real werewolf. He pulled a .38 caliber revolver from his back pocket while in the back of the rig on the way to the hospital. Lucky for me I didn't resemble a werewolf — I had gotten a haircut the day before and thinned my chops. I managed to grab the empty gun and restrain him to the stretcher while he was stuck in a temporary drug-induced trance. For the rest of the trip to the ER, he begged me to go back and shoot the guy with a silver bullet. Needless to say, he ended up wearing a yellow psych gown at Mercy for seventy-two hours.

Lesley advised me that she had too much studying and wouldn't be able to go trick-or-treating with me. I was crushed and made it a point to embellish the regret. She laughed at my poor attempt at sarcasm and told me that she would make it up to me by taking me turkey hunting for Thanksgiving. I laughed it off, though I had always been intrigued by the idea of how allegedly challenging it was to kill a turkey. Apparently they are either elusive creatures or their awareness of impending doom is heightened during the holiday season.

I arrived at work an hour earlier than usual. I had been up since three a.m., still bothered by my visit to the cemetery, and needed a distraction. There were enough specimens in my journal to keep me busy for another year, but they were easily obtained scumbags, walking the streets bravely and unhindered. None of them would do. What I needed was a challenge, a specimen to push me past my limits. This wasn't the first time I had thought about searching for a suitable adversary. Halfway through the summer, the specimens were becoming redundant, offering little satisfaction. Each time I thought I had found a suitable opponent, they turned out to be common street crud.

"So what's on the agenda today, monkey nuts?" Clyde asked from the passenger seat of the rig. "We gonna bash some morons with our clipboard? Kick some homeless ass in an alley?"

I normally wouldn't feed into his idiotic remarks with a response, but today was different. I was feeling overly ambitious, generous even. At least until I found my distraction.

"Come on, Tryke," Clyde continued, "you need to live a little. Unleash some of that inner nerd-rage!" He then yelled out of his rolled-down window and craned his neck toward the sky, howling. It took everything in me not to press the button to my left and roll the window closed onto his defenseless neck.

"All right, all right, get back in here, you nut. It's still early in the day. Where do you want to go?"

He yanked his head back into the rig and slipped on his cheap black sunglasses. "Well, let's see here, we have a couple of options. Pierre Avenue is lovely this time of year."

Pierre Avenue was known as hooker alley, and was also the location of one of the city's many homeless shelters. It was a one-stop shop to get high, a free meal, and an after dinner blow-job — that is, if you didn't mind a salmonella and gonorrhea hangover.

"Why not?" I said. Hell, who knows, maybe I'd find my challenge. It was a good place to start.

"That's the spirit, homo. I knew you didn't have Dave's dildo shoved all the way in," Clyde said, and then twisted the knob on the radio. I was much happier listening to Metallica instead of his obnoxious comments. As short a time as Clyde and I had been riding together, I had already begun mental slash marks every time he pissed me off. Each mark represented a well-placed punch to Dave's right arm once he returned.

I was surprised to see a few walkers this time of morning. I suppose it was Hallows eve, which had to mean something, perhaps a dampening of the human spirit.

"Medic 15, this is dispatch," the radio amplified.

"What the hell, man, we just got here," Clyde grumbled, and then grabbed the mic, yanking it toward his mouth. "Go ahead, dispatch, this is medic 15."

"What's your location?"

I watched as Clyde hesitated with the mic in his right hand. He was contemplating a lie to our position. He did it on our first shift and the supervisor, Jerry, nearly busted us.

"Don't even think about it, Clyde," I said. I usually wouldn't give a shit. In fact, when it was Dave and I, it was always me being warned. What the hell was happening to me?

"Don't get your panties in a wad," Clyde said.

"We just passed medic 3 a few minutes ago, remember? I don't feel like standing in front of Jerry for an hour explaining why you lied about where we were."

"Medic 15, what's your location?"

"Two hundred block of Pierre Ave," Clyde said.

They took longer than usual to respond, most likely baffled by our location. I pictured one dispatcher arching an eyebrow to a fellow dispatcher beside her, whispering, "Pierre Avenue? I don't want to know."

"Disregard, medic 15," dispatch said.

"That worked out better than you thought," Clyde said. "Now let's see what we can find." He rubbed his pale hands together and started his search.

About a mile down, just as we made the bend in the road, Clyde suddenly flung his sunglasses onto the dashboard. "Stop the ambulance!" he yelled, leaning forward and staring intently out the front window like a dog that had just spotted a rabbit.

I instinctively stopped, thinking I was about to hit something I hadn't seen in the road. He flung open the door and darted toward a guy on the sidewalk, leaving his door ajar.

"Where the hell are you going?!" I pulled the rig to the curb, slamming on the brakes to bring his door shut.

The next thing I saw was Clyde tackling the skinny man to the ground. *You've got to be kidding me.* I grabbed my portable radio and exited the rig. In the short time it took me to reach them, Clyde had the man pinned facedown and his hands sprawled on the sidewalk.

"Tryke, call dispatch and get them to send a police unit to our location."

"Now, why would I do that?"

He pulled two plastic bags from the man's pocket, one filled with pills, the other pre-filled syringes. He tossed the two bags at my feet. "That's why." Clyde pulled a roll of Kerlex bandage from the side pocket of his pants and quickly bound the man's wrists and then sat on his back.

After a brief moment of inner laughter, not to mention a subtle hint of admiration for my crude partner, I radioed dispatch.

While we waited for police, the drug dealer struggled under Clyde and spouted out a few idle cursing threats. The words didn't seem to bother my partner. The gleam of self-satisfaction in his eyes shielded any slur the scumbag could toss. I wondered if I had that same look in my eyes after releasing a dirty soul. I knew my battle with the Gamemakers would never be complete, but getting rid of the ones that I had so far, keeping innocents from the grasp of the dirty souls, preserved my ambition to keep going.

Chapter 4

We arrived back in our district following Clyde's morning drug bust. It was just after lunch before we made our first call for the shift. After Clyde's vigilante takedown, I thought his angry demeanor would have been soothed a little, but he actually seemed more agitated than usual. I had left the incident alone, letting it simmer, until now. He was obviously chasing something, and I was determined to find out what. It was time to pry and see what he would reveal.

The MDT mounted in front of Clyde's side of the rig beeped. He lowered his sunglasses and glanced down at the screen.

"Is it a call or just a message?" I asked.

"Call, 445 Fransen Avenue, an overdose."

After flipping on the lights and siren, I began my probe into Clyde's psyche.

"So, what was the deal with that takedown?" I asked.

He hesitated and propped his right foot on the dash. "When we took the turn, I saw him stash the bag in his pocket. Come on, look where we were. Wasn't it obvious?"

"Yeah, I get it, but why not just call it in? Why the vigilante attitude?" I said, glancing to my left and then to my right before proceeding through the intersection, horn blaring.

I must have struck a nerve. He scowled at me, obviously not liking the association with the word *vigilante*. After a few seconds of silence he sighed and said, "Look, when I was a kid I had to watch my mom slowly deteriorate from the stuff. After my dad died, she started dating this guy and the next thing I know she's wasted out of her mind, sun up to sun down. That son of a bitch fed her drugs like it was damn Lucky Charms. I was twelve and taking care of myself. You get it now? Good!" He turned and faced his window.

"Sorry, really, just give me a heads-up next time before bolting out of the rig. Okay?"

"Sure, no problem."

I didn't push any further. I could tell it went deeper, and I knew better than to tug on fragile nerves. I had to slither quietly across my own mom's delicate mind after my dad passed. At one point, I wasn't sure she would ever surface from her deep depression, but she managed to, just long enough to die.

The police had a unit on scene when we arrived. I'd been to this particular neighborhood many times for similar calls: suicides, domestic assaults, but mostly overdoses. Dealers were as common as used needles around this place. I had to keep a close eye on Clyde to make sure he didn't lose it and go on a rampage.

We placed our equipment on the stretcher and wheeled it toward the front door, leaving it parked by the outside stairs. The address was a dilapidated two-story house with near vertical stairs leading to the second floor. I could see one of the officers lingering at the top of the thin stairwell. I grabbed the drug box while Clyde nabbed the heart monitor, and we trekked up the steep stairs, just hoping they were more stable than they looked.

I'd witnessed the scene of an OD, or overdose, countless times and there were a few constants one could count on: an individual lying in the center of a stained mattress in their underwear, drenched from perfuse sweating, mouth wide and gaping with drool, and loud snoring respirations — on the verge of death. Narcotic overdoses are so common we carry an instant reversal medication, Narcan. It works amazingly fast, similar to the speed of the D50 (concentrated sugar) that we administer to hypoglycemic diabetics.

Vigilance is key when dealing with overdoses, and two particular cautions come to mind. First is needles, which could be lurking anywhere; HIV and hepatitis are two bastards you don't want as friends for life. Second, and even more important, is the size of the patient; make sure that you have enough muscle with you to take down the son of a bitch that you are about to wake from a narcotic slumber. A three-hundred-pound man who just lost his very expensive buzz will be damn angry. He will want money or blood, or both.

This guy we were about to piss off wasn't small. I guessed about 6'2 and two-fifty. Clyde stuck a 16-gauge needle in his right AC vein — the man didn't so much as budge when the needle penetrated his skin — and hooked up a bag of saline fluid. We warned the officers of the usual outcome and they both immediately pulled out their Tasers and pointed the red dot directly at the man's chest.

"Just don't hit me," Clyde said, looking back at the more than eager officers. Clyde pulled the vial of Narcan from its package and connected the needle to the prefilled vial. The officers nodded, not wavering from their stiff ready positions. "I'm serious, you ass-wipes. Don't hit me."

I propped myself onto the man's left side and pinned down his sweaty bulging shoulders. The reversal is nearly instant, if indeed the patient ingested narcotics. But there was no doubt in my mind with this guy; multiple empty pill bottles and a morphine patch sitting next to the bed were good indicators, not to mention the track marks along both of his arms.

Even though I had my knees pressed against the man's shoulders, there was really no amount of preparation that could save me from surprise. It was like watching a balloon being blown up by a small child and anxiously awaiting the inevitable pop and the crying that followed. But this was no balloon or child. This was a 250-pound, highly narcotic-dosed man about to rev to life.

Twenty seconds — yes I actually counted — after Clyde pushed the Narcan into the man's vein, he sprung up from the bed, bypassing my futile attempt to restrain him, and took a huge breath. His wide, bloodshot eyes were grasping for an answer to why he was suddenly awakened from a dreamy death.

"Easy, big fucker," Clyde said, standing to the side of the bed, holding the bag of saline attached to the man's arm. "Get a grasp on your surroundings, and fast. See those two officers' at the end of your bed? They're pointing a very high voltage of electricity at your tender nipples."

For a brief moment, I thought the man came to his senses enough to heed the warning. But suddenly he let out a gurgling roar — still having fluid in his throat — and jolted from the bed with surprising agility. He hardly flinched when an electric prong pierced the right side of his chest just below the nipple line. He glanced down at the object in his chest and yanked it from his skin, sending spatters of blood onto the sheet, and my pants.

The other officer immediately fired his Taser, landing a shot on the man's upper chest. This one seemed to stun him, but didn't completely stop his determined rage. Seeing an opportunity to approach, the first officer pulled out his nightstick and placed it firmly against the man's trachea from behind him. The man continued to struggle, until he heard a familiar sound: a .45 caliber pistol being cocked next to his head.

• • •

When we finally arrived at Mercy General Hospital — home to the overworked nurses and doctors of the city, saturated in the deepest and darkest pit of raw medical mayhem — I managed to get the man to tell me what he actually took that had brought him so close to death. Along with a handful of pills he downed with Vodka, he had somehow extracted the substance from his Morphine patch and injected it into his veins. Dr. Hudson didn't seem surprised by the act. Most likely he had seen it before, considering where he'd worked prior to coming to Mercy General.

"If you guys want to kill yourselves so bad," he said, "you really need to find a more secure place to do the deed." The man, still cuffed to our stretcher, didn't acknowledge the advice. Meanwhile, the doctor spouted an order to the nurse for labs to be drawn, and then handed her the chart.

Dr. Hudson was a veteran in the war on drugs and GSW's, or gunshot wounds. He'd transferred here a year ago from Chicago for family; his parents were living in Dallas and he wanted to be able to look after them in their aging years. After leaving a busy ER in Chicago, Mercy General was merely a continuance of his fast-paced medical journey: level-one trauma center, waiting room constantly full, beds in the halls with screaming psych patients, and the ever-present nose curling smell coming from the depths of ER hell that no amount of disinfectant or potent odor neutralizer could touch.

Dr. Hudson and I talked quite often, mostly about patients, but occasionally we'd discuss other things. We'd even grab a drink every now and then after a shift. I asked him one day why he picked Mercy, considering the hospital he had recently left. I would have thought a nice clinic or private practice would be in order after leaving the Chicago trauma center. He told me that chaos was the thing in life that made the most sense to him, so why not embrace it? We all have our perspectives, I thought, even if they are a little twisted. We own them, so why not coddle them?

The two police officers showed up a few minutes later and retrieved their handcuffs. They decided not to arrest the man, mainly because they didn't feel like doing the paperwork, but they also knew he was only hurting himself and was going to be detained in the psych ward for a mandatory evaluation. All suicide attempts get a yellow gown and seventy-two hours.

I was finishing my report at the nurses' station when Clyde nudged me with his shoulder and asked, "They get that druggie a yellow gown yet?" He was returning from antagonizing a few nurses. I saw him out of the corner of my eye standing between two nurses in a "Captain Morgan" pose, attempting to pantomime the delivery of a baby, which I was sure he hadn't done yet. It was entertaining nonetheless, especially when he mimicked yanking on the umbilical cord as if reeling in a fish.

"Yeah," I said. "Are you finished harassing the nurses?"

"I was just showing them a few of my techniques."

"Right, whatever. I dressed the stretcher and put it outside the door."

"I saw it. Aren't you a swell partner?"

"Nah, not really," I said. "I just know how slow you are."

"Pfft," he said, and then turned around and marched off toward the double doors. I stifled a smile and followed him out of the ER.

I was surprised that Clyde had held it together as well as he had on the call, considering the story about his mother. I was half-expecting him to break down when he saw the unconscious man lying on the bed beside a nightstand full of drug paraphernalia. He'd remained calm, but it was only a matter of time before he lost it again. And when he did, how far would he take it?

Chapter 5

I have always preferred smaller crowds, and have kept the same mentality when it comes to friends. Some would even consider me a loner — I've been called one on occasion — though I would prefer the word *selective*. There's nothing wrong with searching out challenging or pleasant companionship. And one companion I was particularly fond of, after my sister died, was my black lab, Gizmo. Sad to say, he died six months after my sister. At the time, I was filled with so much rage and confusion about death that I preferred solitude. Since then, I have slowly allowed myself to inch back into the world.

The decision to get another dog wasn't an easy one. I knew the likely eventual outcome, that I would have to face its death before my own. I searched the pet store, but none seemed to be compatible with me. Next I checked the pound, and that's when I found Earl. The girl working that day was nearly in tears as she explained to me that Earl was just a day away from being euthanized — he had too many ailments for the pound to afford. Earl is a breed of his own, a mutt with a shaggy brown coat and white floppy ears. The reason I chose him was his eyes. I felt they matched my own; deep within, they held a sadness desperately searching for answers to a predicament. He may have been ready to give up, but I wasn't letting him. If I had to suffer this life, then so would he. We'd walk the dark path together.

Earl has recovered quite well since his death sentence. He's almost as elated about life as I am, but he manages to hold his enthusiasm in most of the time, saving his energy for pressing moments such as dinnertime. I can't blame him. I reserve my own for Scotch, particularly one rich with peat from the island of Islay in Scotland. I was enjoying a glass of it in my hidden room when the phone vibrated beside me. Lesley's name lit up on the screen.

I hadn't told her about the secret room I had installed, and for good reason. I needed a secure area to keep my journal and other paraphernalia related to my side venture.

"Hey there," I said, after pressing answer on my phone's display.

"Hey, to you. What are you doing?"

"Nothing really, just sitting back with a drink, reading. And you?"

"Don't mention reading. I hate books. That's all I do is read, and take notes. Then I have to read those again too." She sighed. "It never ends. Remind me again why I left my caring boyfriend to inflict self misery."

The word *boyfriend* used to make me cringe when it was uttered in my presence, but over time I have gradually accepted it. Lesley and I make sense. Most importantly, she doesn't bug me about frivolous perceptions. We both see life as a death trap, a huge dome of darkness filling in the cracks, following paths of least resistance, until it eventually tracks us all down.

"Because you won't be happy until you are dissecting the dead."

"I miss you, terribly."

"I miss you too," I said. I wasn't being sarcastic. Not entirely. I just had some obligations that needed attending to, and they were better done alone. I actually had grown quite close to Lesley. I suppose it makes sense, now that I am calling myself her boyfriend.

"I can't wait until Thanksgiving break," she said. "I'm looking forward to some real food. Did I tell you about the cafeteria lady that cussed me out?"

I laughed, not entirely surprised. "No, what happened?" Lesley is actually a soft-spoken woman, and witty, but once her principles are placed in peril, she can be quite convincing.

"I wanted a salad that day, not having any vegetables for two days because of a fast food binge with my study group. There were no more salads in the spot where they usually were, so I asked very politely if they had any more made in the back. Her exact words, 'Really? How about doing us all a favor, honey, and eat a damn meal.'"

Now, first of all you have to know that Lesley eats. She doesn't pick at her plate, nor does she only eat green leafy vegetables. She's naturally gorgeous with shoulder length black hair and mesmerizing blue eyes, but most attractively, she's humble. She dresses to dissuade the eyes, not pull them in. Of course, she does exercise occasionally, but mainly to release bottled up stress.

I smiled and asked, "What'd you say to her?"

"I simply stared at her, and waited until she brought me my salad. I was attempting to explode her brain with my thoughts, but unfortunately it was protected by years of self-loathing. Did you know that self-loathing thickens the meninges of the brain?"

I laughed again, "I'm proud of you for not feeding the lesser species."

We talked for a few minutes longer, and after I hung up, I wrote down the date when she was coming into town. I had three weeks to find my challenge before she arrived.

• • •

The shift so far had been quite busy, and I wasn't surprised, considering it was the day before Halloween. After a morning of seizures and minor MVA's, the afternoon was filled with elderly dying of old age, or so-called natural causes. Who knows what the Gamemakers are really up to? For all we know, there's no such thing as natural death and we are all implanted with specific detonators timed to go off when they decide.

It was just after midnight, and I was sitting in my favorite flimsy folding chair at the station with the bay door open. The fall air was cool, but not cold. It was soothing to my flustered and anxious thoughts. The specimens continued to build on my pages, and I was being picky. Too picky, in fact. I stared out into the dark, dimly lit street in front of station fifteen. Somewhere out there were more future specimens inflicting their evil on *humanity*. If I didn't find my lurking challenge soon, I was going to have to settle for a lesser specimen. I could not afford to let them roam and breed unfettered for long.

I flinched when the MDT beeped from the passenger side of the rig. Here we go, first call of Halloween. What will it be? Thirty seconds later, the alarm sounded and the female dispatcher's voice amplified over the speakers.

"Medic 15, I need you to respond to 547 Robin Avenue, Pine Lake Nursing Home, for an eighty-three-year-old unconscious female."

I folded my chair and placed it against the wall, and then hopped in the driver's seat. Before I had a chance to turn the ignition, Clyde snapped open the passenger-side door and said, "Woohoo, we got ourselves a gomer first thing in the morning!" He grabbed his hat from the dash and placed it on his head. He picked up the mic and said, "Medic 15 en route." I didn't comment, mainly because I didn't feel like hearing an elaborate rant about how much he hated nursing homes.

I kept quiet most of the short trip to the address, letting the radio do the talking. Clyde was about thirty seconds from pushing me over the edge with his repetitious drum solo on the dash when dispatch interrupted, "Medic 15, we have further information. The patient is not breathing. CPR is in progress." I snatched the mic from the clip and said, "We copy dispatch, we're one minute out."

"Let's get this party started," Clyde said, turning his hat backwards. He began another drum solo on the dash, this time with two ink pens. I assumed he was mentally prepping for the code the way wrestlers slap themselves in the face before a match. When was Dave coming back? Sure, Dave was passionate, sometimes even loud, but rarely was he obnoxious, especially in the middle of the night.

Nursing homes around the holidays remind me of elementary schools: hanging paper decorations from the ceiling, bulletin boards filled with craft projects, and an odd smell that was most likely coming from one or multiple pairs of soiled underwear.

We trekked down the long maze of deserted hallways before finally reaching the room number. As usual, we had no one to guide us. Luckily for the patient, I had been to this particular NH a few times and knew the layout. Down the halls I had to stop Clyde, multiple times, from jumping up and hitting every cardboard pumpkin and bat dangling above us.

The nurses' station for the set of rooms we came to was deserted; where they disappear to, I haven't a clue. One would think they would all be piled in the room with the coding resident, but when we entered, one lone male nurse in white scrubs was doing compressions on an elderly female. He turned toward us when I knocked on the open door, not breaking his stride, and said, "I'm not sure how long she's been down, but I checked on her about an hour and a half ago and she was fine."

The woman of 309A had been alone in the room. Her roommate had either died recently or was out for a nightly stroll. Her face was ashen with hints of cyanosis. She didn't appear to have been dead very long. There was a white foam oozing out from her mouth. Seizure possibly, status epilepticus? Hypoglycemic? Multiple pill bottles were scattered on her nightstand.

Clyde connected their fast pads to our monitor and then took over compressions. As I unrolled my intubation equipment, and while the nurse was shoving air down the patient's throat via a bag valve mask, I said, "Medical history?"

The male nurse said, "The usual, hypertension, high cholesterol. Nothing extraordinary."

"Epilepsy? Diabetes?" I asked.

"No."

"Asystole," Clyde said, after halting compressions and looking over at the heart monitor beside him. The nurse took over compressions while I intubated and Clyde placed an IV. As I slid the tube down her trachea, I noticed a smidgen of white grainy residue on her upper lip. I shrugged it off and secured the tube.

While bagging, I scanned the room for more medications, personal medical devices, or anything unusual that grabbed my attention — a habit I have developed over time. After a while you start to feel like a medical detective out there, attempting to weed through the patients personal items and bystanders' words to find a solution to the mystery. I didn't notice anything that hinted at her demise. I ran through the possible causes of her death that we could fix in the field. She had no obvious trauma. After a lethal heart rhythm, which we were already attempting to treat, I considered her blood sugar.

"Ninety-two," Clyde yelled to me a minute later, referring to her blood glucose level. Okay, that's not the problem.

After another round of Epinephrine, we pushed Narcan, our narcotic reversal drug. Maybe she was a secret pusher or a dealer, working the dark corners of the NH and searching for a buyer. I checked both arms, to entertain my curiosity, but they were clean. Needless to say, the drug had no effect on the steady flat line displayed on the monitor.

As we were loading her onto our stretcher, I noticed an empty glass next to the bed that had the same residue on the rim as she did on her lip. It was probably nothing but I was curious for some reason. Just as I was about to pick it up and sniff the contents, the stretcher shoved back against my leg, nearly knocking me over. Then I heard Clyde yell, "Dude, can't you see we're working a code?! Move!" I looked past the stretcher toward the door. A man wielding a push broom and wearing green overalls lowered his head and shuffled to the side as Clyde yanked the stretcher forward out the door.

I glanced back at the man as we wheeled the dead lady down the desolate hall. When he saw me looking, he ducked his head, hiding his eyes beneath his cap and resumed pushing his broom. At one time or another, we are all curious about death. It is hard to look away when our own mortality is staring back at us.

The nurse, Jeff — offering his name as we wheeled down the exit hall — did compressions for us from the side of the stretcher. After we loaded her into the rig he offered, no, practically begged, to ride in to the ER as a second hand. I didn't feel like returning him back to the NH after the call. Besides, we were likely going to call the code before we pulled out of the half-circle driveway. From the look in his eyes when I said we didn't need him, you'd have thought we had just punched him in the stomach and taken his lunch money.

• • •

Clyde pushed one more round of epinephrine en route with no conversion. After consulting with Dr. Hudson, Clyde called the code in the back of the rig. He yelled to me the time of death through the small opening like I was his personal secretary. He then proceeded to switch off the lights in the back and crank up the radio. Lucky for me, his volume control only worked on the speakers in the back.

In the rearview mirror I could see the top of his head leaned down in a sleeping pose. I guess sitting in the dark with the dead and jamming to rock was his therapy after a code. If the dead lady's soul was following her former prison, I doubted she was still there after Clyde blasted the radio. But, though they are rare, I've seen old rockers before. I laughed to myself when I pictured her floating in the air above Clyde, arms extended, displaying the rocker hand sign and banging her head along with the music.

Once we transferred the dead lady to the ER bed, I pulled Dr. Hudson into the hallway. I knew I was probably reaching for something that wasn't there, but I couldn't shake the curiosity about the white residue. Maybe it was just powder from an electrolyte drink or some vitamin mixture. It wasn't uncommon for the elderly to stay hydrated. But what if it was something else?

"Is it possible for you to run toxicology labs on her?" I asked. "I mean without a direct police request?"

"Yeah," he said. "You suspect foul play is going on at the nursing home? It sure as hell wouldn't be the first time someone has tried killing off the elderly."

"I'm not sure, but something about the whole situation doesn't sit right with me," I said. "I wouldn't normally make such a request, but…"

"No problem, but don't expect immediate results. They do it in house here and those bastards over there are slow. And don't inquire about it, because they'll just hang up on you."

"Thanks," I said. "I could send Clyde over there if you want. At the very least, he'd annoy the hell out of them."

"I might take you up on that if they keep pissing me off," Dr. Hudson said.

That's why he and I got along so well. There was no need for long exasperated reasoning for every move I made. We had a mutual trust between us.

When I came back into the ER — after stretcher duty — I waited for Clyde to finish his report. I plopped down in an empty chair in the nurses' station next to the computer that displayed the CT's and X-ray's. I was bored and in the process of repetitively flicking a paper ghost with my pen when a female's voice said, "I overheard your request to Dr. Hudson."

Chapter 6

I turned in my chair toward the female voice, clumsily dropping my pen onto the floor. I didn't know how to respond to her comment, mainly because of the way she was staring at me, but also due to her alluring dimples as she smiled. After I got passed the dimples and focused on her entire appearance — rectangle lensed black spectacles, dirty blonde hair pulled into a ponytail, long white lab coat, and brightly colored tennis shoes — I was still at a loss for words.

"Huh," I said stupidly.

"Sorry, I'm Kimberly." She offered a hand. It was soft, delicate, no jewelry. "I didn't mean to listen in on your conversation. It's just a hobby of mine."

"I'm Tryke," I said, recovering from my brief moment of distraction. I glanced at the nametag on her lab coat. It read, Dr. Kimberly. No last name. Odd, I thought, maybe her last name was difficult to pronounce. "So, eavesdropping is a hobby?"

"No," she said smiling. "Ever since medical school I've been interested in forensics, but I liked the fast pace of emergency medicine more. Anyway, I keep up with the latest murderers and their weapons." She had my full attention.

"So, what's the latest on poisonings in the area?" I asked.

She wheeled a chair next to mine and sat down. She seemed as giddy as a teenybopper. She smelled good, fresh shampoo, soft scents of a woman. I missed Lesley.

"All right, so get this, ten years ago every nursing home in Dallas was locked down. Why? Ready for the kicker?" I nodded. "The papers named him the Elderly Slayer. Supposedly, for five years straight he terrorized nursing homes by poisoning random patrons. His string of horror begins on Halloween, and continues through Thanksgiving, ending his killings on New Year's Eve."

"What did the toxicology reports reveal?"

"Mostly traces of sedatives and narcotics. It's not that unusual for the elderly to be on pain meds, even sedatives, but they found something else when they dug deeper...cyanide. There's no telling how many more he killed before the police caught on. How many autopsies are performed on the elderly, unless something suspicious is reported? Very few, and even then I doubt many are taken seriously. Most of those poor people don't have family, or anyone who gives a crap about them."

"Did they catch him?" I asked.

"They had a suspect, a man in his late thirties or early forties. I remember seeing his face in the paper. But they had to release him due to lack of evidence." I wasn't surprised. The slippery bastards often slither away. The Gamemakers don't always create idiots; evil comes in many layers of intelligence. Kimberly went on.

"There were a few other murders while he was in custody, which meant he wasn't the killer. After he was released from police custody, the killings stopped. Maybe the Elderly Slayer got spooked, or found religion, who knows?"

"All of the scum I've ever come across on the streets never seem to stop. Either the police or us pick them up on a regular basis," I said.

"Precisely, so, you think the lady you brought in was poisoned? Disturbing, but exciting news." Her eyes were wide and eager, awaiting my response. She was nodding, assisting me with my answer.

"Actually, I'm not sure why, but… yes. Just a feeling I got before leaving her room."

She slapped my knee, clearly excited. She looked at her watch and said, "Halloween has just begun, and the Elderly Slayer has made his first move. We need to get a rush on those toxicology labs so we can head this guy off." She got up from her chair and picked up the phone from across the counter. I wanted to tell her about Dr. Hudson's warning about the lab techs, but I figured she already knew. Besides, she may have some "womanly" persuasion over there that Dr. Hudson couldn't pull off.

"You think he'll strike again? Today?" I asked as she dialed the extension.

She nodded, and then covered the receiver on the phone. "If this is him, then expect to be coding old people all day long." She pulled a small notebook from her coat pocket, tore a sheet of paper from it, and quickly scribbled something and handed it to me. It was her phone number. "When we get the results, I'll call you."

She turned around and began speaking on the phone. I folded the piece of paper and placed it in my pocket. As I began to walk away, the situation dawned on me. How was she going to call me? I grabbed a piece of notepaper, wrote my name and number on it, and slid it next to the phone. She smiled and thumped her head with the base of her hand. The entire situation was innocent, but I still felt awkward handing her my number.

• • •

Back in the rig, my mind was twisting and twirling with so much new information that I felt the need to make a list — something I despised. But I couldn't do it at work. My journal, the place where I placed all of my thoughts and rearranged them into manageable piles, was at home. And currently at the peak of my thoughts was this elderly killer.

He was the specimen that would fit perfectly into the waiting slot. I had never hunted a high profile killer, and the possibilities of the catch were exhilaratingly nerve-racking. This was going to take time, and careful strategy. If this story broke in the news or even amongst the police, there would be officers everywhere, and he could go back into hiding. This had to be done right, and that began with heading off the only one who knew about the killer: Dr. Kimberly. I appreciated the information, but felt I could handle it from there.

Once I had the results of the toxicology reports, I would figure out how to deter the doctor. In the meantime, I could conduct some research on the suspect that the police captured but had to let go. It would temporarily soothe my eagerness to begin pursuit of my challenging specimen. I glanced down at my watch and realized that I wouldn't be off for another five hours. But I was already set in motion, and couldn't wait that long. I wanted to be at home in my hidden room, in front of my laptop, searching the internet in peaceful uninterrupted silence.

I remembered Clyde's laptop, where he constantly surfed Asian karaoke videos on YouTube. He usually had one waiting to be displayed for my viewing pleasure, but I wasn't interested. He obviously had his own issues he needed to sort out. Who was I to intervene and feed his behaviors?

Before turning onto the street to our station, I asked

Clyde, "Do you mind if I borrow your laptop for an hour when we get back?" I was paying attention to the road. When he didn't answer, I looked over at him. He had a wily grin on his face.

"Sure, if you tell me what the hell is on that piece of paper I saw Doctor nerd-tits slide to you?"

"Doctor nerd-tits? Really?" I had to come up with something fast. "Her number, but I told her I was seeing someone. She insisted on me taking it, so I did. Anything else?"

"Don't tell Dave, he'll want his dildo back from you. Damn, you shot down a doc? She may be a nerd, but she's hot. Lesley must be one nice piece of —" I slammed on the brakes in the middle of the road, and now I was seconds from slamming his head into the dash. "Take it easy, you sensitive girl. Use my damn laptop, I don't give a shit."

"Thank you," I said, and continued down the road.

"I thought you had a laptop anyway," he said, attempting to repair his pride.

"Blue screen of death the other day," I said. My laptop was perfectly fine at home, away from prying eyes, and for good reason.

"That sucks. If you need me to pull shit off of your hard drive, I can do it," he said, opening the door to guide me back into the station, "for a fee of course." He slammed the door shut before I had a chance to respond.

• • •

Once I filtered through Clyde's random nude pictures of women, substituted for the default shortcut icons on his home screen, I finally found his web browser hidden behind a pair of rather large Asian breasts. At least he was consistent and obsessed with a specific nationality, and it wasn't just random nonsense to attract attention.

When I typed in "Elderly Slayer" and pressed Enter, the first article that popped up was from a newspaper overseas about an old lady wearing a Slayer t-shirt, obviously a fan of the band. I realized I left off Dallas. Once I typed in the correct name, a local paper that I recognized was first on the list. I clicked on the page. The headline of the article read: *ELDERLY SLAYER LEAVES ELDERLY SPOOKED ON HALLOWEEN.* Who the heck comes up with these headlines?

I skimmed the article. After reading a few lines, I realized that the timeline was before they had a suspect. It basically told me the same thing Dr. Kimberly had explained to me. I needed a picture of the suspect they released.

Though I didn't have the toxicology results, I had to admit that the circumstance fit the profile: Halloween, nursing home, Dallas, multiple deaths. Five years was plenty of time to lay low. Killing random innocents was pertinent to these guys' survival; once they start, they never quit. If he *was* back, why the same area? Personal vendetta? Nostalgia maybe?

After scanning through years of this guy's killings, I found an article with the headline:

SUSPECT IN HOLIDAY SLAYINGS ARRESTED.

The suspect was identified as 48-year-old Duncan Sims. Police say Sims was apprehended in his home Monday evening. They aren't releasing any details at the moment. An officer on scene was quoted as saying, "The elderly of Dallas can sleep better knowing we have him in custody."

From the picture, he looked older than forty-eight; dark grey eyes, face thin and sickly, and the hair he had left on his head was mere strands. Overall, he didn't give off a very threatening appearance, but considering his victims he didn't need to look ominous. Most of them probably couldn't see or hear him coming. He was a cowardly predator. I memorized his face, but even the most idiotic and bold killers disguise themselves in some manner.

I found another article, dated a few weeks later:

*ELDERLY SLAYER STILL ON THE LOOSE, SUSPECT
RELEASED FROM CUSTODY.*
*The police said earlier today that Duncan Sims had been cleared of
any involvement in the holiday slayings. While Sims was in police
custody, two more potential murders took place. Medical Examiner's
office spokesperson stated that although the results were inconclusive,
they still found small traces of cyanide in the bodies. When local
authorities were asked to comment on the Medical Examiner's findings
they refused, stating the case was very fluid and volatile. Local nursing
homes were put back on alert. Despite it being February, elderly
residents aren't taking any chances. Mae Filbers, a resident of Wooden
Glen nursing home said, "I sneak out of my room and check the doors
behind the nurses at night." Local authorities said they were doing
everything in their power to protect elderly citizens, including random
walkthroughs of nursing homes around the city.*

I found an article about Sims following his release. The
article went on to talk about how mistreated he had been
since his arrest, including the days immediately following
his release. He was contemplating a lawsuit against the
police department for wrongful arrest and slander. In the
end, he decided against it. *"Let bygones be bygones,"* he was
quoted as saying. He was probably eager to get back to his
mundane life as a productive citizen in this great city. I
wasn't buying this guy's noble pardon of the police. The
psycho has been resting unhindered for the past five years.
The Gamemakers have called on him to come out of
retirement. Awake, and continue your havoc on the elderly,
you brave, brave soul.

I searched the following year, including the beginning of
the next holiday season:
*ELDERLY SLAYER STILL AT LARGE. LOCAL
NURSING HOMES LOCKED DOWN THROUGH
HOLIDAY SEASON.*
*With no suspects in custody, nursing homes are ramping up security
by hiring off duty police officers. When asked about any leads, local
authorities advised that there were many, and that they were taking*

each of them seriously. We also caught up with the Medical Examiner's office, and a spokesperson for them said they were on alert and would be investigating all elderly deaths in nursing homes until the killer was caught.

I went through as many articles as I could find, every year right up until the present. Duncan Sims wasn't mentioned again, probably because of his threatened legal action. There were no eyewitness accounts or suspicions reported, or none that the police released. This guy was good, or at least good at restraint, stopping while the suspicion was high. If he was starting up again, why tempt fate? He had a clean slate and could have easily started over in a new city.

I typed *cyanide* into the search engine. I knew a little about the chemical, remembering fragments from chemistry class in college, but not enough to give me insight into what this guy was using. I read through a few articles, highlighting pertinent information.

Cyanide poisoning is a form of histotoxic hypoxia. It blocks our cells from utilizing oxygen in the bloodstream, which means it chemically asphyxiates us. Sodium Cyanide, NaCN, was the substance he probably used. Cyanide salts would explain the residue I saw on the woman's lip and the rim of the glass. But none of the articles that I read ever mentioned that they found any residue of the chemical on scene. They stumbled on it during an autopsy when the medical examiner suddenly became nauseous. He said he detected the distinct odor of bitter almonds, indicative of cyanide. While intubating the lady, I didn't recall that aroma. But as I read further, I found out that not all people have the ability to detect the odor; supposedly, only about half of the population carries the gene.

The last article I read was about toxicology of the chemical. Due to the chemical's relatively short half-life, testing for cyanide in the blood has to be quick, within a few hours. After the first hour, half of the cyanide in the blood is gone. If what the nurse told me on scene was correct, we should be okay on time. If it's there, they should be able to detect it in the blood.

I had a restless night, with the unknown grappling with my mind. I needed to know if the killer had been unleashed. Each time I got up to use the restroom I checked my phone for a missed call from Dr. Kimberly. I was tempted to call her a few times, but knew it wouldn't do any good. She would call the second the results were in. Considering her demeanor earlier, she was as impatient as I was, if not more so.

Chapter 7

I sat alone at the table in the station kitchen sipping on my cup of dark-roast coffee. Clyde usually slept another thirty minutes past the bell, which was fine by me, because I needed time to slow my thoughts. Our relief would be there within the hour. I had been so focused on our female nursing home code last night that I had forgotten about the obvious. Though we hadn't had another NH death during the night, another medic unit could have. At the very least, I could see if a pattern was forming in the city while I waited for the results of the toxicology report.

I left the kitchen and sat down in our small office and powered on the station computer that was connected to our local network. I clicked on the call-log icon and filtered the last twelve hours: MVA, assault, seizure, overdose, and a few chest pains. No codes, but that didn't mean anything. The chief complaint that dispatch places on the log is the original call, not what our report reads after; a seizure or fall could turn into a code. I checked the addresses and recognized two of them as nursing homes. I moved the cursor to the right to check the chief complaint: one was a chest pain, the other difficulty breathing. They were only an hour apart, and Medic seventeen had made both of them.

I picked up the phone next to the computer monitor and dialed.

"Station seventeen, Mark speaking."

"Mark, it's Tryke."

"What's going on?"

"Not much, just wanted to ask you about a call y'all went on last night."

"Which of the eight were you curious about?" Mark said, sighing loudly into the phone.

"Damn, sorry y'all got slammed. The nursing home calls, you went on two, right?"

"Yeah, back to back. Wrong place, wrong time. You know the routine." Mark was one of the more honorable medics on the department. If he were near an address, despite just coming off of a call, he wouldn't hide behind the radio and sneak back to his district.

"My girlfriend called me last night and said her grandfather was taken to the ER with difficulty breathing," I said.

The phone went quiet. When he spoke again his voice was soft, apologetic. "Sorry, man, but the two we made were both codes. Tell your girlfriend we tried, but both were Asytole (flat-lined) when we got there. We didn't get so much as a quiver back on the monitor."

I let out an exasperated sigh and said, "All right. Thanks man, I'll call her in a few minutes and give her the news."

"Good luck," Mark said. I hung up the phone.

A few minutes later, while I was in deep thought, Clyde busted into the office, nearly spilling my coffee on the keyboard. With way more energy than necessary this early in the morning, he said, "Let's get the hell out of here. Come on, our relief just pulled in the parking lot." I shifted in my chair and faced him, rolling my eyes in the process. "Damn," he said, "you look like shit. I know what you need."

"Oh really…please enlighten me."

"You need to get your Halloween freak on. The nurses' from Mercy are having a costume party." He started pelvic-thrusting the air. "Come on, you may even see your hot nerdy doc friend."

"I have other plans," I said, "but…you know what, write down the address. I might show up."

"No, you won't, but here it is anyway." He pulled a piece of paper from the printer beside him and scribbled the address down, and then slung it on my lap. I folded it and placed it in my back pocket.

I had no intention of going, but with Lesley off at school it was important to seem social. I knew better than to let suspicions build. Last year Dave informed me about rumored speculations concerning my sexuality before I started dating Lesley. I didn't care about the content of the speculation, but the less I was on anyone's radar, the better. I had to maintain the correct balance of mystery to keep people at a safe distance and from prying. Since the time the rumor surfaced, I've changed my pattern, randomly showing up at places that Dave invited me, even if only for a moment.

• • •

When I got home, I tossed my bag onto the living room couch. I was exhausted. I needed a nap, but my mind would never allow such a span of time to be wasted on sleep, not without some answers first. Until Dr. Kimberly called, I didn't even think my good friend — continuous soft falling rain — could have persuaded my mind to take a break.

I made a pot of coffee and poured a cup. I settled at my desk in the dimly-lit hidden room and opened my journal to a blank page. I began writing everything that I knew so far about my potential new specimen. If nothing came of it, I would at least have it for future reference if he did show up again — never let a good specimen go to waste, I always say.

Eventually, quiet concentration soothed my eagerness enough for my mind to allow me blissful ignorance of my surroundings. My phone vibrating on the desk startled me back to reality. With a crick in my neck, I slowly reached for the phone. I didn't recognize the number, but the text message cleared it up: *Call me, the results are in!*

I looked at my watch. It was 1030. I quickly dialed Dr. Kimberly's number. She picked up on the first ring.

"Hey, they're in! And they're positive!" she said.

I immediately perked up, shedding my groggy demeanor. "What'd they find?"

"We need to discuss this in private. I'm still at work, and I'm getting some strange looks. Positive results aren't usually blurted out with enthusiasm in the hospital. When can you meet?"

"Hmm," I said, lost for words. Meet? Away from work? I didn't quite know what I was getting myself into. "I can meet you within the hour. Did you have a place in mind?"

"How about the coffee shop on Lake Street, Groggys. Eleven-thirty okay?"

"Meet you there," I said, and hung up.

I was intrigued. Why did we have to meet in private? Why couldn't I just meet her in the ER? Most importantly, had she told the police? I didn't know Mercy's protocol concerning positive toxicology results relating to a potential homicide, but most likely it was up to the ordering physician, which in this case was Dr. Hudson. He'd obviously be sent the results, but how did Dr. Kimberly receive them first? I hadn't had a missed call or text from Dr. Hudson.

Though my mind was spinning with rousing questions

and possibilities, I was still moving quite slowly. On my way to the shower I clumsily kicked the bedroom door, slamming the knob against the wall. A familiar rattling sound — one I hadn't heard since I was a child — came from the wooden floor boards. When I was around eight-years-old I walked in on my dad placing a shoebox under the floor in this very spot. After sealing the board shut he sat me on the bed and told me a story about leaving things alone that were never meant to be disturbed. Of course, a few days later while he was at work and my mom was busy in another room, I snuck in there to see what was hidden below the floor. To my disappointment, the shoebox was gone and the space was empty.

I had forgotten about it until now. Intrigued, and filled with nostalgia, I knelt down and felt along the edges until I reached the board that was loose enough to pull away from the others. I stuck my hand down into the small dark space, and to my surprise a shoebox was wedged inside. I pulled it out and wiped the thick layer of dust from the top and removed the lid. Three tattered journals lay in the box.

Part of me wished that I hadn't ever opened that floor board. It was the same part that was with me the day I found my dad's original journal, beginning this seemingly never-ending scavenger hunt. Any bit of exhaustion lingering from work the night before was immediately swept away by an intense force of exhilaration, along with sparse dapples of anxiousness. Why had my dad told me about the one journal and hidden these away? Could it be that he had forgotten about them? That thought quickly faded when I remembered that nothing was ever that easily explained in my life.

I opened the journals one by one and quickly flipped through them. All three were full of my dad's handwriting. I didn't have time to read and decipher, but after skimming a few passages I knew it was going to take some time to sift through these new words. From what I read, it was most likely more rants about the voices and the Gamemakers, but there was this empty feeling in the depths of my gut that warned me not to tamper with them further. I had just recently come to terms with my life, settling into how I was going to spend the rest of my days. I didn't like the uneasy feeling of change that was growing darker around me. I wasn't as eager to decipher these three as I was the first one, but I knew I had to, if only to finally put an end to all the mystery and confusion. Once I returned from my meeting with Dr. Kimberly, I would begin the descent into the pages, slowly.

How could I have been so naïve to think one journal could hold a man's lifetime of troubles? I already had a few of my own.

• • •

The coffee shop was busy. While standing in line to place my order, I found Dr. Kimberly nestled at a corner table facing the window. I wasn't one for drawing attention to myself or others. I was planning on ordering my drink and then greeting her by sitting down at the table. A few minutes later, however, she spotted me in line, then stood and waved enthusiastically. Slightly embarrassed, I lifted my hand in a half-wave, exerting much less energy than her.

After retrieving my drink I sat down across from her at the small table. She had her long dark blonde hair down, covering the left lens of her black rectangle glasses. She was wearing navy colored shorts that revealed long, firm legs, and the same pair of bright colored tennis shoes she had on at the hospital. It was odd, and sometimes disturbing, seeing someone outside of work in their street clothes. I remember the first time I saw Dave away from work. He was sporting denim shorts and a pair of complex leather sandals. After his divorce, his new girlfriend Angie — now his wife — claimed that she wouldn't allow that fashion atrocity to ever happen again.

"You dress down nicely," Dr. Kimberly said. I was wearing a pair of old jeans and boots along with a black and dark green t-shirt.

"Thanks...I guess." I said, wondering what she was seeing. I was going to reply with *so do you,* but held it in, remembering compliments for men and women are regarded differently. If in doubt, shut the hell up.

She smiled and got right down to business. "Sodium cyanide. That's what the toxicology reports found. They also found the sedative Lorazapam. I called the nursing home and got a list of your patient's medications. She was only taking blood pressure and cholesterol meds. This is big time, Tryke. The Elderly Slayer is back!"

A couple from the table beside us peered over their shoulders when she yelled the information. I'm sure a few others turned around, too, but I hardly noticed. I was dazed by her faint perfume and long dark blonde hair. Her legs crossed neatly, and her tight skin. Her deep dimples hovering below her cheeks, teasing me slightly with each reveal.

"Tryke, did you here me?" she said in a lower, but still excited voice.

"Yeah, sorry... I was just thinking. So, what do we do now?" What the heck was I doing? This wasn't right, this feeling, and these damn hormones raging through my nostrils down to my waist and along my inner thighs. I had Lesley in my life. Whoa, big fella, one at a time.

She looked at me, twisting the sides of her mouth from side to side. She uncrossed her legs and leaned in toward me, brushing her hair from her face slowly with her hand. I got a waft of her fresh smelling shampoo.

She said, "I haven't alerted the authorities about the findings." She was waiting on a response from me, a sign to proceed. She had apparently seen something that gave her a reason to trust me, enough to tell me that she had kept the information from the authorities. But why?

I stayed calm, keeping my facial expression to that of understanding, and not surprise. I didn't want to frighten her away. I needed her to reveal whatever strategy she had formed. "What's the plan?" I asked in a hushed voice.

"What do you think about tracking this guy down ourselves?"

I kept my expression stuck in mild suspense, not giving her anything to feed off of. I was truly in shock by her request, a fellow dark soldier wanting a partner to hunt a foul soul of the night. I doubted she had the same intention and plans as I did with the man, but why couldn't she assist me unknowingly? There was one complication hovering in the air surrounding this entire endeavor: we would both be withholding information from the police.

"Before I agree to this, how many know about it?"

"Just you and I. No one else," she said, as if I should have known. She looked tense and slightly offended.

"I'm talking about the results."

She relaxed her shoulders. "Oh, I took care of that. I swiped the specimens from the lab." Naughty girl.

"And Dr. Hudson? Won't they be sending the results to the physician who ordered the tests?"

"I took care of that, too. I erased the orders in the system."

I couldn't stifle the smile that was aching to be released. She smiled back at me, bringing that set of dimples to the surface in full glory. I felt the heat rising in my cheeks. This was going nowhere good, and I had to get out of there.

"It looks like you've taken care of the preliminary work," I said, and forced a yawn. "I need to get some sleep."

"So, you're okay with all of this?"

"I'm in," I said. I slid my chair back and stood.

"I'll walk you out," she said.

I opened the door for her as we exited the coffee shop. She looked down shyly and thanked me. Simple gestures seem to always light up the opposite sex, no matter the intention, and it's something that will forever baffle me. I have always considered it a sign of mutual respect learned from years of watching my dad with my mom.

Before I opened my truck door to leave, she said, "If you get up early enough, I thought we could start tonight." I must have showed my reluctance. "Come on, I have the perfect alibi."

"I'm listening," I said.

"Okay, a few of the girls at Mercy are throwing a Halloween party. I thought we could swing by there, just to show our faces, and then go on the stakeout. I've done some research and mapped out a few of the ones I think he might hit next."

I hesitated, but she already had me hooked. "A stakeout? Hmm, all right. Let's see where it goes. Oh, and one more thing. I have some information about two more possible poisonings last night. I called station seventeen this morning before I left and they told me that they made two codes last night, back to back." Her eyes widened at the news.

I gave her the names of the nursing homes where the two deaths occurred. Then we briefly discussed the plans for the evening and said our goodbyes.

Chapter 8

I fell asleep halfway through the second journal and woke in my chair in the living room. I hadn't discovered any new revelations about my dad from the two that I had gone through. As I suspected, there were more drunken rants and curses, mainly directed toward the voices. However, there was a man's name mentioned a few times that I had never heard him speak of before, or write about — Randal. There weren't many specifics about the man, only brief mentions during rants. I went back and highlighted the name each time it was mentioned. After I finished reading all three journals, I reread the highlights and tried to make a connection, if there was one.

I decided it was best if I met Dr. Kimberly at the Halloween party, and then we would leave from there. The last thing I needed were rumors getting back to Lesley about me and another woman.

Earl was still resting calmly, sprawled out in his bed, paws stretched lazily over the sides. I envied his life at times — his seemingly clear conscience, and the ability to fall asleep in an instant. His only worry was foiling ninja squirrels attempting to sabotage his food bowl.

It didn't take me long to slip a bandana around my face and a worn brown cowboy hat on my head before leaving the house. I found the hat in my dad's closet when Lesley and I cleaned the house after Mom died. I didn't recall him ever wearing it, but I assumed it was there for the same purpose as I was using it for tonight. A gunslinger was the easiest costume I could come up with on such short notice. Besides, I rather liked the idea of the gunslinger in the old West, bringing swift justice to the filth with a pair of six-shooters on his hips slid into well-oiled holsters — no lengthy trials or slick attorneys.

Dr. Kimberly didn't divulge what costume she would be wearing, but advised that I would recognize her easily enough. I wasn't quite sure what she meant by that, but I hoped she was right about spotting her. I really didn't feel like roaming the party and pulling back masks. This was supposed to be an alibi, not an event.

Twilight was just now ending, which meant my doorbell would be ringing shortly if I didn't turn my porch light off. Like an idiot, I hadn't bought any candy to hand out, and disappointed trick-or-treaters can be ruthless. I decided to drive around for an hour so the kids wouldn't think I was home and avoiding them — I didn't want to face a truck covered with raw egg the next morning.

It was a perfectly spooky evening for Halloween: sporadic ominous clouds hanging low in the sky, each brushed along by a cool breeze that allowed winks of a nearly full moon. Dry autumn leaves ruffled along the dead grass and damp sidewalks. Before leaving my neighborhood, the nostalgia of my childhood brought back memories of my little sister. Trick-or-treating was one of my favorite memories of us. She and I roamed the neighborhood as a team for the one year she was old enough, before she died. Every small ghost, princess, or ghoul slinging a plastic pumpkin pail reminded me of that night: her signature giggle, the smell of cheap makeup paint and wax-paper-wrapped caramels, the thrill in her eyes when she rang her first doorbell, anxious, awaiting a trick or a treat. It was a good year though, lots of candy with very few disappointing homemade popcorn balls. I even managed to convince her to venture into one of the neighborhood haunted houses with me. She was scared, but the exhilaration on her face afterward was worth the brief fright she endured. She would have been an adrenaline junky like our dad, wanting over and over again to ride the steepest, fastest roller coaster at the amusement park.

I wiped a tear as it slid down my cheek and took a deep breath, snapping back to the present.

• • •

There were more people than I anticipated at the party. The cars were lined up past the stop sign at the end of the street, leaving me no option but to park my truck a street over. Walking the half-block to the party, I had to remind myself that I was only staying long enough to be seen. I don't consider myself agoraphobic — it's not a fear, but rather a choice. I fit somewhere close to the loners and not too far from the annoyed thinker, but definitely distant from the social attention whores.

When I reached the house I slipped my bandana over my mouth and trudged up to the front door. *Monster Mash*, early buzzed laughter, and fog machine smoke filtered out the front screen door. To my surprise, no one was lingering around the entrance, making out or puking, but it was still early. Though it wasn't a high school party, alcohol doesn't discriminate, and has a way of slyly easing away inhibitions, as casually as the wind blows away fake fog.

My mission was simple: find Dr. Kimberly and get the hell out. If things had only turned out as we planned them.

The second I entered through the screen door I was hit

with a rogue hotdog in the center of my chest. There was something oddly familiar about the incident, but I couldn't quite place it. The black light pulsing to the beat of the music made it hard to recognize anyone, but there was no mistaking the culprit behind the slinging of the wiener. I should have known, Clyde, dressed as a hotdog vendor — but no ordinary hotdog vendor. Wearing an apron and a matching striped hat with an umbrella attached to the top, he was strapped to a small makeshift hotdog cart. As he spun toward me to the beat of Michael Jackson's *Thriller*, I saw his entire crude costume. Behind the cart was a blowup doll leaning its head inches from his crotch.

"What's up cowboy Bob?" he said. "Didn't think you'd show up. Huh, maybe you're not a total suck-dick after all."

"I'm flattered you think so," I said sarcastically.

"Oh, your doc friend is here. And she looks damn hot in —, Hey!" He turned around to face a blonde female vampire, nearly bursting from the skimpy netting surrounding her large breasts. She playfully snatched his striped hat from his head. I laughed as he chased her away, attempting to keep his awkward costume together.

I grabbed a soda from the inflatable coffin next to the kitchen entrance. As I tilted my head back and took my first swig, I felt a sudden piercing in my lower back, and then one more beside it. I didn't move, sure any sudden jerking would only cause further pain. I inched forward and slowly turned around. Black Widow from the Avengers had two guns pointed at me, only her hair was dirty blonde and she wore rectangle spectacles.

"We were about to have ourselves a little showdown, Drawdown," Dr. Kimberly said, sliding her two guns clumsily back into their holsters. "Nice holsters."

"Thanks. I see you went all out. Where'd you find the tight leather?" I said, trying not to stare.

"I had it on hand," she said, leering at me.

I felt suddenly warm, a blushing sensation surrounding

my neck. "So, which nursing homes did you have in mind?" I said, quickly turning the conversation.

"Slow down, you just got here."

"I thought we had a plan — show our faces and leave."

"All right, all right," she said. She pulled me over to the side, next to the staircase, alone. Not that it mattered. No one had a clue about what we were discussing. "According to the articles, he's been known to strike a nursing home more than once. But…he's only done that twice — that they know of. Parkland and Magnolia are the two I have a hunch about."

"Okay, we've made our appearance," I said. "Let's get out of here while we can."

"One dance, and then we go," she said pleadingly, removing her glasses and revealing her bright copper eyes. She slipped them in the front pocket of my jeans.

"I don't dance." For some reason the words left my mouth in a less convincing manner than normal. It almost seemed as if I whispered them.

She grabbed me by the arm and dragged me to the outer ranks of the costumed dancers. I hardly struggled, realizing it would have dampened the mood and most likely blown the effort of the night. I gave in.

The music that had just started playing was a strange mixture of howling winds, creaking doors, and techno. The zombie couple next to us were moving faster than zombies were supposed to move. I was about to comment about them when Dr. Kimberly slyly moved her body close to mine and slung my arms around her waist. Slowly, she began moving her hips, rocking them against mine. For some reason, I couldn't let go of her. I felt compelled to give in. Her exposed lower back was warm, the muscles tensing as she moved seductively to the music, which was now picking up its pace. She turned around and pressed her leather butt snuggly against my hips, leaning over, whipping her hair and gyrating against me to the repetitive beat. The strobe lights pulsed, matching my rapid heartbeat, and the music pounded my eardrums, leaving me temporarily immune to outside forces. I was caught in a trance, unable to remove myself from her grip. She returned upright and pressed her back against my chest, resting her head on my shoulder, continuing to move her entire body like a squirming snake. I felt her slowly run both of her hands on my back, lowering them to the crevice of my thighs. I instinctively pulled away, but she grabbed firmly and drew me in tight. She twisted around and faced me, wielding a luring grin, sweat glistening off her forehead. She continued to stare at me for the rest of the song, appearing to be caught in a trance of her own. The repetition of the dance beat seemed to never end, or change, encapsulating us in a permanent state. Then the pulsing of the lights stopped and the song abruptly ended.

I wiped the sweat from my forehead and snapped back to reality. "That was intense," I said.

"Thank you," she said, running a finger down my chest and all the way to my jeans. She retrieved her glasses from my front pocket.

I didn't know whether to thank her back or run the other way. I was completely conflicted.

"We can go now," she said smiling, obviously satisfied that she got her dance.

"Okay," I said, still a bit dazed. After a few seconds, I slipped my bandana across my face and followed her out.

Chapter 9

I felt kind of silly on a stakeout, considering we weren't cops and I've never had aspirations of becoming one. On top of that, there are more than thirty nursing homes in Dallas, so the odds of us catching this guy were slim. Why had I agreed to this crazy endeavor? I didn't quite know, but as long as Dr. Kimberly's suspicions stayed away from Duncan Sims, I would entertain her little game.

After the odd dance we shared at the party, which was still hovering deep in my groin area, I was more than curious what her ultimate intentions were with this venture. Was she trying to seduce me? Could it be that simple? I doubted it. She had gone too far — erasing orders, keeping valuable information away from the police — for it to be an innocent crush. No, she was more likely living out some sort of fantasy, a vigilante of the night, and I was her sidekick. My initial instinct was to get the information and then deter her from further involvement, but now that I'd seen her willingness to break rules, and even the law, I thought she might be of use. At the very least, she would be a good asset to have at the hospital. I needed to keep her hanging on just enough to satisfy her craving.

The parking lot of the nursing home was mostly bare, with only a few stray vehicles. We tried blending in, parking in between a small sedan and a truck, but anyone halfway paying attention would have easily spotted us.

Sitting in the front passenger seat of her yellow Jeep, I accepted a pair of night vision binoculars that she handed me. She had obviously done this before. I briefly examined them and then raised them to my eyes. "What does a nice young doctor need night vision binoculars for?" I said.

Gazing through her own pair, she replied, "My ex-husband was a bastard. I did my own investigation and busted that son-of-a-bitch at a gas station parking lot with his whore."

"Nice work, Dr. PI. A gas station parking lot? Classy."

"Why pay someone else when it's so damn fun to spy? You get to see their expression when you knock on the car window with your camera. And yeah, if you'd have seen the tramp, you would have understood the locale. He probably discovered her in the outside bathroom."

"Yeah, I suppose that would be satisfying, seeing their shocked faces."

"It definitely was. His whore was just lucky I didn't have my two holsters attached, like I do tonight." She tapped the plastic gun strapped to her right leg and burst out laughing. I smiled along with her, but something told me she wasn't completely joking. If she'd had a gun that day, would she have killed the girl, and her husband, too?

She reached toward my leg and I instinctively flinched. "I'm not going to hurt you," she said grinning. "I need something in the glove compartment." Since the dance at the party, I felt apprehensive. I needed her close, but not in-bed-close.

I relaxed my arms. "Oh, okay, I didn't know," I said, trying to seem embarrassed. I opened the glove box for her and she pulled out a walkie-talkie. "You have a scanner, too?" I asked.

"Yeah, and it doesn't have anything to do with my ex. I just like listening."

"For?"

"Work, usually. I want to know what I have to look forward to before I arrive. I switch back and forth from police to EMS." She switched the power on. The police chatter was immediate. Halloween was always a busy night for us all. I thought about the idea of a scanner for myself — for certain obvious occasions — but I liked to keep things simple. Besides, noise irritates me and I preferred quiet in my lab.

As the dispatchers conversed back and forth with the officers, I set the binoculars on the seat next to me and treaded carefully with my next words. "So, what are your plans if we do happen to run into this guy?"

She continued to stare forward, binoculars in hand. "I thought we could have a little fun with him." My thoughts exactly...wait...what? I didn't say anything. I was waiting for a punch line.

"How do you mean?"

She lowered the binoculars and slowly removed her glasses. "Well, what do you think about giving him one of his own potions?"

I turned away from her and faced my window. I couldn't yet tell if she was serious. Suddenly, I heard a burst of goofy laughter and then a snort.

"Come on, Tryke, you should have seen your face. You looked like somebody ran up to you and stole your shoes."

I smiled and forced a laugh. "Did you just snort?"

Embarrassed, she covered her mouth. "Oops, I guess I did. Anyway, I really didn't have a plan. I just thought it would be cool if we caught this guy before the police."

"So, you want to one-up the police. I get it. How long were you planning on waiting until you informed them?"

"I thought we could decide that together." She glanced toward the floor, awaiting my answer.

I wasn't sure where she was going with this "together" thing, but as long as I was part of the decision-making, I was okay with it. I needed to keep the police in the dark, too, until I had this guy in my lab.

"Okay, sure," I said. "We can both keep an eye out at work and do a few stakeouts. We'll give it a couple of weeks and decide then about alerting the police."

She looked up at me with a smile. "Perfect," she said, clearly excited.

I switched the scanner over to the med channels and listened for my comrades. She seemed interested to find out how her own colleagues were faring. After a few minutes, we were both glad to have the shift off. By the sound of the reports, it was psych night and seizures. It seemed an odd combo, if you didn't consider the particular night of the year.

I stared out the window into the darkness, phasing out the dispatcher's voice. I should have brought coffee. The previous night was wearing heavily on my eyelids, and just as I felt my eyes begin to shut —.

"Did you hear that last transmission?!" she asked, as she turned the volume up on the scanner.

I stretched my eyes and looked around. "No, what was it?" I asked.

"Magnolia Trace, medic ten. Do you copy?" the dispatcher's voice said.

"We copy, dispatch, place us en route," medic ten responded.

"Do you know where that is?" she asked.

"Yeah, it's a few miles up the road. What's the call?"

"Unconscious, unknown."

"It sounds like it could be our guy," I said. "What are you waiting for?"

"Oh...right. I wasn't sure you wanted —" She placed

the Jeep in drive and squealed the tires out of the parking lot.

I grabbed ahold of the "oh shit" handle above me and quickly snapped my seatbelt on with my free hand. "Take it easy, medic ten is on the way, too," I said as she flew through a stop sign. "That would be a nasty collision, not to mention we'd be dead."

"Sorry," she said, and eased off the gas pedal, but not as much as I had hoped. On our next turn, I could feel the top-heavy Jeep sway and lift one of its tires from the pavement.

When we finally reached Magnolia Trace Nursing Home, Dr. Kimberly slowed down and pulled into the parking lot casually, as if we had just arrived to visit grandma after a nice stroll on a Sunday afternoon.

"We beat medic ten," she said proudly.

"Of course we did, Flash."

She smiled and felt around for her binoculars, which had fallen down onto the floor board. "Do you see anyone suspicious?" she asked, finding the binoculars and raising them to her eyes. She started looking around frantically.

"No, just us," I said. "Have you ever heard about killers who hang around their own crime scenes for a peek at their work?"

"Yeah, a lot of them do that, from what I've read. They like seeing the aftermath. I hadn't really thought about it with this guy. You think he — " She lowered her binoculars and glanced over at me as if she just had a sudden revelation. "Hey, yeah, this could be good for us. It'll be easier to catch him if he lingers around the scene of his crime."

"Maybe. It's something to think about." A little nudge was okay. It kept hope in reach. I had no idea if he liked to hang around, but that was irrelevant. It would keep her busy staking out NH's, and hopefully not treading back toward the original suspect, Duncan Sims. He was my territory.

Less than a minute later, medic ten pulled their rig under the tall round overhang, gathered their equipment, and placed it onto their yellow stretcher. They typed the entry code into the keypad and proceeded in through the front double glass doors. I pushed the scan button on the radio, allowing us to listen to the other med channels. I wouldn't know which hospital they were going to until they advised dispatch — unless it was a code, because then they would choose the closest.

"We'll soon know if it's a code," I said. She had the binoculars held back up to her eyes, alternately jerking her head from one entrance to the other.

"Come on, you son of a bitch. Leave!" she said.

I admired her passion, but doubted she would have it in her to actually hunt down the guy and kill him. She was like most people, a spectator eagerly waiting to witness justice. If hangings were still done in the town square, she would be in the front row watching, but not on stage pulling the lever. The Gamemakers had smiled at us when we stopped the public executions, which gave the criminals more rights than the innocent citizens, and added conflict to the chaos.

The radio remained quiet for the next few minutes.

"What's going on?" she asked, breaking the silence. "They've been in there for at least ten minutes."

"Who knows? Sometimes there're obstacles: wrong information, incompetent aide, no patient in the room…the list is endless."

"They're coming out the front door," she said, leaning forward, binoculars pressed hard against her glasses. "Son of a bitch! They're doing compressions!"

"Huh… really?" I said, hurriedly lifting the binoculars and peering through them. "The patient must have coded on their way out."

"I was about to say. Don't y'all usually work them in the nursing home and call the code on scene?"

"Yeah, usually. If they coded on the way out, it probably wasn't our guy. Cyanide works too fast." Unless he actually *was* watching and administered the dose when he heard the sirens.

"Yeah, you're probably right," she said, disappointed. "What were our odds of actually seeing the guy anyway?"

"Probably slim, but we were close enough to witness a code. So who knows." Though she was feeling let down, I could see a glimmer of hope lingering in her eyes. "He'll make a mistake, don't worry."

"Do you think we should wait around a few minutes, just in case it was him? See if he leaves from the back door?"

"If you want, but I don't think this was *his* work."

She nodded and sighed. "All right," she said, and handed me her pair of binoculars. We watched medic ten's strobe lights fade off into the distance. "What now?"

"I guess back to the party so I can get my truck."

"Okay… unless you have any ideas?" She looked over at me with hopeful eyes, eagerly waiting a new direction.

"I don't," I said. "Sorry. But this was a good start." She turned the ignition, sighing quietly to herself, and started driving back toward the party. "Did you ever check out the two codes I told you about that medic seventeen brought in?"

"No, not yet," she said.

"It may help with planning our next stakeout. You know, some sort of pattern."

"Yeah, I could do that. Who knows, maybe he'll even show up at the ER tomorrow night. Change it up a little."

"I doubt it. These guys are creatures of habit."

"But a girl can dream, can't she?"

"Sure, just don't let them turn into nightmares." She didn't respond to my remark, and seemed to have slipped into her own private, internal world.

A strange dream to desire, but I suppose it fit, considering what we were out doing that night. I wasn't sure how far she was willing to take this obsession of hers, but at least she would be busy looking into the two codes the next few days. It would give me time to stalk, alone.

When we turned back onto the street of the party, I noticed that it didn't appear to be waning anytime soon. Costumed drunks had flooded the house and filtered out onto the front lawn. Empty beer cans and smashed pumpkins overflowed the two trashcans in the driveway.

"Looks like we're missing a hell of a party," I said. "My truck is one street over. Take a left here."

"Maybe we should've stayed."

She parked behind my truck, turned the radio down, and said, "So, are you headed home? Or…do you want to have a drink at my house, talk some more about our next move?" She pressed a small black button on her radio and displayed the time. "It's still early."

I was caught off guard by the offer. I didn't answer immediately. "I can't —"

"I'm sorry," she said, quickly turning away. "I'm being too forward."

"No…it's just, I'm exhausted."

"I understand," she said, clearly disappointed. "You didn't sleep last night. Maybe another night then."

"Definitely," I said reassuring her. Little did she know that I needed her as an asset, and not as the fantasy sidekick she needed in me. I opened the door and said, "Don't forget to look into those two codes. And call me if you find something."

"I will. Be careful driving home. Goodnight."

"Goodnight," I said, and shut the door.

It wasn't just an excuse. I really was tired. But I still had another journal and a half to filter through.

Chapter 10

Part of me feels responsible for all that has transpired in my life. I assisted them on their quest to their ultimate path, my destruction. I allowed them in and offered them coffee and a nice warm place to stay. I can't help but wonder what things could have been avoided if I had never opened the door. How many cells could have been spared the torment?

My dad's passages didn't become any clearer as I skimmed over them on my days off. The only continuity was the name, Randal. I had my speculations about his identity. However, the possibility that it created would mean that my dad's letter to me was merely a distraction. But why, and who was the distraction meant for? The only other person who knew of its existence was my uncle.

Until I could make the connection, I held everything neatly together. I was good at unraveling my world, but not until everything was in place and ready.

Dr. Kimberly called me last evening about the two codes medic seventeen worked. I didn't know to what extent she went to determine that they weren't part of the Elderly

Slayer's work, but she assured me that it was done with great caution. The entire conversation made me wonder if I should keep any further discoveries to myself. I had already begun to push past my comfortable limits with her.

Dave was coming back next shift, meaning this would be my last shift with Clyde. Though he'd been a crude and vulgar pain in my ass, I had reluctantly grown to put up with his antics. I wouldn't go so far as to say that I liked him, but after hearing his story and witnessing his tenacious resolve, I couldn't help but feel for the guy.

We had just stopped off at the bookstore at Clyde's request. He wanted the Steve Jobs biography. I was pleasantly surprised by his interest, but I wouldn't be completely convinced until he had the purchase receipt in his hand.

"Man, I'm gonna actually miss seeing your lame face," Clyde said, plucking the book from the shelf.

"Yeah, really? I'm flattered." With the palm of my hand, I muffled the radio traffic that was amplifying from the portable radio clipped to my hip.

"Don't think I'm gonna massage your uterus or anything," he continued. "You have Dave for that. I'm just saying things could have been worse."

"Well, I suppose you're not as big a douche as you make yourself out to be."

"Come on," Clyde said, "let's get out of this place. The nerds by the graphic novels are gazing at my junk."

"After you," I said, laughing at his delusional paranoia.

At the cash register, he pulled a debit card from his wallet and purchased the book, though his eyes lingered a little too long on the modestly-covered nudie magazines that were displayed behind the counter.

"Are you sure you're done shopping?" I asked, staring toward the cluster of magazines.

He jerked his head back toward the young cashier. She pursed her lips, holding in a smile. His face turned multiple shades of pink. Without speaking, he ignored the receipt in her hand and walked briskly toward the exit.

"He's so timid," I whispered to the cashier, and then shrugged.

Before we had time to open the doors of the rig, dispatch called our medic unit number. Through the window, I could see Clyde pouting with his arms crossed. I grinned and keyed the portable radio. "Dispatch, this is medic 15, go ahead."

"Medic 15, we need you to respond to 453 Charles Avenue for an unconscious female, unknown age."

"We copy, dispatch, place us en route."

The address was a well-known hole for addicts of all kinds to meld as one huge sludge pile. I could care less about their drug use as long as they didn't drag it into the realm of children.

Clyde hadn't uttered a word on the short trip to the address. As much crap as he constantly slung around, it most likely wasn't my comment at the bookstore that was keeping him in deep thought. There was something else poking at him.

Though the afternoon had just begun, time had no relevance to the residents of the house on Charles Avenue — any time was a good time to be high. The tattered couches and chairs perched on the front porch were filled with hunched-over, drooling zombies, all traveling through the mind's abyss and thoroughly detached from the living. It was the easy way out of this torment.

Before reaching the front door, I could actually hear Clyde's frustration and anger building behind his constant audible sighs as he pushed the stretcher through the dirt-filled yard.

"Wake up!" Clyde yelled, snatching the jump bag from the stretcher. When no one acknowledged him, he proceeded to stomp on the rotting wooden porch, rattling the flimsy structure. As a result, I was sprayed with dust and other debris from above. I wiped my shirt and silently thanked him with a curse. A middle-aged man was slumped against the front door, impeding our entrance. After Clyde's initial yell, the man shuffled his head in the opposite direction, revealing a pool of drool on his ragged t-shirt. "What a fucking waste," Clyde said, pushing the door open and knocking the man over. The man didn't seem to mind, placing a hand under his head and settling in where he had landed.

When we entered the quiet dwelling, the front living room was empty except for a few plastic crates and a twelve-inch rat that scurried along the far wall and jammed itself into a hole. Usually on these calls there was someone alert enough to guide us in the general direction of our patient. We didn't have enough Narcan in our drug bag to treat a mass overdose. Most likely the one who dialed 911 had taken off, guilty of causing the overdose in the first place.

"Is there anyone in this shithole who's not fucked up?" Clyde yelled.

I wasn't expecting a response, but a male voice from a nearby room said, "In here." He sounded sluggish, as if he were struggling to stay awake.

We entered the bedroom. The male, whose voice we had heard, was hunched in the corner, his head down on crossed arms that were wrapped around his knees. He was rocking back and forward. A female, no older than fourteen, was splayed out on a mattress in the center of the room. From the strong ammonia smell, we knew the stains on her pajamas were most likely urine. Her face was pallid and lifeless, her breathing shallow. I immediately went to work.

While pulling out the airway equipment, I asked the rocking man, "What did she take?" He didn't answer. I slid the ET tube down her narrow trachea.

Clyde bit his bottom lip, suppressing the rage that was

building. He powered on the heart monitor, slinging the cables onto the floor. I heard him whisper, "son of a bitch" and then he picked up an empty bottle and chunked it toward the man. It shattered against the wall next to his head. "He asked you a question. What did she take!?"

The man stopped rocking, looked up with glazed crimson eyes, and said, "Easy man, I don't know the name of the stuff."

Clyde shook his head in disgust and attached the leads to the young girl's chest. He started an IV and then slammed a vial of Narcan into the vein. The medication didn't faze her.

"Are you the one who called? How'd she get here?" I asked, continuing to squeeze the BVM, giving her thirsty tissues the oxygen they were craving.

The man continued his rocking, and with his head still pressed against his arms, he said, "She's my sister."

I felt a sudden twinge in my gut. "How's her heart look?" I asked Clyde.

"Sinus," he said. "It's steady at the moment."

"Take over bagging for a second, please." Clyde stared at me, but didn't question my request. He took my spot at her head. I calmly walked toward the man in the corner and stood over him. "Get up," I said in a calm, stern voice. When he didn't move I said it again, but with much more vigor. He looked up at me, his young eyes were confused but not afraid. He couldn't have been more than eighteen. He stood, awkwardly, hovering a few inches above me.

Since my first year as a medic, I have learned to control my anger — to an extent. "I'm going to ask you one more time. What did she take? It's your sister, man, we need to know so we can help her." But he wasn't going to tell me. I could see it in his eyes.

"I said I don't know. I didn't give her anything. She took it herself. I called 911, isn't that enough? Do your damn job!" He clenched his hand and tensed his shoulders, unaware that he just revealed his next move. He lazily swung his fist toward me. I stepped back and grabbed his arm, shoving it violently behind his back. With my free hand I grabbed his greasy hair and slammed his head into the sheetrock. I yanked him around so that he was facing me. His nose was oozing blood.

"You can't do this to me! I didn't —" he said.

"Yeah, you did," I said. I dragged him by his hair to the mattress in the center of the room.

I kicked the back of his legs, bringing him to his knees, and then shoved his head down inches from his sister's face. "Look at your sister! Look! This is your fault! She looks up to you, and this is how you treat her! Sober your ass up and get to Mercy Hospital! She'll need you, if she lives. If I don't see you up there before I get off shift, I will personally hunt you down. Jail will be a pleasant experience compared to what I have waiting for you." I released my grip and he shuffled back toward the wall like a frightened animal. Then he grabbed his head and slipped back into his original hunched-over pose.

"He means it, you piece of shit," said Clyde. "We better see you up there. We have your name and address." Clyde lifted the girl and carried her out the front door to the stretcher while I bagged her airway.

"Nice touch, adding the name and address," I said.

"No problem. Damn, man, I got a boner listening to you threaten that little shit."

I smirked. "Just keep it to yourself."

• • •

As I sat in the rig in Mercy's ER driveway waiting for Clyde to finish his report, my anger finally subsided. I had been too worried about Clyde losing it, not paying enough attention to myself. I knew better than to let my furies be revealed, and was fortunate that I'd been surrounded by the incapacitated, as well as a partner willed with equal rage.

But I couldn't expect to always get away with losing my temper on scene.

The incident hit me close. My sister often crossed my mind, and I still blame myself for her death. Though I feel her soul is safely guarded, I will never be satisfied until I am beside her again. I need to tell her I'm sorry for leaving that day. I need to hold her and see her eyes forgive me. But I know that won't happen until the Gamemakers are finished playing. I must somehow meet their expectations before they will allow the reunion.

After learning that my dad had more hidden journals, I realized that this game went deeper than I could have imagined. There were more players. And some of the current players' roles had changed.

Something was dragging me toward discovering the identity of Randal. I had a hunch he was the missing piece. At the very least, he was someone who could guide me in the right direction. I needed to understand my dad's scattered rants.

Chapter 11

Before Clyde and I ended our last shift together, we made a short trip up to Mercy to inquire about the condition of the teenage girl OD, and of course to see if her brother had actually showed up. Clyde was more persistent about the matter. Though I was curious, I had said what I needed to say on scene.

I found the brother in the waiting room. I watched from afar, not letting him see me. He appeared to be sober, no longer cradled in a corner rocking back and forth. His sister never came out of her drug-induced coma. She coded early that morning and they were unable to revive her. According to a nurse when we arrived, the brother had just been told the news.

As I watched him stare down at the floor, I relived each of my family member's deaths. I relived the anger, the pain, and my mind's inability to grasp anything tangible. I didn't pity him. He made a decision to bring his sister down his destructive path, and now she was dead. I briefly pondered his being my next specimen, but decided against the idea.

He would punish himself; the guilt would eat at his soul until he was dead.

Welcome to the game.

After waking from a nap following my shift, my first sip of afternoon coffee was interrupted by a knock on the door. I wasn't expecting to see Dave's well-rested, smiling face until the following morning.

"How's life been?" he said, still wearing his honeymoon attire: loud, loosely-fitted button-up plaid shorts and his awful leather sandals, which I felt hopeful his new wife Angie would eventually burn. In fact, if I remember correctly, she had told Lesley that it would be one of her first duties as his wife.

"After the initial annoyance of my temporary partner subsided, not too bad," I said.

He offered his hand and I politely shook it back. Unexpected guests arriving at my door two years ago would go unanswered. My solitude life has been dwindling a little every day since, but I have yet to take the full plunge. I have only inched out enough to cause mild anxiety. So far, I've managed to handle it okay.

"Yeah, sorry about that. Hope it wasn't too awful," Dave said.

"Nah, I'm just giving you shit."

"Hey, how about some light in this dungeon?"

"Sure, open the curtains, but not all the way," I said. "My fangs will retract into my skull if you do."

He smiled. "I'm not looking forward to being up all night again. Not after resting peacefully every night listening to ocean waves and drinking a beer anytime I felt like it. Speaking of, do you mind if I grab one from the fridge?"

I nodded, "If you can find one that you left over here. I don't drink the weak stuff."

"I know, I know, only the hard stuff. It's pointless taking your time getting to the point. Blah, blah."

"I'm just saying."

"Whatever."

He found one of his cheap cans of beer and popped it open. He then sprawled out on my couch.

"Shouldn't you be home with your new wife?" I asked.

"New wife, new rules," he said, taking a swig of beer and placing one arm behind his head. "She trusts me around you for some reason. She even insisted I come over to see how you're doing since Lesley's been away at school."

"How thoughtful, but I think I can manage," I said. His last wife would never have let him roam unassisted. If he had, once he arrived home, she would have gnawed on his spleen until he lost consciousness. I always had a feeling, since the first time I met her, that she was hiding something very dark and deep within. I was just glad Dave divorced her before she revealed it completely.

"How are you handling the long distance thing?" he asked.

"Good. I stay busy as usual."

"Busy with your secret life. The hidden world of Tryke is legendary amongst us mortals."

"Mwahahaha, give me a break. I have a damn girlfriend, and a dog. What do I need for all the spectators to lose interest, a potbelly and a kid? Well, forget it."

If he only knew how right he was. What's more perfect than a sarcastic secret life? Pretentious mystery seems to be where others think I have taken myself. I suppose they've arrived at this conclusion since I've become involved in a relationship, without changing my habits. Actual mystery loses its appeal once a woman attaches, or so I've been told. I was attempting to achieve the opposite when I set out to battle the Gamemakers. I was trying to avoid attention, especially a romantic encounter.

"Speaking of Lesley, Angie said she'd be in town for Thanksgiving," Dave said. "I overheard them on the phone and they want all of us to be together. What do you think?"

"Sure, I guess."

Surprisingly, our days off fell on Thanksgiving and Christmas. Since my entire family has been eradicated from this place, the holidays are simply another day, and I'd rather be working. I prefer walking among the other tortured souls, patiently waiting their turn to shed.

We talked a while longer, mostly about the details of the holiday. Dave conveniently pointed out that my house had the most space, considering Angie moved into his small apartment. In the end, I reluctantly agreed to hold it at my place. How lucky for me. I just hoped Lesley knew how to cook a turkey; my skills peaked with grilled cheese sandwiches.

• • •

The next morning I arrived at work before Dave, as I normally did. I enjoyed the quiet alone time with our rig, slowly sipping on a fresh cup of strongly brewed coffee. At times I even considered it therapeutic: the creaking of the sliding doors, the squeaking of the shocks as I slid on the bench seat from shelf to shelf, the low hum of the radio. We whispered to one another — the rig and I — the secrets of our patients; each scream, every cry of agony, was melded into the walls. We had an understanding, a sad truth about the actions we take — his quick speed and loud sirens, my swift and methodical hands — how they rarely had the intended impact of helping the dying. But we can never stop trying. We have an obligation to continue the battle. My job is my hunting ground, and my lab is the releasing room.

"Hey, man," Dave said, stepping up into the rig. "Tryke, you there?"

I looked back at him, "Yeah… I was just adding up our saline inventory in my head."

"Did you already go over the entire rig?"

"And restocked what those two morons used last night

and forgot to put back."

"Thanks. I still think they do that crap on purpose," he said.

Little did Dave know, during our first year together, I was the one switching things around on the rig. It was amusing to watch his tantrums. He has since learned to accept some degree of chaos. I have tried to persuade him to embrace the mayhem of our job and fight it with more chaos. He usually frowns at my attempts, but I think I'm breaking through and slowly getting to him.

The bell sounded in the station, and a few seconds later a male dispatcher's voice amplified over the rig's radio as well as the station speaker. "Medic 15, we need you to respond to 290 Birchwood Boulevard for a welfare concern."

Dave placed us en route via the MDT in the front seat. While slipping on his uniform shirt over his t-shirt, he said, "The dead, first call back, great."

"It's probably nothing," I said. "It's a weekday." Welfare calls on weekdays usually turn out that either the person is out of town or they're staying with a family member. Sunday morning, however, when the family can't get grandma to answer the door to go to church, that's a different story. Then, more often than not, grandma is found stiff as stale bread.

Dave jumped into the driver's seat and started down the road.

"I didn't read the information when I placed us en route. What's it say?" Dave asked.

I scrolled past the address on the screen in front of me. When I read the notes dispatch had written below the address, my speculation of nothing wrong quickly changed.

Call came in from property manager: pest control unable to gain access to residence for several weeks, neighbors complaining of strong odor.

"Pest control can't gain entry, neighbors complaining of

smell," I said.

"I think you're wrong on this one. Weekday or not, it sounds like this one's been dead awhile."

The pest control guy was leaned against the hood of his van when we pulled up to the townhouse. We spoke to him briefly. He told us that the property manager was on her way to unlock the residence and then he left in a hurry.

"I guess he didn't want to hang around and see the end results," Dave said.

"Guess not."

A few minutes later, a small white sedan pulled into the parking lot and stopped next to our rig. A lady in her sixties with stringy blonde hair and bright red heels got out and flashed her keys toward us. Two police units arrived on scene behind her.

"The police must be bored this morning," Dave said, shutting the rig's back door after sliding the jump bag over his shoulder. I nodded and grabbed a handful of blue masks from the side compartment.

We followed the property manager to the front door. "I don't know what this is about, but these units have to be sprayed," the lady in red heels said, clearly irritated. She then proceeded to rap on the front door.

"Do you know the resident?" Dave asked her.

"Mr. Frank! Ms. Stella! Are you in there?" she yelled, her face inches from the door, and pressing the doorbell rapidly. "I know *of* them. Met them once. Okay, I'm unlocking the door." She looked back at the two officers who were now standing behind us. They nodded in unison toward her.

Once she unlocked the door we moved aside and let the officers enter first. A horrible but familiar smell wafted out the door as they eased it open. I took a step back and to the side. "Police! Anyone home!?" the officer yelled. No one answered. As he pushed the front door the rest of the way open, he quickly covered his nose and mouth. "What the hell is that smell!?"

I looked over at Dave. He was cringing, with his right hand covering his mouth and nose. I said, "That, sir, to put quite simply, is shit. More precisely, human shit if I had to guess. But I sense a hint of sweat, and maybe piss, I can't be absolutely sure."

The officer turned pallid. He appeared to be moments away from adding vomit to the aroma. I handed him a blue mask after placing one on myself. Dave had his donned before anyone. "Shall we?" I said, motioning for the officer to lead the way.

"Thanks," the officer said, quickly shoving the mask on his face.

"Here, this helps too," I said, tossing him a small bottle of hand sanitizer. "Smear some under each nostril."

The bottom floor of the townhouse was immaculate: the carpet still had lines from the vacuum, the couches covered in factory plastic, the kitchen virtually untouched.

We came to the stairs leading to the second floor. Before proceeding, one of the officers yelled up the stairs, "Police! If anyone is up there, identify yourself!" They both drew their weapons. A few seconds later, a female's voice answered back from the top floor.

"Frank, is that you?"

"This is the police, ma'am, we're coming up the stairs. Are you alone?"

When she didn't answer back, Dave and I cautiously made our way up the steep stairs behind the two officers. The smell intensified, penetrating my flimsy blue mask. My eyes began to water and burn slightly.

One of the officers guarded the partially closed door in front of us while the other checked the adjacent room. A few seconds later, he emerged and said, "Clear."

The two officers stood on either side of the door, weapons drawn. One of them said, "Ma'am, do you have any weapons on you?"

"No, sir," she said. Her voice was shaky and sickly.

We waited outside the door until the officers cleared the room. Seconds later they both emerged, nearly knocking Dave and me over. As they leaped down the stairs toward the front door, one said, "She's all yours."

Dave and I looked at each other, shook our heads, and then entered the dark room. She was lying supine in the center of her queen size bed. I couldn't quite see what I was stepping on, but it crumpled like paper. With one boot in front of the other, I slowly made my way to the window on the other side of the small room.

"Who are you again?" the woman asked.

"EMS, ma'am. Ambulance folk," I said.

"I thought you all were the police."

"We came with them. They left."

"Oh, well, I'm feeling okay. Who called y'all, was it Frank?"

"No, ma'am, the property manager."

When I pulled back the dark curtains, the entire room was brought to light in all of its nasty glory. I quickly ducked from the army of cockroaches that scurried into the wall vent above my head. Under my boots was layer upon layer of piss-covered newspaper. On the dresser was an array of gel deodorizers, drained dry, most likely dying instantly when first cracked open. Empty fast food bags and boxes of snack cakes littered the top of the small television, as well as the end of the bed. At least twenty medication containers, covered in roach feces, were scattered on the bedside table.

Dave had been silent since we entered. I glanced back at him. He was wide-eyed, and still standing at the door. "What the fuck," he whispered.

"What was that?" the woman asked, hearing Dave.

"Nothing, ma'am," Dave said quickly.

I yanked open the one stubborn rusted window in the room. I don't think it had ever been opened before that day. "Ma'am, do you mind if we take a quick set of vitals?" I asked.

"I don't know what for, I feel fine," she said, lifting a flyswatter from beside her and swatting the air. "But I suppose I don't see any harm in it, so go ahead if you must." When the light from the open window hit her face, I noticed she didn't appear quite as old as her voice. She looked to be in her early sixties.

"Thank you," I said. Dave tossed me the stethoscope and the BP cuff. When I hunched over — straining to avoid contact with the soiled bed — the horrid smell intensified immensely. She leaned over and lifted her arm in my direction, giving Dave a full view of the situation.

While I pumped up the BP cuff, I stared over at Dave. Above his mask, I could tell he was grimacing as he looked down under the woman. I imagined him saying, "You've got to be shitting me." He stumbled back a few feet.

"Two-forty over one-eighty. Have you been taking any of your medications?" I asked, knowing the answer was no.

"Honey, if you could hand them to me from the side table, I'll tell you my medicines."

The conversation was going nowhere. Dave cautiously made his way toward me. His forehead was sweating profusely. He whispered, taking short breaths, "Roaches… crawling from under her. And shit, actual shit, all along her back and bed. It's horrible, man." He nudged me out of the way and slung his head out the window. The next thing I heard was heaving, and then a volley of chunks hitting the ground outside.

I wiped the crud from the outside of one of the many medication bottles. I managed to decipher her name: Stella Jordan. The medication had expired two years prior. "Ms. Jordan, we need to get you to the hospital," I said. "Your blood pressure is way too high, and this place is just not sanitary. Do you live alone?"

"What's that? My blood pressure is high?"

"Yes, ma'am. Do you live alone?"

"No, Frank takes care of me."

"Who is Frank?"

"My son."

My disgust quickly turned to anger. I closed my eyes and rotated my neck, attempting to control my temper. I clenched my hands, cracking my knuckles. Deep, calming breaths were not an option in this place. Unless this Frank guy was mentally disabled, I had an empty slot waiting for him in my journal. His offense moved him rapidly to the top of my list, even ahead of Mr. Slayer of the Elderly. Besides, I still had some homework to complete on my high-profile killer friend.

Chapter 12

It took us another thirty minutes, after placing on protective gowns and a second pair of gloves, to move Ms. Jordan down the steep stairs. On the way to the ER, she told me that she hadn't been out of bed in at least three months because of body aches. Once we actually removed her from the bed and onto our backboard, I got a glimpse of the mattress and her underside. She had been sitting in her own shit for so long that it had eaten her flesh down to the bone and the mattress down to the springs.

Dementia, and the trust of her son, had blocked common sense, leaving an old lady vulnerable – along with her Social Security check, I suspected.

Before leaving the residence, I glanced into the other bedroom upstairs. The son's room was neat and tidy compared to the nightmare of his mom's room. She was a money mule, treated as a nuisance. By not refilling her meds and pumping her full of fast food and snack cakes, he was speeding up her death exponentially. As sick as the act is, it's not rare for a child to prey on the parent's retirement income long after their death. The imagination of these filthy souls can be quite malicious.

I managed to find an old photo ID of her son, Frank, in his bedside table. Ironically he was a sanitation worker for the city. Forty-five years old, shabby looking, full head of unkempt thick hair. I had a clever event forming for his release.

While Dave started an IV in the back of the rig, I told him I would handle informing the police of the situation. I told the two officers, who were sitting safely in their cars, that the hospital would handle social services being called. They thanked me for saving them from tedious paperwork.

It bought me time from the police, but the hospital would notify social services after reading Dave's report. The question was, how long would it take them to follow through and track down Mr. Jordan, or at least call him? I had to head this guy off before they scared him into hiding. If my suspicions were correct about him, he would run.

When I got off the next morning, I called Mr. Jordan at work.

"This is Frank."

"Yes, sir, this is Dr. Jimmy at Mercy Hospital. I was calling to inform you about your mother, Stella." I paused to see how he was going to respond.

"I'm busy, doctor. What's the news?"

"She had a spell of hypertension and we're going to be keeping her for observation a few days. She wanted me to call so you wouldn't worry. She said she'll call when she is ready to be picked up."

"Is that it? Can I get back to work now?"

"Sure you can," I said. It sounded like he slammed the phone down when he hung up.

His apathy was so damn sickening to listen to, it was hard for me to hold my tongue. He was tormenting his mother's mind — feeding her dementia with false sentiments like deodorizers, and her diabetes and hypertension with intoxicating snack cakes and fried foods. It was just another form of torture.

After lunch I sat and watched his townhouse. He arrived home around 1600 hours, backing his dilapidated nineties station wagon in front of his address. He was shorter than the picture showed, but still as shabby in his work uniform. I reclined my truck seat after he entered his house, expecting to be there for awhile. I opened a *Popular Science* magazine I had in my backseat and started reading an article on dark matter.

I only got a few paragraphs into the article when out of my peripheral vision, I saw him prop open his front door. He opened the back of his station wagon and ran back into the house. I set my magazine down and placed the seat back upright, removing my sunglasses. I watched as he shoved two full black trash bags, along with a suitcase, into the back of the wagon. He then got into the driver's seat and took off, squealing the tires.

I wasn't expecting him to run so soon. What tipped him off? Social services wouldn't have called that fast. It didn't matter. My brief thought of binding him to his mother's mattress, face down for an evening, wouldn't be realized after all. My only concern was getting him inside my lab.

I followed him to the outskirts of town, where he filled the car with gas and dumped the two black trash bags into the dumpster around the side of the station. I wanted to stay and see what was in them, though I was pretty sure it was just the trash from his mother's room. He was attempting to cover his tracks, unaware that they'd already been seen. After leaving the gas station, he drove back into town, stopping at a house a few blocks from his address.

I pulled past the house and parked, keeping a direct line of sight to the front door. I cracked the window and ducked my head out of view. He rang the doorbell, nervously glancing over his shoulders. A man answered wearing bright yellow gym shorts and no shirt. They exchanged a few words and then the man started yelling at someone in the house. From the sound of the exchange, it was most likely the wife. Mr. Jordan threw up his hands and then marched back to his vehicle in the driveway. The man followed him, apologizing.

Mr. Jordan seemed to calm after they talked out in the driveway over a cigarette. "I'll leave by morning," I heard him say, before getting into the back seat of his station wagon.

You'll be gone well before dawn, I thought to myself.

• • •

Mr. Jordan was neatly exhibited on the metal table in front of me, his steady heartbeat displayed on the monitor on the shelf above his head. An IV of normal saline dripped slowly into his right AC vein. I was waiting patiently in my chair for him to rouse from the cocktail I had shoved into his jugular vein while he slept in the backseat of his wagon. The soft hum of the generator was quite soothing, muffled behind the closet door, relaxing the simmering anger still residing inside me.

As I have become acclimated to my new way of life, my lab has become more efficient and reliable: sturdier metal table, a pulley system for the restraints, better lighting, and mounted cameras perched in each corner facing the table, along with one outside, above the back door, for obvious reasons. In the past, I'd had to leave my specimens unattended due to unforeseen circumstances, trusting — hoping — that the medication wouldn't wear off before I made it back. Now, thanks to an application on my phone, I can easily tap into my cameras and watch from anywhere.

Mr. Jordan started waking, squirming around on the table while attempting to make sense of his surroundings. When he saw me out of the corner of his eye, he made eye contact with me and let out a moan of garbled sounds behind the bandage stuffed in his mouth. After a few seconds, he finally stopped when he realized I wasn't going to entertain his unrecognizable words. I stripped off my outer navy colored overalls, revealing my work uniform. I pulled two syringes I already had prepped and ready from atop my duffel bag and slid them into the right pocket of my shirt.

"Mr. Jordan, my name is Tryke Harper. Though you do not know me, we have a mutual interest." My voice was calm, my mood shifting to work. His eyes darted from one side of the room to the other. "It's only me here, I assure you. Before we proceed I wanted you know that you will soon be free. No longer will you be able to feed off the silent screams from your mother. She will no longer burden your dirty soul. There will be no more need to torture her or yourself." Once the information processed, he started thrashing around on the table, again attempting to curse me through the wad of bandage in his mouth.

I knew they were watching and waiting, eagerly rubbing their grubby hands together and realizing that once this one was released, another would quickly takes its place — most likely even more vicious and clever. There was a time not long ago when I wasn't sure if our organic suits had pilots. But the idea of a pointless suit made no sense to me, even before seeing my sister leave her body. If there's one thing the Gamemakers have made clear to me, it was that their players always have a mission — none roam aimlessly in their world. I didn't care how many they bred, I was going to continue doing my part. I know the battle will come to an end someday when they grow weary of me. At that time I will not struggle. I will be ready.

Continuing his huffing and puffing through the bandage, Frank stared toward the camera at his feet. It was one of the original two cameras from the beginning, the one I didn't smash into pieces. I said, "That particular camera was there to catch sight of the dirty soul once the organic suit was shed. That was back before I knew the game, when I was chasing the afterlife. It's now there as a reminder, a symbol of the past." He writhed in place, attempting to threaten me again with muffled words, not accepting his imminent fate. If he didn't calm down, I was afraid he wouldn't reach the important bargaining stage before he was released. He needed that stage of grief to ponder his choices. I gave him a few minutes, but his anger never abated.

"Let's proceed, shall we?" I said.

Once the medication hit the cardiovascular system, it wasn't long before the alarm bells from the monitor started ringing. I silenced them. At a time not long ago, I attempted to coerce the soul to reveal itself. I went through the process of resuscitation: a shock here, a shock there — all pointless, of course — but that was before I realized my mission. If I were to let on that I know the visions are real and not a mental distraction the Gamemakers would change the rules. I'd be back in the same place I once was — lost, attempting to piece my life together, trying to decipher what was real. I was nearly defeated, left to drown in the mind's bottomless depths, but somehow I had emerged, and the truth was brought to fruition.

Once the rhythm on the monitor settled to a steady flat line, I switched the power off and unhooked the IV line. Mr. Jordan's soul left quietly, not showing itself; nothing, not so much as a chill in the air. I was surprised, considering the frequency of sensory observations during my latest releases. Not to mention the graveyard incident, in which an entire apparition was revealed. Maybe this was another tactic. They may be attempting to lower my guard, so as to strike harder next time. What if they decided to reveal brief glimpses of my dead family?

Chapter 13

I woke up with an intense headache and a fiercely beating heart. The dream felt eerily real. Alone, in a vast meadow, I stood below a crimson sky. The clouds were black and yelling screams of thunder from afar. The hot wind stung my face as if I had just opened the door of an oven set to broil. By my side, I felt the hilt of a heavy broadsword. Suddenly, sheets of rain fell from the sky, causing steam to rise under my feet.

I wasn't alone for very long. When I turned, after feeling a powerful gust of wind from behind, an army of grey/black souls was silently hovering fifty yards away. I didn't wait for an introduction. I pulled the heavy sword from its sheath and took off running in the opposite direction. The rain pelted my face, obscuring my view of the vast emptiness in front of me. Having nowhere to hide, doom and helplessness quickly overwhelmed my existence. I felt like a lone king on a chessboard facing an entire board of queens. After a long and tortuous trek, as my legs failed and my lungs shrieked for air, I finally woke. The slow motion, glue-like feeling was horrifying, especially because there was nowhere to hide and I was being chased by an army of souls wielding whispers of torment.

My dreams have never been pleasant. I have never roamed the skies on a soft cloud or saddled a unicorn and rode off into the sunset with a beautiful girl. They are constantly filled with worry and anxiety over the hellish truths of the world surrounding me and beyond. Did I believe in foresight, the ability to see a future me? I sure hoped not. But I can't help but wonder what the playing field is like on the other side. Would it be fair? Would it be just? Would another ability replace free will?

The phone vibrating on my side table startled me. Lesley's name lit up on the screen. I slid my finger across the display and answered.

"I didn't wake you, did I?" she asked.

"No, I got up a minute ago. What time is it?"

"Four in the afternoon. Are you okay? You sound a little rough."

"Eh, I'm all right, just a bad dream." I cleared my throat. "What's going on?"

"I was just calling to make sure you haven't forgotten that I was coming in tomorrow."

"No." I yawned. "In fact, I tidied up yesterday for you."

"Thanks, Mr. Clean. Look at you. A host. I never would have thought."

"I try." A text came through, vibrating in my ear. It was Dr. Kimberly, alerting me about another possible lead on our guy.

"Do you need to get that?" she asked.

"What? Oh, that was just Dave asking me if I'd talked to you about Thanksgiving."

"So, he told you about my request?"

"Yeah, I'm okay with it. I told him we could have it over here."

"Thank you so much, Tryke. That was nice of you."

"Hold off on thanking me. I only said I'd provide the location. You have to do the cooking."

"Of course I will. I'm excited actually. I've never cooked Thanksgiving dinner before. Wait, come to think of it, I've never even cooked for you."

I pictured her beautiful smile and her entrancing impassioned blue eyes. When she got excited, her eyes brightened, giving off the impression I was staring into a beaming blue sky. It was the closest I would ever come to a good dream.

"I'm looking forward to it. Actually I'm relieved. I don't have time to order a turkey from Gordon Market this late."

"I'm just glad we'll finally be together. I miss you."

"I miss you too," I said.

"My parents are calling. I'll see you tomorrow, okay? Tryke… okay?"

"I'll be here, don't worry."

After I hung up the phone, I brought up Dr. Kimberly's text, reading the extremely long message in full. From the contents it was obvious she had been on the internet all morning and listening nonstop to the scanner.

Holy cow, a lot of people die every day. I won't bore you with the numbers but… really? My scanner has been nonstop, I don't know how y'all do it sometimes. So… I've been on the phone with every hospital in the city practically, searching for leads. With everything I've gathered, I think I have his Thanksgiving visit narrowed down to a couple of nursing homes. Call me.

I wasn't convinced, and besides, I had a holiday to host. She would have to manage this stakeout without me. I was behind on all of my endeavors. And once Lesley arrived tomorrow I was gridlocked until she went back to school. The thing that was bugging me the most was identifying Randal, and his connection to my dad. Until Lesley arrived, that was my focus. I would handle the Elderly Slayer after Thanksgiving. There were still two more holidays remaining, and Dr. Kimberly's fantasy detective work wasn't a threat to this guy.

A row of frowning faces was followed by a few exclamation points when I texted Dr. Kimberly back, advising that I wouldn't be joining her. I told her I'd make it up to her after the holiday and she replied with, "You better" and a smiley face.

Knowing coffee wasn't strong enough to keep me awake while reading, I popped open an energy drink and began the long and strenuous quest through the journals. I started by circling every passage with the name Randal in it, intending to reread them later in hopes of discovering his connection to my dad.

By three in the morning I was exhausted, my eyes were burning, and I was ready to trash the entire lot. I was no closer to figuring out how this Randal guy fit into my dad's life. When I tossed the three journals onto my desk, one fell over the side onto the floor. I got up from my chair and stretched my aching back. When I bent down to snatch up the journal that had fallen, a scribble caught my eye on the inside back cover. I picked it up and examined it. The handwriting was not my dad's. I couldn't believe it when I first saw it. I stretched my eyes, focusing on the cursive. It was my mom's handwriting. My eyes were so fatigued I must have overlooked it.

Jake Randal, Fortune 322.

With a sudden burst of energy, I pulled up Google maps on my computer and typed in the address, 322 Fortune. Fortune popped up but not a three hundred block. Maybe it was in another city. I broadened the search. Still nothing. I was stumped, my brief bout of energy quickly fading. Sighing, I propped my feet up onto the desk, closed my eyes, and placed both hands behind my head. What now?

After a few minutes of sulking, I opened my eyes and laughed out loud at myself. My exhaustion had numbed my brain, keeping the obvious at bay. I typed in Jake Randal in the Yellow pages. None of the results matched the Fortune street address. Fortune may have been something else entirely: a phrase, a wish, anything. I wrote down each of the addresses for Jake Randal. At least it was a start.

• • •

I managed to get two hours of sleep. Lesley said she'd be in by five, which gave me eight hours to find Jake Randal. I put each of the addresses that I had found into the GPS on my phone while waiting for the pot of coffee to finish brewing. A cold front was moving in and with it came rain clouds that threatened an ice storm — an added complication to my already difficult situation. I slipped on my jacket, grabbed my Styrofoam cup of coffee, and set out to the first address.

I could feel the nerves rattling around in my stomach with each sip of coffee. I wasn't sure what I was going to uncover, if anything. I was reluctant to open new doors, but something was urging me forward. Lesley arriving today definitely added to my anxiety. It had been a few months since we'd seen one another and I didn't know how I was supposed to act, having never dated anyone long-distance before. What if she's changed? She sounded the same on the phone, but in person, face to face was the real test.

The first address was an apartment building in a part of town that I'd normally not venture into without some sort of weapon by my side. Thankfully, probably due to the weather, no one was outside this early. I rang the doorbell and stepped back and to the side — a habit I've learned since becoming a medic — you never know what might be hidden behind the other side of locked solid doors.

Through a cracked open chained door, a young woman peered out and said, "What do you want?"

"I'm looking for Jake Randal. He's a friend of my parents."

"There ain't no Jake living here." She slammed the door shut and immediately slid the deadbolt into its slot.

Okay, one down.

I had no luck at the next two addresses either, though the rudeness was a little less severe. One was a widow, the other a man in his twenties. I guess I was lucky people were even answering the doors. I figured the reason was that it was the day before a holiday. Most families were expecting relatives to arrive from out of town and the lonely were hopeful an unexpected guest would come knocking. In my experience, the holidays either made people really happy or really pissed off.

On the way to the next address I stopped by a gas station to refill my coffee. It was already after lunch and I had two addresses left, leaving me a few more hours remaining on the clock.

The next address was located in a gated community. When I approached the gate, a man in his fifties exited the guard shack with a clipboard in hand. I rolled down my window and smiled. "How are you this cold morning?" I asked.

He greeted me back with a friendly smile. "Fine, sir. Where ya heading?"

"755 Willow Bend, Jake Randal's house."

He scanned his clipboard and said, "Sir, I don't have a Jake Randal at that address. Are you sure you have the right neighborhood?"

"Yes," I said. I lowered my head and sighed.

"Sir, are you all right?" he asked, stepping closer to my vehicle.

I shook my head and lowered my voice, slowly lifting my head and staring out my front windshield. "My dad recently passed away and left this address in an old notebook of his." I turned toward him. "I didn't get to know him while he was alive and I was hoping to find out more about his life."

He seemed to be mulling over my words. A few seconds later he said, "All right. You got ten minutes and if the owner of the house at that address hasn't contacted me at the gate, I'm coming looking for you."

He smiled but I could tell he was serious about tracking me down. "Deal. Thank you very much."

He nodded and waved me through. People loved a heartrending story around the holidays, and a search for further meaning of a dead loved one even more.

A white Oldsmobile that looked like it hadn't been moved in years sat in the driveway of the address. I parked behind it and made my way through a path of dead potted plants surrounding a rusted wrought iron railing to the front door. So far the place didn't look too promising. I rang the doorbell, unable to hear the familiar tone beyond the door. No one immediately answered, so I knocked, thinking the doorbell might be broken. Still no answer. I leaned over, peering through the open blinds, but was unable to see much through the grimy window.

With only one address left, I wasn't ready to give up easily. I looked down at my watch. I still had five more minutes before the security guard would come looking for me. I knocked and rang the doorbell again. Through the door I heard a man's voice.

"Hold your horses. I'm coming." The deadbolt unlocked, and then the door swung open. An elderly man was standing behind a screen door, wielding a metal cane and staring at me through a pair of thick glasses.

"How can I help you?" he asked in a friendly but stern voice.

"Are you Jake Randal?" I asked, stepping closer so he could see my face.

"Who's asking?"

"Tryke Harper, sir. My dad was Henry Harper. He was a friend of Jake's."

He squinted through his spectacles toward me, and then nudged open the screen door with his cane. I moved down the short steps, giving way to the door. He eased outside and said, "He doesn't live here anymore. Supposedly, he went nuts and killed his wife and daughter years ago. Violently, I was told, but I didn't push for specifics. I got the house cheap, as you can imagine."

I didn't know what to say. Though I didn't know this Jake Randal, I was shocked by the news. I still wasn't sure if this was the same guy that my dad knew.

"That's…" I sighed. "I don't know what to say. That's horrible news."

"Not much one *can* say about things like that."

"I don't suppose you could tell me what happened to him, you know… after?"

"Not sure. I reckon he's in jail if I had to guess. If it'll help you I've received a few pieces of mail over the years with his name on it, forwarded from another address."

"That *would* help. Do you mind?"

"Not at all. I hope it helps you find what you're searching for. Come in for a minute and get out of the cold."

I stepped inside and into the entryway, letting the screen door creek slowly shut behind me. The walls were barren and the wooden floor I was standing on looked like it hadn't seen oil since it had been placed there.

"Give me a second to find it. I'll be right back," he said, moseying toward the next room over.

"Thanks," I said. I felt a little creeped out as I pictured the violence that occurred in the house. I didn't know where the killings took place, but I was sure each of the walls held their own stories of violence, their own hollow screams of the innocent. When I peeked around the wall into the dining room, I thought I saw drops of blood on the baseboard, but it was probably nothing. There are people who clean murder scenes of this magnitude for a living, and they wouldn't leave something so obvious. But… people are sometimes sloppy and careless. I was curious. A few steps into the room I heard his cane thumping the floor, drawing closer. I quickly stepped back into the entryway just as he rounded the corner. He handed me a small piece of paper with an address scribbled on it.

"Here you go, son," he said, opening the screen door for me to exit.

"Thanks again," I said. Before I stepped out into the cold, I glanced down at the address. I stifled a smile. I recognized it as an office complex, but that wasn't what had me going. It was the 322 written next to Suite.

I thanked the guard before leaving. He waved and let out a boisterous "Happy Thanksgiving" as I drove off.

• • •

After roaming through the labyrinth of office buildings, I finally found the correct one. I placed my truck in park and switched the radio off. This was it, another diverted path to travel down. A part of me didn't want to venture any further. I could go home and burn all of the journals, and that would be the end to all of this. I could then live out the rest of my days as I had been doing this past summer. But that wasn't me. I couldn't continue with my laid out path knowing that more pieces of this constantly changing puzzle were out there somewhere. I needed to know, if only to keep my sanity.

The elevator music was a pleasant distraction, but I couldn't say the same for the horrible cologne the suit beside me had slathered on. I held my breath to the third floor, and with full cheeks of air, nodded to the man before exiting the cramped space.

314, 318, and there it was, suite number 322. Before entering, I read the plaque beside the door: Dr. Leonard Fortune. Well, that explained the Fortune part. Now to find the missing piece, Jake Randal. There was no abbreviation on the plaque beside his name, leaving me clueless as to the type of doctor this guy was. I assumed, due to my dad's bout with cancer and heart disease, that this Dr. Fortune was some sort of specialist.

No turning back now. I was committed. I turned the metal doorknob and entered. The waiting room appeared normal for a doctor's office: an elderly lady covered her mouth with a tissue, a young boy about the age of eight sat alone and playing a handheld video game, and an eclectic mix of magazines littered a small table in the corner.

A female receptionist looked up from behind a piece of glass and slid it open. "How can I help you, sir?"

"Uh, yes." I cleared my throat, stepping closer to the window. "I was wondering if I might speak with Dr. Fortune."

"Did you have an appointment?"

"No, ma'am. I just need a moment of his time."

"Dr. Fortune is very busy, sir. If you want to see him, you'll have to make an appointment."

"Can you just give him a message for me? And if he still doesn't want to see me, I'll make an appointment."

She sighed loudly and pulled a pen from inside her globe of puffy hair. "What's the message?"

"I was a close friend of Jake Randal. I want to make things right." I didn't know if it would work, but the message was vague enough to hopefully spark curiosity.

I sat next to the young boy and waited. I noticed that he hadn't looked up once since I entered the room. He was completely oblivious to his surroundings, totally immersed in the safe world of his video game. I envied him as I anxiously waited for a response from the receptionist. I glanced over at the stack of magazines, but I was too nervous to read. I just stared at the ticking clock on the wall, watching the seconds waste away. It was already four o'clock, which left me one hour before Lesley arrived.

A few minutes later, the door beside the sliding glass window opened and a tall man who looked to be in his sixties entered the waiting room. He was wearing a boring brown tie and loafers to match. He had a thick head of brown hair that I was sure was a toupee. He pulled his round spectacles down to the bridge of his nose and stared toward me.

"Sir, come back please," he said, holding the door open for me. "Second office on the left."

The room was peaceful: soft lighting, full living room set of furniture, and an inlayed bookshelf set against the far wall and overfilled with various books. I sat down on the worn leather couch and he took a seat across from me in a dark red chair under an overhanging glass lamp.

"Can I get you something to drink?" he asked in a soft voice.

"No, thank you."

"So how did you know Dr. Randal?" he asked while crossing his legs. "Were you a patient of his?"

"No, but I believe my dad was. After he died, I found several of his journals and Dr. Randal was mentioned quite often in them. My dad had cancer and a few other ailments in the end. There were some discrepancies in his diagnosis and I was hoping I could get in touch with Dr. Randal and clear them up."

Denial can be a fun game, right up until the words are uttered to yank you back to reality.

"You do know what type of doctor Jake is, don't you?"

"I wasn't sure, no."

"Psychiatrist."

Chapter 14

When Dr. Fortune said the word "psychiatrist," I felt a
sudden heaviness in my chest and a swirl of dizziness
surrounding thoughts that were sprinting in multiple
directions. The news changed everything, but also nothing
at the same time. Actually, all it did at the moment was
cause mass confusion. I managed to quickly regain my
composure, shuffling in the chair and staring out the
window.

"Are you all right?" Dr. Fortune asked. "Are you sure
there's nothing I can get you? Some water perhaps?"

"No, really I'm fine. Thank you for asking." I turned
back toward him, attempting to steady my words. "I was
just thinking… It explains a lot, him seeing a psychiatrist."
But it didn't. It opened up an entirely new journal of
questions. Not to mention angry slurs toward my dad for
writing me a false letter. What was he thinking? More
importantly, what was he hiding?

"A lot of people see us when they are facing terminal
illnesses such as cancer. I only have a few minutes, but

maybe I could answer a question or two for you. First, I have to assume you don't know what happened to Dr. Randal. Why else would you be here looking for him?"

I wrinkled my brow, attempting to appear confused.

"Well, this may be hard to hear, but Dr. Randal was accused of killing his family."

"Whoa! Really?"

"It was all over the news. I'm surprised you didn't hear about it. A tragedy in every sense of the word."

"Well," I leaned over and lowered my eyes toward the floor, "I wasn't expecting to hear news like that."

"I don't expect many people do. So, what questions might I try and answer for you, Mr. Harper?"

I didn't reply immediately. I was stalling. "Did you two share patients and office space?" It was all I could come up with at the moment. I knew what I wanted to ask, but there was no way he was going to give me patient records. Still, it was a valid question. What if he did treat my dad once or twice while Dr. Randal was out sick?

"Patients, no. Office space, yes, for many years. We actually went to medical school together." He stared toward the window. I presumed he was remembering Dr. Randal from a time before he decided to murder his family.

"I don't suppose you could tell me where Dr. Randal's patient files are."

"I'm afraid not. But you could ask him yourself."

"Huh? He's not in jail?"

"God knows he should be for what he did. No, he's doing his time in the Boland Asylum on Gregory Street. Here, I'll get you in." He went to his desk and retrieved a prescription pad. I took the folded piece of paper from him. Odd, I thought, how readily he handed me a pass to see Dr. Randal. Maybe he sensed my desperation. "Give this to the nurse over there. They'll let you visit him, briefly."

"Thanks, this is very decent of you."

"Tell him George will be over soon."

"Sure thing."

• • •

I made it back home just before five. Thankfully, Lesley was running a few minutes late because of last-minute travelers on the road. As I waited at the kitchen table in silence, my stomach knotted with anticipation. I dreaded change. And since Lesley was part of my life now, change in her was not welcome either. What if things were different between us? Also wiggling around, nestled alongside that uncertainty, was the recent disturbing news that may end up changing what I knew about my dad. I had to keep things in perspective, handle one thing at a time, or I'd lose all control.

The doorbell rang. I avoided answering it as long as possible. When I opened the door, Lesley set her suitcase down and lunged toward me, squeezing her arms around my neck and lightly kissing the lobe of my left ear. I thought the familiarity would return instantly. I thought I would experience the good feelings I felt after our first date. But there was a strangeness about the embrace that I couldn't explain. Was it her? Was it me? Or was it the time spent apart? We just needed time to reacquaint ourselves, get back in a groove. I was sure that was it.

She sensed my apprehension, holding me at arms length. "What is it? Aren't you happy to see me?"

"Of course I am." I quickly pulled her in for another hug.

"Okay..." She removed her coat. "You seem distracted. Are you sure everything is all right?" She stared at me with her captivating blue eyes, studying me.

"I'm fine." I kissed her, longer than I normally would, so I wouldn't have to explain further.

"Okay, then." She changed the subject and walked toward the kitchen. "Let's see what you have in your perpetually barren cupboards, and we'll make a list for the store." I grabbed her suitcase and purse and placed them in my bedroom. She continued talking to me from down the hall, in the kitchen. "I talked to Angie and told them three o'clock. I hope that's okay with you."

"Fine with me," I said as I rounded the corner to the kitchen. "You're doing the cooking, remember?"

"Yeah, but not alone. I thought we could do it together." She spotted my reluctance. "Come on, at least part of it. It'll be fun."

I agreed to play a small role in the cooking process. Maybe I'd baste the turkey, or put the rolls in the oven. I think I could manage that without screwing it up.

• • •

After we returned from the store and prepped everything for tomorrow's dinner, it was time for drinks. I was pleasantly surprised by how well we were getting along. We seemed to adjust to one another quickly after the initial shock wore off. I joined her on the couch in the living room and handed her a glass of port.

She took a soft sip and then set the glass on the table beside her. "So, what do you want to do?" she said.

I shrugged, "We could have one of our deep discussions, you know, for old times' sake." She didn't seem interested. She was expecting me to say something else. But what? Here we go again with these games of mind reading in which I fail every time. I thought we would have been past this stage by now.

She shook her head and smiled. "Keep going."

"Keep going? You mean… guessing what *you* want to do?" She nodded. As I sat there staring at her, attempting to unravel her riddle, I couldn't help but think how flawlessly beautiful she was: her dark shoulder length hair outlining her perfect pale face and round cheek bones, the curves of her hips in her jeans, down to her recently manicured toes painted blood red and drawing me in. I missed her soft wet lips caressing mine and guiding me.

"Well?" she said, taking another sip from her glass.

I downed the rest of my drink. "I haven't the slightest." But I did have an idea, though I wasn't completely sure it was what she had in mind. If I started stripping her clothes off, she might think I was some sort of pervert. I thought women liked to take their time, wanting us to move in slowly. That's what I'd learned so far, or what I think I learned. But with all the times I've been wrong in the past, I also knew there were no absolutes when it came to the opposite sex.

She stood and grabbed my hand, lifting me to an embrace. She rested her head on my chest and began slow dancing. There was no music playing, but I went along with it anyway. The familiar scent of her milky flesh caressed my senses, sparking memories of us together. I don't know why I hadn't noticed it during that first hug when Lesley first arrived. The nerves must have blocked my senses.

She began kissing my neck and then ran her tongue lightly up to my ear and whispered, "How about now? Any ideas?"

"A few," I said, closing my eyes, feeling a tingling down my legs and back up my spine as she continued softly breathing in my ear. "But I think they're best relayed to you in a more private setting."

"Nah, Earl is watching the back of his eyelids. I don't think he'll mind if you scream a little."

I smirked as she leaned in to kiss me. I had my right hand lightly gripping the back of her hair. I weaved the strands through two of my fingers and firmly pulled her lips onto mine. She yanked her head away, wielding a devious smile and said, "So, it's like that tonight? Okay." She slapped me on the back of my thigh and slung off her shirt, exposing her black lace bra. She abruptly covered her breasts with crossed hands and took off toward my bedroom. Before I pursued her down the hallway, I glanced down at Earl and shook my head at his unwavering ability to relax and ignore all others. He lay on his back, his eyes firmly shut with all four paws hanging lazily in mid-air.

• • •

The next morning Lesley got up early, around six, and put the turkey into the oven. I stayed up with her, drinking coffee at the table and reading the news on my laptop. I couldn't sleep anyway, not with the information I'd received less than twenty-four hours ago. My dad had gone through the trouble to write me a letter, seal it, and hand it to my uncle with instructions to not give it to me until I was ready. Only to tell me he never sought help for the voices, and that it was okay for me to do so. But why? None of it made sense.

After Lesley thanked me for a wonderful night, reminding me it was my turn next time to do the screaming, we spent the rest of the morning in deep conversation about what we had been doing the last few months. It was mostly her talking about medical school and me listening to her animated stories. I heard about her dorm mate, Darcy, who constantly got on her nerves. Supposedly, she was stuck in the "80s Valley Girl" phase and used the word "like" and the phrase "as if" in every sentence, usually while whining about something. But by far the most annoying phrase she used was "gag me with a spoon." I laughed when Lesley imitated a few sentences.

Then she began her tales about Gross Anatomy class.

"You know how we always talked about the soul being trapped in these waste disposal systems?" she said.

"Yeah."

"Seeing the inner workings is quite amazing, don't get me wrong. But once it's empty, the body looks like a dilapidated haunted house."

"Great analogy," I said. "It *is* kind of odd and creepy.

One second we're reminiscing, the next we're floating off to another dimension and leaving our capsule behind."

"Crazy," she said, glancing over at the clock on the wall. It was just past noon. "Well, if we're going to dive into one of our lengthy philosophical conversations, we'll have to wait until later. I need to get dinner ready. You know Dave, he'll be early."

"Okay. We have all night."

"Yes, we do," she said smiling, and gave me a long kiss on the lips. "I'm glad we're together."

"Me too."

As Lesley predicted, Dave and Angie showed up forty-five minutes early. When I opened the door, Angie greeted me with a hug and handed me a small bag with a pie inside. Dave gave me a firm handshake after handing me two bottles of wine. Coddled under his right arm was a twelve-pack of his favorite cheap beer.

"Come on, man, not even on a holiday?" I said, shaking my head at the beer. I looked over at Angie. "Thanks for bringing the wine and pie."

"You're welcome. You know him and his cheap beer. I can't pry it from his hands," Angie said. "I've tried, and my dad did too, earlier. He offered him a twenty-year-old Scotch and Dave turned it down."

"You should have invited your dad over here and left Dave with your mom."

"Come on, man, cut me some slack," Dave said, shoving the beer into my hands and taking back the two bottles of wine. "Put it on some ice, will ya? Thanks."

Wearing my mom's apron and with her dark hair pulled into a ponytail, Lesley emerged from the kitchen. She was beaming, completely unaware of her intoxicating beauty. Dave scaled past me and greeted Lesley with a huge hug, hovering a little too long. Lesley looked over at Angie while Dave had his hands wrapped around her, and whispered "Sorry." I laughed, but Angie didn't seem as amused by

Dave's overt flirting.

"Ignore him," I told Angie. "He's just trying to get a rise out of me."

"You wish," Dave said.

"Anyway, it smells wonderful in here," Angie said.

"Thank you, but I had help," Lesley said.

"She's just being modest," I said. "Lesley did everything. All I did was put the rolls in the oven."

"However it came together, thank y'all for doing it," Angie said, following Lesley into the kitchen.

Dave and I moseyed into the dining room and talked over a drink.

Thirty minutes later, Lesley placed the golden brown turkey in front of me on a silver platter. My mom had used it on every holiday since I can remember: turkey, smoked ham. Dave and I helped bring the rest of the fixings from the kitchen, along with the chilled wine.

Dave stood and tapped his wine glass, which was filled with beer, and said, "I'd like to make a toast before Tryke butchers that beautiful turkey Lesley cooked to perfection." He glanced over at Lesley and raised his eyebrows up and down and then lifted his glass in the air. "To my wonderful wife and our awesome friends. May our holidays be forever cheery."

We all raised our glasses and toasted him back. "Thanks, Dave, for that… insightful toast," I said.

"You're welcome. Now carve the turkey already, will ya," Dave said.

I had never carved a turkey. After my dad passed, my mother stopped cooking on the holidays, never allowing me the honor of carving the bird. I stood up at the end of the table, recently sharpened knife in hand, and hovered over the turkey while planning out a cutting strategy. My phone vibrated on the buffet table across the room, breaking my concentration. It was a short, single vibration. A text. I ignored it and kept my focus on the bird. Halfway through the first cut — which I decided would be the leg for no other reason than because there were two of them, just in case the first one didn't go so well — my phone vibrated again, this time twice in a row. Lesley got up from the table and picked up my phone. I continued cutting, now on the second leg. I was proud of my first cuts.

"I didn't mean to look at the message, but I couldn't help but notice the name, Kimberly," Lesley said with a tenseness in her voice. She set the phone back down on the counter.

"Great," I said, sighing. "I told her not to text me over the holidays."

"Who is she?" Lesley asked, but something in her voice was hesitant, as if she didn't really want an answer.

I looked across the table. Dave and Angie were both staring intently, as if waiting for the climax to a movie. Lesley was standing a few feet to my right, hands by her side. They weren't yet on her hips, thankfully.

"She works at Mercy," I said. I didn't know what to say. Nothing had happened between us. Why was I so uneasy about revealing a simple friendship? I didn't know what the message said, but I was pretty sure it wasn't incriminating in that sense.

"And, is she someone I need to be worried about?" Lesley asked.

"Of course not. I mean, worried for what?" I said attempting to sound dumbfounded by the entire event.

The phone vibrated again. I cringed inside. What the heck could be so damn important?

"Don't you think you should check the message?" Lesley said, now clearly irritated.

"I do," Dave chimed in. Thanks, Dave.

She tossed me my phone. Four messages from Dr. Kimberly. I had missed one from earlier.

I think I was right. I don't know what I should do. Call me soon, please.

Crap, where are you?
He saw me.
If you don't hear from me in an hour, come look for me!

What the hell was she up to? I had to control my expressions, they were all staring at me. Lesley was attempting to analyze my response. If she had only seen the first message, it could easily be explained as a curious patient we brought in. She had to buy my reason, and I had to be quick.

"She was excited about a patient is all. We brought a man in a few weeks ago, in a coma. And supposedly he came out of it," I said.

Lesley looked over at Dave for assurance. He could save me with one phrase. But it wasn't his place to save me, nor should he be put in that position.

"Dave was still on his honeymoon when I brought the patient in," I said quickly. Dave looked relieved, blood returning to his pallid face.

Lesley sighed.

I shrugged and tossed the phone to her. As it hovered in the air, I heard it vibrate once more. I was doomed, no matter the content of the text. If I explained about the Elderly Slayer, everything would be exposed, including Dr. Kimberly and me averting the law. I would have to take this one in the gut. But what was my story? How would I explain the other texts? She caught the phone and scrolled through the messages.

She placed the phone on the counter, ducked her head, and walked away. I was stuck in place, unable to move. My instinct was to go after her, but I couldn't. Dave's head was pointed at his empty plate. Angie stared at me pleadingly, waiting for me to take off after Lesley. Angie didn't wait long. She marched into the other room to search for her distressed friend.

I picked up the phone and read the latest text:
I need you.

I didn't have a witty explanation. I had to take whatever was coming. It was pertinent to my survival.

"Man, is that the blonde at Mercy? The doctor?" Dave asked.

Sighing, I said, "Yes. But it's not what Lesley thinks it is."

"Then tell her."

"It won't do any good. It's… complicated."

"Oh. Well, in that case, I don't know what to tell you," Dave said.

Standing with her suitcase in hand next to my front door, Lesley stared at me with aching wet eyes, awaiting a last-second explanation. I hated seeing her upset. If only I could sit her down and explain it all. I felt the ripping and tearing inside that everyone whined about. I felt the emptiness absorbing me with each tear rolling down her face. I wanted to reach out for her. But I just stood there in the hallway, pathetically helpless, and didn't utter a word. And neither did Lesley. She turned and walked out the front door.

Chapter 15

Like everything else in my life, it all happened quickly and coldly. I sat at the table, alone, just me and the untouched Thanksgiving spread. Dave and Angie left immediately following the incident. I told Dave we'd speak at work.

Halfway through a glass of Scotch, I remembered the cause of the entire ruined event — the texts. I had been diving so far into the depths of self loathing that I completely forgot about them. Why not pile on the shit and see where it leads me? I dialed Dr. Kimberly's phone number.

"Where have you been? I almost got myself killed," she said, answering immediately before the first ring ended.

"Hello to you, too," I said. "Wait, what? How?"

"My hunch was right. I decided to go inside and scope the place out before the stakeout. I figured I could get away with it being Thanksgiving. Well, I found the bastard. I caught him in the room about to administer the damn cyanide!"

"How did you know it was him?"

"I saw the vial in his hand. He was about to pour the substance in a man's glass on his bedside table."

"What did you do?"

"I froze in place. I could literally feel my legs shaking. Tryke, you should have seen the stare this guy had. It was cold, emotionless. I have never been so scared in my life."

"Did you get a good look at him?"

"You mean before I took off running? Yeah, actually I did, but most of his features were covered up. He was wearing a janitor's uniform with a baseball cap, the brim hovered over a pair of thick glasses. I didn't see enough of him to make an ID."

"What color was the uniform?"

"Color, why?"

"I'm not sure yet. Do you remember?"

"Green, I believe."

He was there that day in the nursing home. Clyde had to nearly push the guy out of our way. He must have dialed 9-1-1 and then gave the medication minutes before we arrived, watching as we attempted to revive the elderly lady. So, he *was* a voyeur. I hadn't seen the guy's face very well either that day. I couldn't remember if he was wearing glasses or not. It didn't matter, because once I saw him in person, there would be no mistaking. I remember his build and demeanor, two things not easily disguised, especially when one isn't trying to deceive, but is relaxing in their residence.

"Well?" said Dr. Kimberly. "Did it ring any bells?"

"No, nothing. Where are you now?"

"Home. With all my doors locked and the alarm set."

"So, are you done playing detective?"

"Alone, yes. But I'd still be up for it if you were to come with me."

Hmm, tenacious. She wasn't giving up. I thought she only wanted to see this guy and then let the police handle it. Whatever she was up to, I had to go along with it until I had time to catch him.

"Did you call the police?" I asked.

"Yes, and gave a brief statement. Dammit, I knew I shouldn't have, but I panicked."

"You saved somebody's life is what you did."

I had to act fast. The police would begin digging and most likely reopen the case, depending on what was found at the scene.

"I guess you're right," she said.

"Did you mention anything to the police about the Elderly Slayer case?"

"I'm not that stupid, Tryke."

"I didn't think you had. I was just curious because you said you'd panicked earlier. You might have slipped."

"I can assure you I didn't."

"What *did* you tell them?"

"Just that I was visiting a friend and some creepy guy was harassing me."

"I take it the guy was gone before the police arrived, and they didn't catch him."

"I doubt it. He most likely took off out the back hallway door when I screamed and ran."

Relieved that she hadn't alerted the police, I laughed and said, "Little Ms. Stakeout ran screaming. I don't believe it."

"Well, believe it. It was freaking scary."

We talked a while longer. I told her about my failed attempt at Thanksgiving, not relaying that it was her text that caused the situation to crumble. A "spat" is the word I chose to describe the situation. When I mentioned Lesley, she seemed to shrug off the idea that I had a girlfriend. When I told her that Lesley left angry, she offered womanly advice, telling me to let her be, meaning alone. I suppose it was sound advice. It was my plan anyhow, though I suspect her intentions were much different.

Before I hung up, she relentlessly pressed me to join her

for an early dinner. I finally gave in and met her at a nearby Oriental restaurant.

• • •

The restaurant was surprisingly busy. I guess we weren't the only lonely people out there.

"Thanks for coming," Dr. Kimberly said, removing her coat and setting it in the booth beside her. "I didn't feel safe being alone. I would have invited you to my house, but I thought you might feel a little weird after what just happened to you."

"I'm fine with this," I said. I wasn't really hungry. My mind was too cluttered, causing unease and queasiness. At the top of that clutter was Lesley leaving. I wanted her to call. I wanted her to disrupt this meal. But I knew that would never happen. Things like that only happen in the movies.

"This place is busier than I thought it would be," she said.

"Because this life is a plague."

"That's a dark way of putting things."

"All right, Miss Rays of Rainbow Bliss. What's your take on the world?"

She smiled and shifted her dark blonde hair to her right side. "I've *had* my share of disappointments in life. In fact, things were very dim for many years."

I took a swig of the diet Coke that our waitress had just set down beside me and anxiously awaited her tale. "What dimness was in your life?"

"Well, to start off, I was adopted by a wonderful and wealthy couple when I was very young —"

"That doesn't sound so horrible. Sorry, go on."

She smiled, "Anyway…when I was in high school, they traveled to Europe. While they were over there, they were killed in a train wreck."

"Okay, now *that* is horrible."

"So, the next year after they died, some man calls me out of the blue and tells me he's my father. Of course I didn't believe him…at first. But then he told me some things that made sense about my adopted parents. Long story short, he told me my mom died giving birth to me and he wanted to be part of my life. Once I did some digging and found out he was my real dad, I was excited that I would get to meet him."

She didn't seem to want to finish her story. There was something aching to come out, but she wasn't ready to share it. Not with me, anyway.

"I take it y'all haven't been living happily ever after as a family?" I said.

"Let's just say that after the newness wore off, he wasn't some brave knight riding in to save his daughter."

"Okay, so it's been a little rough for you. But you still haven't explained your positive outlook, the secret to a gleaming life of joy."

"There's no secret. I just don't let the bad times take over my life. Why should they be more powerful than my desires?"

"I see your point, that is, if everything is in the past. But what if the battle is still waging?"

"I have more dark tales, believe me, and some are still going on. I take them as they come." She shrugged. "I guess I really don't think about things as much as I used to."

"Brave of you, not letting them in. I wish I could do the same."

I'd tried many times in the past to ignore the Gamemakers, but they always seemed to find a way back in. Finally, I just accepted their challenge.

"You can." She reached her hand across the table. The waitress saved me by bringing our meals.

"Thank you," I told the waitress. Dr. Kimberly didn't appear as thankful to receive her food. She forced a smile when the waitress put the plate of food in front of her.

"So, what's *your* darkness?" she asked, unfolding her napkin and placing it in her lap.

I have a lab where I release dirty souls. I've been in a constant battle with the Gamemakers ever since they stole my entire family. And that's just the beginning.

"My parents were also taken from me, along with my sister."

"So we're both hitchhikers on our way to a better place."

"I hope so." And I did. I have always pondered the other side, desperately desiring a fair battle one day.

We finished our meal, then stood outside under the blue and white awning of the restaurant. The temperature had dropped and the dark clouds that were farther to the east when we arrived had sneaked overhead and began slinging a mixture of rain and sleet down, thumping the canvas above us.

"So, what now?" she asked. "Are you going back home to a cold and lonely house?"

"I have Earl, my dog. He's not much for conversation, but —"

"Come on, we can have drinks at my house by a roaring fire," she offered, pulling her coat snugly around her, teeth chattering.

"Tempting, but... I have to —, sorry, one second." I pulled my vibrating phone from my pocket and read the page-long text sent by Lesley.

I'm sorry for leaving without talking, but what could I have said? You left me no choice by staying silent about the text. I am hurting and stressed and... I really don't know what else. Confused, I guess. Maybe it's better I stay away for a while until you figure out things. Bye for now.

The words were cold, harsh, and they stung. I was definitely not an expert, nor slick when it came to women. I didn't have a sly comment to keep her going. If she wanted to stay away, fine. I placed the phone back in my pocket.

"Do you have Scotch?"

• • •

Dr. Kimberly's home was modestly decorated for someone on a physician's salary. I was expecting marble floors and huge paintings on the walls; maybe even a tapestry or two. Instead, it was quaint and very… orange. She shed her jacket and placed it on the wooden coat rack next to the door, and then proceeded to remove mine before I had the chance to object.

"I take it you like orange," I said, stepping into the living room

"I like fall, the whole pumpkin thing, leaves… you know anything in a patch."

"Sure." If you wanted to live inside a pumpkin, then, okay.

"I'll be right back. Make yourself at home. On the rocks, I presume?"

"Yeah, thanks."

She left the room. When she returned a few minutes later, she was carrying two glasses. One was a frilly cocktail.

"Have a seat on the couch while I light a fire." She leaned down and turned the gas knob next to the fireplace. She pulled a canister from atop the mantle and retrieved a long matchstick from inside and lit the logs.

"Do you always have logs already in the fireplace?" I asked, and then sat on the corner seat of the couch.

"Most of the time, yes. I like to be prepared for cold nights. A good book, or… conversation," she smiled and then abruptly looked away, "completes a warm, crackling fire nicely." She laughed. "Sorry for being cheesy, but I'm a nerd at heart."

"Nah, I get it. A cozy fire is nice."

She moved the small coffee table off the brown and orange rug and sat on the floor next to the fireplace.

"Come down here. I have an idea."

"Okay…" I said, edging off the couch and then onto the floor, trying not to spill my drink. "What are we doing?"

"A game. More precisely, a drinking game."

"I'm listening." The sleet and rain mixture was really coming down outside, now steadily tapping on the windowpane.

"The rules are simple. We guess something about the other, and if the person guessing is right, then the other takes a drink. If the guess is wrong, then the person who asked the question drinks. Got it?"

"Okay, simple enough. But I don't think the drinks are equal," I said.

"Sorry, you chose your drink." She raised her eyebrows and shrugged. "I'll go first. House rules." She smiled and curled her legs under her, prepping for her first guess. "You've been a loner since you were little, frowning down at the world."

"Not exactly, but close enough," I said. I took a drink. "You have never given yourself enough credit."

"Too vague."

"Okay, you have never thought you were good enough as a person." She took a drink.

"We're starting a little deep. Let's lighten the mood," she suggested.

I shrugged. "Okay."

"You go out of your way to intimidate women on purpose." I shook my head. "So, it's not an act? Interesting." She took a drink.

"You secretly want to be a bad girl. Tattoos, biker, stripper maybe."

"Hmm." She raised her glass and stopped just before her lips. With her free hand, she removed the pin that was holding up her hair.

"No?" I took a sip from my glass. Without asking, she got up and went to the kitchen and returned with two bottles, one for me and the other her premixed drink. She poured me another, and topped off her own. "Thanks."

"Where were we? That's right, my turn. Let's venture back down a tad deeper." I shrugged again, beginning to feel the warmth of the first drink running along my veins. "You wanted to be a cop, but the structure didn't suit you."

I had to think about that one. The structure part was correct, but being a cop, no. Maybe a rogue detective. "Drink," I said.

"You like the dead. That's why you became a doctor." She stared at me, the flickering flames reflecting in her glasses. She mulled the words carefully, attempting to read me. "Drink," she said.

I took a sip. It definitely wasn't Scotch. "What is this stuff?" I flipped the bottle around. I had never heard of the brand. It was some cheap rot-gut whiskey.

"Sorry, that was the last of the good stuff."

"What are you trying to do to me? You know I still have to drive home."

With a devious smile, she shrugged and said, "We'll see."

I had an idea where she was heading with that smile, but I ignored its true meaning. I said, "I'm serious."

"All right, all right, one more round. Then we can take a break," she said.

I nodded. "My turn. Hmm…let's see. You have daddy issues." I blurted it out without thinking it completely through. I had already forgotten about the story she told me earlier about her father. Though she didn't elaborate about it, I should have known it was a sensitive issue. She lowered her head, resting her glass on the rug. "Sorry," I said. "I forgot. I didn't mean to —"

With her head still in a downward pose, she shifted her eyes up at me and lifted her glass to her mouth. "Don't be so intimidated by a girl." A smile slowly unfolded on her face. I smiled back, still unsure. "Yes, it's the same old story. Never good enough for father. I'm over it, but I do get tired of seeing the movies portray that it's only sons who can't live up to their fathers' standards."

"I guess that's one I never had to face." Lucky me, right. Not quite. A secret world hidden from me since childhood is far more elaborate of an issue to face.

She let go of her drink, letting it rest on the surface of the rug, and inched closer toward me. Through the window, twilight was drifting away and the sleet had slowed to a steady soft sprinkle. Thunder rumbled softly in the distance. My inhibitions were dangling somewhere outside in the cold.

The next thing I felt were wet lips pressed against my own. I tasted sweet cherry and rum. I felt her soft hands around my neck. I ran my hands through her silky hair, giving in to the seduction. She leaned back and slung off her glasses, whipping me gently with her hair, flinging floral scents of her perfume and shampoo into my nose.

She slid her legs smoothly over mine, placing herself firmly on top of me. She leaned back shoving my head into her breasts. Lifting my head with a soft grip of my hair, she pressed her cheek next to mine and moaned in my ear, gently sliding her tongue along the lobe. Just as her hands slid down my back and moved slyly around my waist to the front zipper, I said, "I can't."

"Sure you can," she whispered in my ear, obviously feeling the part of me that hadn't paid attention to my objection.

I grabbed her shoulders and held her out at arms' length. "I'm sorry. You're a beautiful woman, but this is bad timing."

She pushed me away with intense force and then stood up. Quickly tying her hair up in a knot, she said, "Get out."

I stayed seated, caught completely off guard by her sudden shift in mood. "Really?" She continued to glare at me. "Okay," I said, getting to my feet. I picked up my glass.

"Leave it."

"Kimberly, I didn't —" I should have strolled silently out the door when she first told me to.

"Didn't what? Mean to like me? Mean to kiss me and not love me? Mean to stay? Get out of my damn house!"

Chapter 16

Dr. Kimberly obviously had an issue with rejection that I was in no way suited to solve. I had never seen a woman that angry before. She was shaking mad. I didn't stick around and argue with her, thinking if I did, she might have strung me up in her dungeon, a place I felt sure was already overflowing with guests. Once again, we were alone, the Gamemakers and I, no family to distract and no women to answer to. My thin strand of stability, the strand once placed there by my mom and recently held together by Lesley, had now been yanked out from under me. I felt lost, as the influx of riddles flooded my head.

The next morning, I was distracted at work. Before I left the house, I was close to calling in sick so I could visit Dr. Randal at the asylum. I needed something, anything to put me back on some sort of track. I felt myself drifting into the Gamemakers' grasp. I pictured them smiling and rubbing their hands together during my brief moment of weakness.

Dave broke the awkward silence in the rig.

"Thanksgiving went like it was supposed to. Awkward

stares and angry outbursts."

I wanted to laugh, but I didn't have the energy. "Yeah, sorry about that," I said. "Did y'all get something to eat somewhere?"

"Only after Angie consoled Lesley for about an hour. We ate leftovers at my parents. And you?"

"I wasn't hungry."

"Yeah, about that. So…" I could tell he was thinking hard on how to proceed with questions about the texts that had started the whole mess. "What's so complicated about this Dr. Kimberly? And before you answer, just know I'm on your side, man."

"Thanks," I said. "It's actually not that complicated. I *innocently* gave her my number because I was curious about a coma patient I brought in. She called me a few times after, random things, and we became friends. And after the incident at Thanksgiving, I cut it off."

"That's it?" He smirked, obviously not believing my story. Maybe Clyde had said something to him. "How'd she take it?"

"Who? Dr. Kimberly?"

"Yeah, isn't that who we're talking about?"

"She didn't seem too fazed by it. She understood." I wanted to laugh at my own words as they left my mouth.

"Good then, so it's settled. I'll tell Angie to talk with Lesley and get y'all back together. I don't like being the third wheel around them two. And Christmas is right around the corner."

"I appreciate the offer, but I'll handle it in time. She needs to cool off a little while." And I needed time to sort things out.

"Man, you go from mysterious questionable sexuality, to man-whore."

"Friends, man, that's all it was. It's over now anyway," I said. "A man-whore, really?"

The MDT beeped. I looked down at the screen and read

aloud: "1711 Gilbert, Jumping Joy Daycare Center."

Dave sighed and said, "What for?" His apprehension was palpable. I could almost see the scenarios forming in a bubble above his head.

"A fall. Three-year-old," I said.

"All right, I think I can handle that."

Like Dave, I too get antsy when a call comes in at a daycare center. But not from being intimidated by having to work on a hurt child. Mine arises from the darker side of suspicion. Not *what* caused the injury but *who*.

A few minutes later, we arrived on scene and parked the rig under the awning where the parents pull through, like at a fast food joint, to pick up their children after work. I grabbed the pediatric bag while Dave carried the papoose board. Basically a smaller backboard with the ability to keep children restrained, keeping them from moving and further injuring themselves. A daycare worker met us at the double clear doors with a panicked look on her face.

"In here. Hurry! She looks like she's about to stop breathing!"

Dave's face instantly turned pallid and his hands began to tremble. "Go ahead in, Tryke. I'll grab the airway bag and monitor."

The smell of a daycare doesn't bring back nostalgic memories from my youth. Nor does it bring a smile to my face to see rainbows painted on the walls and white bunnies hopping aimlessly through a meadow. I see one thing: a distraction for a lurking monster methodically placed here by the Gamemakers.

The small room I was led into was relatively quiet, except for the audibly pained respirations coming from the hurt child sprawled out on the floor. Three female employees were on their knees, holding hands and surrounding the small girl. They looked as if they were performing some sort of séance. All three glanced back at me when I entered, desperate silent pleas seeping from their eyes, begging for help.

Dave came barging through the door and nearly knocked me to the ground. Through exasperated breaths, he said, "What happened?!" The three women quickly stood and moved to the side. He knelt down at the girl's head and began unwrapping the airway equipment. I grabbed the monitor and placed the fast pads on the child's small chest and back.

All three women began their spiel at once. "One please," Dave said. I did a quick trauma evaluation. There were no obvious injuries on the surface.

A female's voice — not one of the three kneeling on the floor — appeared from the corner of the room. She had black and grey stringy hair. "I was in here when it happened." I hadn't noticed her when I entered. Her voice sounded hoarse and forced. She was fidgety, clutching her necklace and speaking in short bursts. "I only turned around for a minute… she climbed onto the TV stand and fell off."

I glanced over at the TV across the room. The stand stood three feet above the thin grey carpet. Before Dave placed a c-collar on the child, he examined the rear of her head. He shut his eyes and seemed disgusted. He then motioned for me to look. The back of the head was matted with blood. When I shoved aside the light brown hair, the wounds became obvious. There were multiple contusions and lacerations, including one behind her right ear.

Dave placed a c-collar on the little girl and quickly intubated her. After everything was secured, I glanced over at the monitor. Her heart rhythm was steady and normal. Before leaving the room, I walked over to the spot where she supposedly fell. The woman from the corner watched me closely. I didn't see any blood. "Are there cameras in here?" I asked. She glanced around the room nervously. And for good reason. Her story didn't make sense.

"No, sir," one of the three women on the floor said.

"Tryke, let's go," Dave said. I glanced around the room for another explanation. While bending down to lift the board, I noticed a small red stain on the door handle of a cabinet. It was the correct height if the girl had been standing.

Before shutting the driver's side door of the rig, I was stopped by one of the three kneeling women. "I needed to tell somebody," she said, holding my door open.

"What's that?" I said.

"Clarissa, the little girl. She's mentally challenged. But that's not what I came out here to tell you." She glanced over the hood of the rig to make sure we were still alone. "Ms. Walters, the woman who witnessed it." She lowered her voice. "I think she did this to her. She's always yelling at her, and I saw her slap Clarissa across the face one time, too. She shakes her… hard."

"Why the hell is she still working here? Didn't you tell someone?"

"I did, but she's related to the owner. They didn't believe me, and threatened my job if I told the parents. And the little girl, well, she doesn't understand. I was hoping that if someone like y'all told the right people, then someone would investigate." She was on the verge of tears. I felt my own emotions building.

"I'll handle it. We'll get it to the right people. Don't worry, Ms. Walters will get what's coming to her. And as far as Clarissa, we'll do what we can for her. I promise."

She grabbed ahold of my arm and said, "Thank you." She wiped her eyes with a tissue and walked off. The guilt had already begun eating her soul, and to slow the gnashing of its teeth, she was desperately reaching out for justice.

• • •

I wasn't looking forward to facing Dr. Kimberly, but it was inevitable that we'd eventually run into one another. I just wasn't expecting it this soon. She was typing away on a computer at the nurses' station when we arrived at Mercy. Thankfully, she was facing the other way. I thought that if I kept quiet, I could get in and out before she noticed me. If I were lucky she would be trying to avoid me also. And I warned Dave before we arrived not to attract attention if she was there. I told him I just didn't feel like discussing things further with her at the moment. He nodded and seemed to understand.

We had made it down the hallway past the nurses' station without being seen. So far so good. We quickly unloaded the girl in trauma bay three, where a team of surgeons were eagerly waiting our arrival. Dave relayed the girl's story to the ER attending physician, Dr. Carlyle. While I watched them unwrap her head, I felt the tension building inside me. The look on Dr. Carlyle's face as he whispered to the surgeon intensified it further. It was a look of desperation and horror, mixed with anxiety and anger. The senselessness penetrated the occupants of the room, spreading one by one and evoking different emotions. I had to get out of there. I could feel the walls closing in around me.

I wheeled the stretcher out into the hallway and leaned against the wall to catch my breath. While placing the leads to the monitor back inside the pouch, I remembered Dr. Kimberly. I glanced nervously down the hall and peeked around the corner. She was no longer seated at the computer. Cautiously, I wheeled the stretcher toward the doors. It was only about fifty feet away. With my head down, I made my way toward the double doors leading to the rig. I glanced up just so I wouldn't slam into anyone coming inside at the same time. Dr. Kimberly appeared out of nowhere and perched herself in front of the doors, blocking my exit.

I gripped the handle of the stretcher to keep from running her down. I also prepared myself for a yelling match, or a knife thrown at my face; it could have gone either way. I briefly thought about my options now that I had lost momentum with the stretcher. I could turn around and run, leaving the stretcher as a barrier. But, considering her instability the other night, she'd most likely chase me through the halls yelling, "Psych patient loose!"

I spoke first. "Dr. Kimberly."

"Tryke," she said in a surprisingly calm voice. The calm before the storm perhaps? She slowly removed her glasses and placed them in her front lab coat pocket. "Look, I was out of line to kick you out of my house."

"No, it was —"

"I'm trying to be decent here." She pressed her lips together tightly and stared at me with a furrowed brow. "We obviously have different ideas. Let's leave it at that, okay?"

Shocked by her relatively composed manner, I lifted my hands in surrender and said, "Okay." I could see in her eyes that she was boiling inside, and wanted to rip my limbs from my body. Or at least yell at me for a few hours while I was restrained. She marched off down the hall and into a patient's room, slamming the door behind her.

If that was her peaceful approach, I dreaded her vengeful side.

• • •

Before visiting the asylum on my next day off, I stopped by the daycare and waited until my next specimen, Ms. Walters, left for the day. I got what I needed: the make of her vehicle and her license plate number. The rest was easy to obtain.

There was already a list of things to do. I had two specimens to release and an insane psychiatrist to visit. Not to mention a confrontation with Lesley. That is, if I hadn't damaged us to the point of disrepair. If we did talk again, I didn't know how to handle it. An apology wasn't enough. She would expect more, an explanation I couldn't give her at the moment.

Before arriving at my destination, I reminded myself about keeping my expectations low. I might not even get past the entrance doors, and if I did, I wasn't sure Dr. Randal would even speak to me.

BOLIN PSYCHIATRIC HOSPITAL. The brick sign was crumbling. Dr. Fortune was obviously still living in a time when they called them Lunatic Asylums. Back then, these places merely confined their patrons, separating them from society. Eventually, after many years, they did begin treating them: shock therapy, lobotomy, hypnotism, and many rumored practices from experimenting physicians. I recall numerous sinister stories about the place over the years, most of them from childhood: ghosts, screams in the night, power surges to nearby neighborhoods. It was mostly kids' campfire embellishments to scare one another, passed down and distorted over time. But still, many terrible things happened in these places, and you had to wonder how many were actually based on some degree of truth.

The outside of the hospital *did* give off an ominous vibe, with its gothic architecture and a wrought iron entrance gate covered in vines. As I stared up at the three-story building, I shuddered to think what the interior walls had witnessed over the years. How many innocents had been tortured because of the Gamemakers' afflictions?

I was met in the entrance foyer by a brutish female Nurse along with two henchman dressed in all white. The place looked to be somewhat updated, but there were still remnants of its once dark past lingering in the huge paintings of past wardens lined up along the walls. After being thoroughly questioned, I was led into a side room not far from the entrance. They apparently didn't like guests venturing too deep inside, which was fine by me. The farther inside the building, the farther I was away from the exit doors. But it did leave me wondering what they were hiding down those poorly lit hallways. I pictured a drooling, highly medicated Dr. Randal, recently lobotomized, banging his head repeatedly on the thick metal door of his room.

The room I was waiting in was empty, except for a few Victorian-style high-backed chairs and a tall, narrow, frosted glass window. At least I think it was frosted; it may have just been really grimy. The bare walls were peeling, revealing a blood red color underneath the blue paint. An eerie feeling came over me, like someone, or something, was watching.

I jumped when the door slammed open. The henchmen escorted Dr. Randal inside, sat him in the chair in front of me, and then made their way back toward the door. Dr. Randal had a full head of brown and grey disorderly hair. He wore thin black glasses and dark purple scrubs. He held his hands together with interlocked fingers, and stared toward the floor. He wasn't drooling, nor did he appear to have had a recent lobotomy, but he did have a look of disconnection from the world. After a moment he looked up at me, not talking. His head remained still but his eyes moved quickly, searching the room.

The henchmen stood at the closed door facing us with their arms crossed. One said, "You have ten minutes, sir." I nodded to them in understanding.

Dr. Randal was now staring past me toward the peeling wall. He had a peculiar look on his face, his hands now resting on his knees. "Dr. Randal, my name is Tryke Harper. I wasn't a patient of yours, but I believe my dad was. He wrote his thoughts down in journals before he died, and I found your name written several times. I couldn't find a connection."

"There used to be a Van Gogh hanging on that wall," he said. His voice was calm and soothing, not matching his disheveled appearance. "A Wind-Beaten Tree, I believe. Did you know —" He stopped himself and switched his gaze to me and squinted. He then lowered his head and stared at the floor again. "I apologize for my mindless absence. This place tends to make one dream of a different place." He looked back up at me, his eyes now seeming to focus. He shuffled around in his chair and crossed his legs, appearing as if he had never left his practice. "What was your father's name?" I felt as if I were one of his patients lying on a soft leather couch, my eyes shut, about to spill my entire life story.

"Henry Harper."

After another moment of silence he said, "I don't forget my patients, Tryke. Henry Harper was never a patient of mine."

"Are you sure? It's not that I don't believe you, sir. I just don't know why he would write your name down if you weren't his doctor."

"Sounds curious to me also." He was now staring past me again into the wall, losing focus. "What were his ailments?"

"Voices. Disembodied voices."

"Did he write down anything specific? Things they may have told him."

"Many things, and among them were thoughts to hurt his family."

"Did he follow through?" he asked, slowly turning his gaze back to me. He stared deep into my eyes, eagerly awaiting my answer. His gaze was unwavering, and this time I was the one shuffling nervously in my chair. It was as if he was willing me to say yes, and wanted me to elaborate about the manner in which my dad hurt them.

"No!" I said. I looked up at the two henchmen at the door. They shifted in place, switching arms and crossing them back, continuing to look our way. I sat back in my chair and took a deep breath. Dr. Randal hadn't so much as flinched at my words. He was still waiting for more information. "Sorry for yelling, but no, he never laid a hand on his family. He resisted the voices until the end, eventually dying of cancer."

"I'm afraid I can't help you, son. I didn't know your father." He stood and started walking back toward the door.

"He mentioned something else in the journals," I said. He stopped, not turning around. "He spoke about... Gamemakers."

Now Dr. Randal turned, his eyes wide as if he suddenly remembered a long lost secret. "Now, *that* does ring a certain bell... I believe I do remember who your father was. I met him a few times at my office. He was married to one of my patients, Sylvia Harper."

Chapter 17

I was trembling inside at the mention of my mother's name. It couldn't be. *She* was the patient? Memories of my childhood flooded through my head. Birthdays, holidays. I didn't recall anything that hinted to her being plagued with disembodied voices. But, now that I think back on my dad, there wasn't much there either. I only remember his drinking. My mom didn't have any vices that I can recall. It didn't make any sense… She was so sturdy, so firmly set in the world.

Dr. Randal sat back down in the chair in front of me and moved in close. He sensed my bewilderment and pain, his eyes suddenly revealing their own deep aching.

"How is your mother?" he asked.

Though I was still processing the information, I had to stay cool. My time with him was limited and I needed answers, now more than ever. I took a deep breath and said, "She died. From a brain tumor."

His hands started to shake. "I'm… sorry," he said. His voice cracked, riddled with anguish. "She was a good woman… she and I… we had a connection." He lowered his head and grabbed a fist full of his hair.

"Dr. Randal? Are you all right?" I asked. We had given one another equally shocking news, though he didn't appear to be handling his very well, externally. Mine was currently circling around my insides, scraping its sharp teeth against my intestines, tempting me to yell out in pissed-off agony. I was frustrated and tired of being left in the dark about my family.

"I fight them… constantly." He grunted, continuing to clutch his head. "I want them gone! I need them…"

The two henchmen were paying close attention now. I didn't have much time before they snatched him away.

"Dr. Randal, I need you to focus, please. I need to know if you kept any files on my mother." He unclenched his hair and was now rubbing both of his knees simultaneously in a clockwise motion, staring at my feet and attempting to control his breathing.

"I never get rid of my patient files."

"Would it be possible for me to see them?"

He looked up at me, his eyes watery and streaked crimson. He whispered, "Before I was conquered, I purchased a garage to store my records and a few other possessions, were I ever to return. Two-four-five. It's on Torrent Street." He stood up from his chair and ran both of his hands through his damp hair, regaining his composure.

"Thank you," I said.

"I don't have a key, so you'll have to break in."

"I can handle that."

"Time's up, Dr. Randal," one of the henchmen said.

The doctor waved his hand toward the men, pressing for an extended moment. "Your mother was stronger than me. You have her strength, I can see it. And her eyes. Take care, Tryke Harper." He turned around and walked out the door, his two guards in white following closely behind.

• • •

It would have been easier if I could have had more time with Dr. Randal and asked him the questions I needed answered. I had many, including what sort of connection he and my mom shared. When I spoke of her death, it triggered something. I had my suspicions, that there was something lurking inside of him, a darkness creeping around and taking peeks out of his tired eyes. It was the same darkness that made him kill his family. But why would it arise at the mention of my mom?

I needed time to think before proceeding to the storage facility. I had to put everything in perspective and understand what the hell was going on. Now that things had taken a wicked turn, I was back in a dark cellar of the unknown, more confused than ever. Why would my dad write my mom's thoughts down as if they were his own? And why bother writing me a letter?

After returning home, I used my frustration to fuel my next endeavor, which was to search every book in the house from cover to cover, and every possible crevice. I needed to be sure there were no more journals. I wanted every damn thing out, with no more surprises, before I opened my mom's file.

After a few hours of continuous searching, I was now sitting in my library, surrounded by a plethora of open books, physically and mentally exhausted. Thankfully, my search had turned up nothing. I had just leaned back in my chair and propped my feet up when the doorbell rang, interrupting my brief moment of relaxation. Earl stayed firmly in place, curled up next to the fireplace.

"Don't worry, I'll get it," I said. "I wouldn't want you to act like a dog and warn of approaching intruders. How silly of me." He turned over on his back and yawned, stretching his front paws.

I glanced down the hallway toward the door. I could faintly see an outline of a cowboy hat through the small circle of frosted glass. I quickly threw the pile of books into the storage bin I had pulled them from, and straightened the books on the shelves. Then I opened the door.

"Uncle Frank, sorry it took a minute to answer the door. I was in the restroom. So what brings you to this side of town?"

"I tagged along to serve a warrant a few blocks over. Thought I'd stop in and see my nephew. How are you?"

"Not too bad. Come on in." He wiped his boots on the mat outside and slipped his cowboy hat off. My dad's brother, Frank, was a homicide detective for the city of Dallas. He knew about my little sister's sickness, and (my dad's) supposed sickness. He was the one who had handed me the sealed letter from my dad after his death. I wasn't sure if knew the truth about my mom. If he did, he could possibly have the answers I needed, but until I had everything in order, I wasn't ready to confront him.

"How was your Thanksgiving?" he asked. "I'm sorry I didn't show. Thanks for the invitation, though." I forgot I had left a message on his voicemail, inviting him over. He was the only family I had left.

"You didn't miss much. It was actually a disaster," I said.

"Oh? How's that?" he asked, making his way into the dining room.

"Lesley and I had an argument and well… let's just say it was over before it began."

"I'm sorry to hear that. She's a lovely girl. I hope y'all work things out."

"Yeah, maybe." I wasn't feeling optimistic, not after reading the message she sent to me after leaving. He sat down at the dining room table. "Can I get you something to drink?"

"Nah, I'm fine," he said. I sat down across from him.

"So, what's on your mind?" I asked.

"Just work, putting away the misfits. I see you've

rearranged a few things in the house. Looks good." He peered around the room and into the kitchen.

"I didn't have a lot of stuff in my apartment, and besides, I didn't want to change too much. There are plenty of memories I'd like to hang onto. I can still hear y'all clanking around poker chips in here, and my dad's loud laugh."

"He was always a loud mouth," said Uncle Frank, laughing. "Those were good times." I could tell he wasn't just thinking of my parents, but also his wife. It was the four of them, every Friday night, playing poker until well after midnight.

"I miss them, too," I said.

"Did I ever tell you about the time your dad nearly got us banned from Peter's grocery?"

"Is it the one about the bathroom incident?"

He laughed, "Yeah, he lit one of those cherry bombs in a toilet. Luckily, we made it out the back door before they knew what happened." He stared at the wall, reminiscing, I suspected. "Man, he got us into some real jams back then, but somehow we always managed to avoid getting caught."

"I doubt they would have let him work there if y'all had gotten caught."

"Probably not." He shook his head. "You know, growing up, I would have never guessed he had that sickness growing inside of him. Nothing bothered your dad. He was always the one that was surefooted, helping *me* grasp things. Heck, he even scored the prettiest woman in town. It was his charm, I was told by your mother on several occasions. I don't understand this life sometimes."

"If it helps, you're not alone in that. I'm just as lost, if not more, than the rest. He hid it well, didn't he?"

"Yeah, he was always a proud man. He held it in as much as he could, I suppose." Thankfully, he had your mother to help. That woman was a saint, I swear. How have you been? You know… anything out of the ordinary?"

He meant the sickness. Have I had any symptoms? I promised him that I would seek help if any were to arise. I had seen blurs and glitches in this dimension, even dark souls of the released. Never voices though. Only visual distractions to throw me off track.

"I'm clean," I said. "No distractions in my life." He stared at me as if penetrating my mind, using his interrogating techniques to read me. "Honest."

"All right, but remember I'm here for you if you need anything."

"I know you are, and I appreciate it."

He stood and grabbed his hat from the table. "I need to get back to the office." He walked around the corner and into the living room, taking the scenic route to the front door. "Well, you've done good taking care of the house here." He stopped when he reached the library I had transformed.

"A little tribute to my dad. He liked his books," I said.

"That he did." He stepped into the room and walked around, stopping in front of the shelf that held the framed picture of my family at the lake. He took his hat off and leaned in closer to examine the photo.

When he reached out his hand toward the frame, I asked, "Do you remember this?"

He lowered his hand, inches from the frame, and turned his gaze toward the object I had in my right hand. It was a small ceramic owl that my dad kept on his desk at work.

"No, but I knew he had a fascination with owls since he was a child." I could feel my heart rapping on my chest wall, my ears burning red. He turned back around toward the photo on the shelf.

I quickly put the owl down and wiped my forehead, tapping it repetitively to a count of five. Stop, I told myself, breaking my next set of OCD counting before he saw me. I suppressed a heavy sigh when he placed his cowboy hat on his head and began back toward the front door, never touching the frame.

"Remember to call me if you need anything," he said.

"I will."

I watched as he drove away in his brown sedan. That was way too close, I thought. I hadn't been that close to having a panic attack since, well, my first full-blown one last year in my lab. I'd managed to dodge them ever since, but they were always close. I knew never to get too comfortable.

I made a sandwich and ate in peaceful silence at the dining table, going over in my head the plans for Ms. Walters — the daycare worker who had an appetite for beating mentally impaired three-year-olds. This woman's nastiness moved her to the front of the line, knocking the Elderly Slayer down one notch. There were still a few weeks until Christmas, which gave me enough time to find him before he ended his holiday slayings. Besides, I still needed to research his moves further. He was like no other I had stalked in the past. He didn't operate on a whim or sudden rage. He was methodical.

• • •

Ms. Walters was a widow. Her husband died a few years back, unknown cause. He was much older, and from the picture I found, much smaller than her. I wouldn't have been surprised to find out she killed him also, slamming him repeatedly against a wall until he was no longer breathing.

It was almost six o'clock. I watched from across the street of the daycare for Ms. Walters to exit the building. She filed out last, alone — not surprising considering one of her coworkers divulged incriminating evidence to me behind her back. Before getting into her vehicle, she pulled a small baton from her purse and smacked a cat from off the roof of her car. I watched the smile unfurl on her face as the injured animal limped down from the hood and fell onto the concrete. After getting into her vehicle, she rolled down the window and looked around before squealing her tires and mowing down the defenseless feline.

I followed her to a small complex of townhouses. I recognized the name on the dilapidated brick sign on the entrance. When she stopped at the community mailbox, I pulled ahead to her address and parked under the carport. I waited in the shadows behind the tattered wooden fence surrounding the small patio. She was brave, not giving a second thought to the darkness she had just wandered into.

• • •

Once Ms. Walters was secured to the table, I flipped the switch on the front of the generator, revving my lab to life. I slid an IV into her arm and prepped the rest of the room. Before setting the alarm on the stairs, I realized I had forgotten my phone.

"Be right back," I told Ms. Walters. She continued to snore softly.

I snatched my phone from the console of my truck and noticed a missed message on the screen — a text from Lesley.

How are you?

What was I supposed to do with this? How am I? I could just respond with, *Good and you?* But that would invite more conversation. Why couldn't she get to the point? Damn women and their vagueness. They enjoy planting small devices in the form of words in our heads to hijack us later. If I said *this* I'm screwed, if I said *that* I'm more screwed. I needed to return to my former self, before I became versed in romantic relationships. Well, I'm not really versed. Maybe *acquainted* is a better word. I would never be versed. I'm convinced that every woman's neurons are connected, so that they can scheme new ways to torture the opposite sex.

I sat, flustered in the front seat of my truck. Damn you, Lesley. Why couldn't you leave things as they were? I was content sulking, thinking I was the victim. I had every intention of trying to resolve the incident later, after I was finished with all of my endeavors, after the holidays. I texted her back.

I'm okay, not great.

That should suffice until I finished with Ms. Walters. I hurriedly placed the phone in my pocket. Before I reached the first step to my lab, I felt the vibration of a return text.

I miss you.

What the hell? I missed her too, but why tell me now, when we haven't even spoken about the incident? I really hated texting, attempting to express an immediate emotion behind a phone miles away. It seemed cowardly and lazy, but I couldn't dismiss its usefulness at times. In this case it was frustrating. How was I supposed to respond without appearing desperate and weak? I countered vagueness with more vagueness.

Miss you too.

I slipped the phone into the front pocket of my overalls. I decided not to respond to another text until I was done with Ms. Walters. Seconds later it vibrated again, but this time it didn't stop after a short burst. I sighed and pulled the phone back out. Lesley was calling. I wasn't in the mood to talk, but if I didn't answer, I would look timid and afraid.

Just as I was about to press Answer, I heard a crashing sound from the top of the stairs, followed by a loud scream.

Chapter 18

"Shit," I whispered to myself. "How the hell did she get loose." I shoved the phone back in my pocket, not answering, and cautiously peered up the dark stairwell to the entrance door to my lab. The door was cracked open, emitting a beam of soft light, but she was still in the room. I didn't see any shadows along the stairs. After the initial crash and scream, all was silent. She may have just flailed around on the table and knocked over the IV pole or monitor. As for the door, I may not have closed it all the way.

Wishful thinking. When I got to the top of the stairs, I peeked through the open crack, inching the door slowly open. I could see the end of the table from where I was. She was loose; the restraints were empty. This was the first one to break free. I began running my usual routine through my head, making sure I remembered to empty her pockets. A missed cell phone would not be good. I assured myself I did. But, still, I felt a wave of nausea wash over me. What if —. My worries stopped abruptly when the door slammed shut, knocking me back. My wrist twisted, causing immense pain as I tried to steady myself from tumbling down the steep stairs. Son of a bitch, you've got to be kidding me.

"What do you want with me!?" she screamed from the other side of the door. There was more anger than fear in her voice.

I didn't answer. She was holding the doorknob, desperately attempting to steady it. I had removed the lock for this very reason. Now, only a padlock would work, and it was in my... I searched my pockets. "Shit," I whispered. I must have left it in the room. No matter. She obviously hadn't found it. But there was one more potential issue I just remembered: there was a syringe with a few milliliters of substance in it on the arm of my chair. Would she be smart enough to find it and use it? Doubtful, but...

"I'll kill you! Do you know who I am!?" She yelled again, still struggling to steady the doorknob. No, but I know *what* you are.

I couldn't wait for the situation to escalate any further. I stood, bracing my hands against the walls, cringing through the pain in my wrist. I lunged my right boot hard into the door and slammed her against the wall. I didn't hesitate. I pushed open the door after it swung back my way. There wouldn't be another struggle. She was slumped over, knocked unconscious. This confrontation could have gone much differently if she'd been smart enough to grab the syringe and not been so loud.

I cleaned up the mess from the IV that she pulled out and placed another one. I fastened the restraints a little tighter than before, and then sat in my chair and waited for her to arouse.

An hour later, she regained consciousness. With her gagged, we had our brief conversation.

"This must be new for you. Being the one lying helpless on a hard surface, having *me* stare down at *you*. At least you have the ability of sight. That three-year-old didn't, not after you damaged her visual cortex, slamming her repeatedly against that cabinet." Her eyes were full of hatred as she stared up at me. She had been discovered and now the darkness was angry. "Now that I think about it, it was probably a good thing that she didn't have to watch as she slowly deteriorated. She died the next morning after a night of slow and steady bleeding. It eventually covered her entire brain." I searched her for any signs of remorse, but there was not so much as a twitch when I spoke of the child's death.

"Don't fret, because very soon you will have another set of eyes. And when you see the Gamemakers, you can ask them why your mission was to harm children. It wasn't I who placed you here. I am only the releaser."

As the substance did its job, the organic suit fought back, but only briefly. It soon gave in and released the darkness inside.

• • •

Lesley didn't leave a voicemail when she called, and I didn't call her back because I didn't have a clue what to say. I wasn't ready to fix things just yet. The situation needed time to sit and stew with us both. Of course, I was biased toward the waiting period, because I had a slew of unfinished business demanding my attention. And the obvious. I didn't have any idea how to fix our dilemma.

Back at work on our next shift, while moseying down I-635, Dave asked me, "What do you say we have a drink at your house after work? For old times' sake." I had been rearranging the digital books on my phone. I looked up at him. "Whaddya say?" I could almost hear the cry behind his fake smile. He needed the one-on-one beer time. I'd seen the look before, only this time it wasn't quite as desperate.

"Okay," I said. "Why not… I could use a drink myself." I paused during mid-sentence, which alerted Dave. He was about to ask me to elaborate on why I also needed a drink, but dispatch saved me just in time.

"Medic 15, this is dispatch."

I picked up the mic and said, "Go ahead, dispatch."

"What's your location?"

"I-635 approaching Fulton Ave."

The MDT beeped, relaying the call information.

"We need you to respond to I-635 westbound at Greenway for a male and a female, both unconscious in the roadway."

"Place us en route," I said.

"During the day, on the interstate?" Dave said. "There has to be more to it. What's on the MDT?"

"Nothing, just that a motorist called it in." Dave flipped on the lights and siren. We were still a few miles away from the location, but the traffic had already started to slow.

"Medic 15, police are on scene. They are reporting that bystanders witnessed the couple jump from the overpass."

The traffic had now come to a near stop. Dave pulled along the left side of the interstate and followed a police unit to the scene.

"Copy, dispatch, we're two minutes out," I said.

"A suicide couple. This is new," Dave said. His hands were mildly shaking as the adrenaline forced its way through his veins. He managed to steady the wheel of the rig, skillfully maneuvering around vehicles. "I wonder if they're still alive."

I shrugged. "Let's hope not. Suicide that fails is never a pretty scene. We wouldn't want Romeo and Juliet to end up in a nursing home, comatose and drooling."

"That would suck," Dave said, parking the rig behind a pair of police units.

"Medic 15 on scene, dispatch," I said, peering out my passenger side window at our two patients. The couple were side by side, motionless, hands sprawled out as if they were making snow angels on interstate tar. Bystanders were lined up along the median, their vehicles pulled over. The police were attempting to get them to leave, but a seemingly romantic death was more compelling than the threat of the brief jail time that might come from disobeying an officer.

The fall from the overpass only looked to be around 12-15 feet, but then I realized the vantage point of the victims — they must have jumped from the second level of the three-level interchange, making the height around thirty feet. I also noticed an eighteen-wheeler jack-knifed a hundred feet ahead, with skid marks leading back to the two jumpers. Witness, maybe?

"I'll take the female," Dave said, snatching the airway bag from the back of the rig.

They appeared to be in their early twenties. No wedding rings on either. Both were unconscious, but the female's chest was moving slightly. "Sure, leave me with the dead one."

I glanced over at Dave while I did a quick examination of the male. He was suctioning the female's mouth frantically, and pulling shards of teeth out with his hands. Dave yelled over to me.

"Do we need another rig?"

"I don't think so," I yelled back. "One second." The male was pulseless and not breathing. I lifted his head from the pool of blood beneath him, revealing a massive open wound. "No, just the coroner." I slung one of our yellow blankets over him and motioned for one of the officers to help keep him covered. I think most people know what the blanket means once it's placed over a victim, but our brains have a tendency to not accept it immediately. The bystanders were watching intently. Some were clearly horrified, cupping their hands over their mouths as the yellow blanket waved in the wind, allowing glimpses of the dead body.

I knelt down beside Dave and the female patient.

"What do you need?" I asked.

"The crich kit," Dave said.

While I dug through the airway bag for the kit, I unclipped my portable radio from my belt. "Dispatch, this is medic 15."

"Go ahead, medic 15."

"If you had another rig headed this way, you can cancel it. We have one patient we'll be transporting to Mercy. Police will notify on the other."

"Copy, medic 15."

A needle cricothyrotomy is a procedure we rarely perform in the field. I had yet to do one, and I wasn't aware of Dave ever telling me of his experience. If he had, I would have known about it, believe me. Placing a huge needle through the neck and into the trachea is a huge bragging right for the pedestal medics. They stand high above the rest, boasting, with their prized bloody needle held high for all to see.

"Damn," Dave said, "her teeth are bent back. I can't suction fast enough. Pieces of teeth and blood are everywhere."

"Let's do this then," I said. "Have you ever done one?"

"No," he said, "but I'm about to." Conviction. I liked it.

"It can't be that hard. How does her head look? I'm only asking because her friend has part of his brain exposed." I prepped her neck with iodine.

"No, it's weird. The only injuries I found were on her face, especially her mouth." The gurgling was getting worse. Her long autumn hair was splayed out on the pavement. I had an instant image of my sister's hair — the same color — floating in the clear pool water.

"Tryke."

"Sorry... okay, what next?"

"Putting it in the right spot." His hands were surprisingly steady. "I'm not letting her die. I don't know why she jumped, but He isn't taking her today."

Dave making a challenging remark? Ready for a duel?

"Let's see what you got then," I said, fueling his resolve.

Dave methodically and flawlessly slid the needle through the cricothyroid membrane, and then secured the tube. I was impressed with his confidence and conviction. He'd always had passion, just not in the form of a challenger.

"Nice, man," I said.

"Thanks. I think she might live." His expression wasn't grim, which it usually was during these types of calls, where the survival rate is nearly zero. He was proud of his accomplishment, but not in the same way he once would have been. There was a change from his former boasting self. I thought he might finally be catching a glimpse from our side of the game-board.

"Maybe," I said. Who knew what the Gamemakers had in mind for *this* one. Who was she? Could she have been a soldier of theirs who wanted an early release?

· · ·

Once we arrived at Mercy, I spoke with one of the officers who'd been at the scene. He explained to me that the couple were brother and sister. Why did they jump? Only the Gamemakers had the answers. The eighteen-wheeler on scene that had a trail of skid marks along the interstate *did* play a part. Supposedly, the driver slammed on his brakes when he heard the thud hit his trailer. Through his side mirrors he saw the two of them flopping on the interstate. When they jumped, the woman must have leaped a second after her brother, probably having second thoughts, leaving him to hit the truck's trailer, and not her.

I finished my brief report on the dead male while sitting in the rig. I was writing in there and not inside the hospital because of the person standing next to Dave at the nurses' station — Dr. Kimberly.

I sighed when I returned ten minutes later, annoyed that they were still in the same position. I was going to have to interact with her again. They were facing in the opposite direction, leaning on the counter. As I approached from behind, Dr. Kimberly snorted, letting out an annoyingly loud laugh. She then proceeded to rub against Dave's shoulder with hers. It wasn't the ducking of the eyes, lightly-brushing-hands type of flirting. She was trying to draw attention, probably waiting for me to intervene.

I cleared my throat, hoping only Dave would turn around. When neither of them acknowledged me, I said, "Dave." They turned around in unison. "Come on, man, there's a call a few blocks away. I think you'll want to take this one." Dr. Kimberly sneered at me and then whispered something in Dave's ear.

He smiled shyly and asked, "What's the call?"

"Pedi code." His smile disappeared, replaced with alarm. As much as he dreaded making that kind of call, his conscience wouldn't allow him to dodge it.

He handed his report off to the nurse and waved goodbye to Dr. Kimberly. When she reached out and lightly touched his shoulder, I shook my head in disgust. She looked past him and toward me, wielding a sardonic grin. I smirked at her failed attempt to provoke me. The most she was getting out of me was a head shake.

"What's the address?" Dave asked, putting the rig in drive and flipping on the light bar.

"There's no call."

"Seriously? What the hell?"

"I had to get you away from Dr. Kimberly. There's something not right about her."

"What? She's harmless. Not to mention cute, too."

"Don't fall for that innocent mask she wears. She's only trying to piss me off. Let it go."

"You really are full of yourself. Don't worry, I'm not stealing your girlfriend. It's harmless flirting, man. Nothing more."

"Whatever. Just do me a favor, will you? As my friend

— don't talk to her if you can help it."

He looked over at me. "Really?"

"Yes, and you know I wouldn't be asking something so frivolous of you if it wasn't for your own good."

"My own good?" I continued to stare at him, not replying. "All right. Sure, no problem." He looked like I had just taken away his favorite toy. If Dave could only see that it was he who was the toy.

As we pulled out of the ER driveway, I realized that I had called him my friend, aloud, for the first time.

Chapter 19

The next morning after work, Dave and I sat in my living room, him sipping on his cheap beer, me on my Scotch. I wasn't sure what was on his mind, but when he popped open his third beer, I knew he was about to open up, too.

"Come on, man, what is it? I know you have some news," I said. "You look like a sick dog about to spew chunks."

"That obvious, huh? You know I've never really been good at hiding things. Probably why my ex ran all over me."

"That, and her psychotic nature," I said.

"Yeah, that too. You know, I still worry about my daughter inheriting it." He grinned, but the sullen aching underneath couldn't be disguised. "Anyway, look —" He sat his beer down and took a deep breath, letting it out slowly. "Angie's pregnant."

"Already? You work fast. Congratulations."

"Don't congratulate me. This wasn't planned. In fact, it—"

"So your daughter will have a sibling. What's the problem? I thought you liked kids."

"I do, but that's not it." He leaned over, clutching his beer can. "Tryke," he said, lifting his head. He was trembling. "I had a vasectomy after my daughter was born."

"Okay... that changes things." I took a few sips of my drink, trying to come up with something to say. "Well, let's think this through. I'm assuming she doesn't know about your vasectomy?"

"No, it never came up. We never discussed having kids. I know I should have, but... I don't know. I loved her so much, I didn't want it to harm my chances with her in the beginning. And then it just never seemed like the right time to tell her."

"I don't think you have to worry about that anymore," I said.

"Thanks a damn lot."

"Sorry, but she did it, not you."

"I know, but it doesn't make it easier." He was now hovering over his empty beer can, staring down into its aluminum rim.

"How far along is she?" I asked, moving the conversation and not allowing him to linger.

"She didn't tell me."

"Have you decided what you're going to do? How you're going to confront her?"

"Not sure yet. Honestly, I don't know what to do. What should I say when I confront her?"

"You know what I would do." He waited for my answer, staring at me with silent anticipation. He knew where I stood on things like this, but he wanted to hear me say it. "I'd send her packing and get a damn annulment. Start over again, man. You don't need to take care of someone else's kid. Not on these terms."

He mulled over my words. It wasn't his style to go into a

situation with guns blazing. He was more of a let's-wait-and-see-how-long-I-can-stretch-this-shit-out kind of guy. Getting him to leave his cheating ex-wife was like prying embedded nails out of a wooden coffin with a nail file.

He popped open the beer beside him and downed it, setting it next to his rapidly-building collection. "I guess you're right. I just don't know why the hell this keeps happening to me."

I wanted to say: we all suffer my friend, to the very end of this game. "I don't know, man," I said instead. "Maybe you should take a break from the marriage thing for a while."

"You know, I'm not good at being alone like you are. I guess I'm a loser, unable to face this cruel world on my own merits."

"You're far from a loser. It's easy being alone. Now, holding together a relationship, that's much harder. Trust me." What was happening to me? When did I suddenly become an expert and start giving motivational guidance on relationships? Was I now in that group of heart- bruised men offering up cynical advice?

"Well, I suck at both, then."

"You're getting better. Trial and error. You'll get it right one day."

"But, at what cost? My sanity? I don't know how much more I can handle." He slid back on the couch, pathetically, and covered his head with his arm.

"Remember your dream about owning a boat while you were married to your first wife?"

"Yeah, what about it? Knowing my luck, Angie will probably get that in the divorce settlement."

"I was simply bringing up the fact that you found a way out last time."

"This is different. Angie didn't try to control my life like Claire did. Actually, she was the opposite. Maybe I married her because she was so different than Claire. See? I'm cursed. Damned if I do, damned if I don't."

Okay, that didn't work. I thought that bringing up his boat might trigger what worked for him last time. I regretted the next words before they even left my mouth. "If you want, you can stay here in the spare room. But just until you figure things out."

He abruptly sat up with newfound energy. "Are you sure? I know how you like your privacy."

"No, I'm not sure, but I'm okay with it. Take it while you can before I retract it."

Maybe it was the alcohol, or the pitifully desperate look on his face, that caused me to make such a bold offer. He quickly accepted my proposal. He didn't give me a timeframe on when he was going to confront his wife, only that it would be soon. I figured I had enough time to finish a few things before he moved in.

• • •

When I turned onto Torrent Street, the storage facility was easy enough to find. I wasn't sure how I was going to proceed, especially if there were too many prying cameras. But, as I neared number 245, I was relieved to see that it wasn't inside the climate-controlled area. There were only a few sporadic cameras outside guarding the cheaper units, and none close to where I was going to be. I wondered, grabbing my bolt cutters, if this particular unit was chosen for that reason.

The rusted lock fell apart without much effort. I cautiously raised the rusted metal door and stepped back, letting the dust settle. The small area was surprisingly neat and orderly, as though he were recreating a memorable space: two large grey file cabinets set against the back wall, a mahogany desk partially covered in thick plastic along with a variety of fake plants sat against another. A leather couch, also wrapped in plastic, was positioned in close proximity to a wooden chair, giving the impression it was meant for patient/doctor interaction. The space looked vaguely familiar, though I couldn't quite place it at the moment.

The file cabinets were the obvious place to start. I opened the first one and found that it was crammed full of files, thankfully in alphabetical order. I found my mom's file easy enough, although it was thicker than I imagined — probably due to the "connection" that Dr. Randal mentioned. I slung off the plastic covering on the desk and set the closed file down in front of me.

Attempting to avoid reading the files, I opened the top desk drawer and fumbled around with the contents. For some reason, I was more nervous now than I had been after finding the second set of my dad's journals. With everything still processing, I wasn't ready to read an outsider's opinion of my mom's thoughts. But it had to be done. I needed answers, and hoped they'd bring closure to this entire charade.

The drawer was mostly filled with loose papers and pens, and a few bent paperclips. There was also a pill bottle, without a label. From the clean smooth exterior, it didn't ever appear to have had a label on it. I dumped the few pills that were left into my hand and examined one. It was small, round, and cream-colored, not much bigger than a 325mg aspirin. There was an imprint code, P-001, but no logo on the pill. Curious, I opened the medical application on my phone and did a search. I didn't find any results that matched the code, so I did a quick internet search. No results there either. It was most likely some generic pain medication that he put in a blank pill bottle, but I couldn't afford to discount anything at the moment. I placed the pills back in the bottle and slipped it into my pocket.

Finally, I took a deep breath, flipped open the file, and began to read:

32-year-old female seen for auditory hallucinations. Visit attended by patient and husband.

Patient reports "voices" began approximately one-year prior. The frequency has been sporadic until two weeks ago when they became fairly continuous, telling her to harm her family, advising that they were plotting against her survival. Attention and appetite decreased, organization good until last night.

Denies symptoms of mania. Neurological: no headaches. All other systems were reviewed and are negative.

I skipped down to medications.

Patient adamant on not taking antipsychotic medications, wishes only to have therapy sessions with doctor. Next visit in one week.

I flipped through the weekly visits, but nothing stood out. The thoughts weren't much different than those my dad described in his journals. I didn't know what I was expecting to find. I suppose I wanted to see it for myself, have definitive proof that my dad deceived me. And it *was* truly my mom who had the sickness.

After a year, the visits became more frequent.

Eventually, I found my name mentioned on a particular visit — the reason I recalled the makeshift room I was sitting in. The place was actually a recreation of Dr. Randal's office. I had been there before, when I was a child.

Follow-up. Visit attended by patient and five-year-old son, at my request. Patient, on last visit, mentioned multiple depression symptoms and auditory hallucinations, specifically mentioning a threat to her son five years prior while in the womb. When asked specifics about the threat, she refused to elaborate, becoming suddenly irate. I didn't press the matter.

A threat to me while I was in her womb?

Mother and son interaction organized. Son's speech appropriate for age, and when asked questions about family and home, responded with above average replies, showing high levels of perception regarding his environment.

So, I'm developing normally. Okay.

I flipped through the years of their visits and came to a specific section of my mom's file that was even stranger than what I had read so far. He named the file Revelations. His notes on my mom became intertwined with his own perceptions.

For the first time in my career, I have connected with a patient on a multidimensional level. She referred to the auditory hallucinations as being placed there by the Gamemakers, a name I had given to my own givers of deceit. For a reason I cannot explain, I feel we have had this conversation before.

I skipped over a few pages.

Today I revealed to her my own encounter with the Gamemakers. Her response was actually one of elation. She expressed relief in not being the only one trapped in their game.

We aren't alone in this dimension; this is their domain. They slip in and out of multiple dimensions at will and poison us, one at a time. Together, we must form a plan and carry it out to conquer them.

A few more...

Recruiting is going well. The subjects are complying. The next step is to begin our search.

A few more...

Sylvia seems cynical about furthering the recruiting. She has also refused to be hypnotized, blaming her recent bout of insomnia on the sessions. I have agreed to continue our sessions without hypnosis.

Insomnia, a foe I knew all too well.

A few more...

I don't know how, but the dimensions from which they travel seem to have multiplied. They must have figured out our plan. The influx of transmissions has increased to phenomenal levels. I don't know how much more I can handle. Sylvia has stopped coming to sessions. She will not return my calls. She doesn't yet realize how vital she is to my survival and our mission.

A few more...

I was thrilled when Sylvia finally contacted me. I received a phone call from her at three a.m. Her daughter was having visual hallucinations. Advised her to bring daughter in for evaluation the following afternoon. We can finally get back to the mission. Things have been dim without her. The sense of losing control and giving in to the voices has become unbearable recently. I need structure or my family's death is imminent.

The next day.

Sylvia did not show for her appointment. I attempted to contact her residence, without success.

I stared at the date of the entry. That was the morning my mom lay down because of a migraine. That was the morning my sister drowned in our swimming pool, during the few minutes I left her alone while in our tree house. Suddenly, I started having trouble catching my breath. My rapid heartbeat was drumming in my ears, and sweat began beading rapidly down my face — I knew immediately that I was having another anxiety attack. I threw the file from the desk and slid out of the chair, sitting down on the cold floor next to the filing cabinets. I pressed my back stiffly against them and began slow, repetitive counting. It was the only act I knew that would put my mind back on track.

After a few exhausting minutes, I managed to control my breathing. Memories of that day had always triggered confusing emotions, especially guilt. But knowing my little sister was suffering and was going to be subjected to this guy was even more frightening. Had my sister lived, what would have come of her treatment by Dr. Randal? What were his end plans with my mom? I had yet to find a treatment plan. Recruiting. Hypnotizing. None of it made sense.

A gust of wind rattled the metal door, reminding me to finish what I had come to do. I stood to gather the scattered files, and sat at the desk to continue where I had left off.

After several phone calls the next few days, her husband responded to me. Their daughter had been in a terrible accident and was taken from them. I fear Sylvia will not return. I am lost without her.

The rest was indecipherable. Just scribbles and pen marks pressed hard into the paper. That was the last entry he'd placed in her file. The date was right before he murdered his wife and daughter. Then, a male voice interrupted my thoughts, startling me.

"Howdy, neighbor!"

Chapter 20

I quickly shut my mom's file and raised a hand above my eyes, blocking out the sun's glare. I couldn't make out the face, but his voice sounded raspy, like that of a smoker. I cautiously got to my feet. Though his tone was friendly, one could never be too careful.

"I didn't mean to frighten you there," he said, not yet stepping past the line of the door.

"What can I do for you?" I asked.

"I'm a friend of the doc, two spots down."

The broken padlock was lying on the desk a few feet in front of him. He had to have seen it. "Oh, I was just —"

"You must be from the state. I was wondering how long it'd be before y'all found this place. Sorry, I'm being rude. My name's George Cedar." He stepped into the unit and held out his hand for me to shake.

"Bob Chance," I said, shaking his calloused hand. He looked to be in his late fifties, well pronounced gut, jeans tucked into a pair of brown work boots. "I was sent to recover a specific set of files. The rest will be confiscated by tomorrow evening."

"It don't make no sense to me how a man like that could do something so horrible."

"You knew him well?"

"I guess not," he said, shaking his head and staring down at the floor. "He came out here often. Very friendly man."

"I take it y'all talked a lot."

"I'd come over to his storage or he'd stop by mine. He liked my choice of beer and my setup." George lowered his voice, placing a shielding hand next to his mouth, and said, "It's my get-away from the wife."

"I see."

He let out a bellowing laugh, rattling his gut. "I'd go mad if I didn't have this place." He seemed to be convincing himself, the guilt seeping out from his pores.

"Did Dr. Randal ever tell you why he recreated his work space in here?"

"The quiet, mostly. He said his office was too loud. He'd read for hours on that couch, most of the time his files, but occasionally he'd read a book or a magazine. Always ones about psychological mumbo-jumbo."

"Makes sense," I said.

"He once told me it was safer here, but I didn't understand what he meant. I assumed he meant away from his patients. You know...all the crazies." He was making circles in the air around his right ear. Morons like him didn't bother me. My mom wasn't crazy. She was tricked by the Gamemakers and her so-called psychiatrist. But she never let either of them win. This guy was cursed with something way worse and much more widespread. He was ignorant.

"Yeah, you have to be careful," I said. "They're everywhere, some closer than you think." I remained expressionless while he stood there silently, attempting to read me. By the look on his face, he didn't know whether to laugh or run. I slammed my knee against the desk drawer next to me, ramming it shut. He flinched, taking a step backwards. After an awkward few seconds of letting him stew in uncertainty, I slowly unraveled a wry grin.

"You had me going for a second," he said, letting out an uncomfortable laugh. He lowered his hands from their defensive pose.

"I can't lie," I said, turning my head and gazing around the small room, "this place gives me the creeps, too."

"Well, uh, I've taken too much of your time already. I ought to be going. The wife gets a little suspicious if I'm not home by dinner time. Nice talkin' with ya, Bob."

"Same here."

After he left, I pulled open another file drawer. I was curious about other patients the good doctor had treated. I wanted to know if the connection with my mother was an isolated incident. After scanning over a few of the numerous files behind my mother's, I hadn't found any more narrative that was consistent with my mom's, but there were way too many files to dismiss the possibility. I decided to move to the next cabinet. When I opened it, I noticed immediately that it was much different from the other. Instead of being jammed full of thick manila folders spilling their contents, this one was strategically neat. There were two dark green hanging folders. The first one contained one thick manila folder inside, and the other, much wider, held an assortment of manila folders.

The first green folder was labeled "War Plan". My heart plummeted down into my bowels when I read the name. I opened the file and began reading. It read like the label: a formulated plan, all typed and neatly structured. The opening sentence read:

The Gamemakers are a formidable force with one purpose in mind: to cause debilitating diseases to their victims. They must be stopped at all costs.

Gamemakers
Recruits

War

These three words seemed to be the premise for what followed. I flipped through and read each of the stages. The detail was incredible. It must have taken him quite a long time to devise such a meticulous plan. In summary: The Gamemakers were an entity responsible for causing whatever affliction the patient possessed by sending their minions to actually implant the sickness inside them. The minions were disguised as everyday people, even family members or friends. The patients he was recruiting were all ailing with some type of audible or visual disturbances. Once the recruits were primed and ready — after his hypnotherapy — they were to wage war by seeking out and killing the minions. Once the minions were dead, their sickness would be eradicated.

On the last page of the file, I found out what Dr. Randal did with any recruits who disobeyed his orders:

In the event of a rogue recruit:

I will first attempt to erase the recruit's memory and release them from the program. If this fails, I will have to delete them permanently.

There was no elaboration as to how he would delete them, but I had a pretty good idea. The next green hanging folder, the one holding the collection of manila folders, was labeled Recruits. There must have been forty to fifty files, with first and last names written in bold black letters on each of the tabs. My mom's was first in line.

The file was much thinner than the one from the first cabinet, as were all of the others. There were only a few pages in my mom's file, all neatly typed. Essentially, the pages said that she had passed as a recruit with high marks. Thankfully there weren't any orders for her to kill, but for my own sanity I needed to be completely certain. I needed to thoroughly go through her two files and compare them with the journals at home, in quiet. I glanced down at my watch and realized I had been there over four hours. Dusk was approaching.

Along with needing quiet, I needed privacy. I couldn't risk any more storage neighbors stopping in for a friendly chat. I gathered all of the "War Plan" files. I also grabbed a random selection of files from the first cabinet in an effort to form a better understanding of his thought process. That is, if I could get past the irrational rants.

Before shutting the storage unit, I stood at the entrance and stared into the small space. This was his war room, a place where he planned and strategized. He used his patients, strategically choosing recruits with a previously instilled inclination to harm someone or themselves. They willingly allowed him to hypnotize them and he preyed on their vulnerabilities. My mom must have either realized his intentions or got lucky that Dr. Randal held a soft spot for her when she refused further hypnotherapy. I didn't see anywhere that he attempted to erase her memory or permanently delete her. If his plan had been consistent, his initial goal would have been for her to kill her family.

How many had he already killed? How many family members had been murdered on his orders? And could he still potentially be operating from behind the asylum doors?

• • •

When I got home, I settled down in my hidden room to thoroughly go through the files and the three journals. I wanted to compare dates and notes. I needed everything in chronological order so I could rule out the possibility that my mom had been instructed to kill.

I pulled the pill bottle I found in the storage unit out from my pocket. I placed it in the desk drawer where I was planning to keep the files once I was done with them.

Starting with the journals, I marked dates I recalled from what I had already read. My mind drifted, and I wondered why the journal my dad had faked seemed more harsh and threatening than the three originals. Maybe his thinking was that if she ever did follow through with the voice's demands, his journal would be enough to deter the authorities from questioning anything else. He was just protecting her. Considering how honorable he was, it made sense. My dad obviously hadn't known about Dr. Randal's plot, because if he had, Dr. Randal would have been in jail, or worse, before he had a chance to kill his family.

Before setting the journals aside and picking up the files, I focused on one of the later entries. I found my mom's heart-rending words of regret a few days after my sister drowned:

I should have known they would go after my sweet Katy. They told me I would regret ignoring them. Katy, I'm so sorry, baby —. The "Y" in "baby" stretched across the page.

I imagined my mom crying and my dad setting his journal down and abruptly leaving his chair across from her, pulling her close and squeezing her tightly until the tears subsided. I know what it's like to battle a constant force rivaling your every move. That, on top of the death of my sister, must have been a tremendous heartache for them to deal with. I don't know how they survived for as long as they did. She blamed the Gamemakers for my sister's death in the journal. But like me, she probably partially blamed herself.

The term "Gamemakers" may have been strategically placed in the recruits' heads by Dr. Randal, but my mom — according to the notes — actually mentioned the name to him first. In fact, it was the revelation they shared. They had both begun referring to the ones responsible for their afflictions as "Gamemakers," before Dr. Randal's plot ever came to fruition. I checked the dates in her journals just to be certain, and sure enough she mentioned them before the date in her file.

While searching the dates I was nervous, dreading the potential outcome of discovering that Dr. Randal planted the name. Ever since I adopted it from my dad's letter, it has served as a connection to him. From now on, it will be a connection to both of my parents. Dr. Randal knew the truth, that the Gamemakers are responsible for placing evil in the world, but he twisted it to satisfy his own deep desires and hurt the innocent. Dr. Randal and my mom might have shared a name, but not their principles.

When I got to the typed files of the recruits — the War Plan folder — I laid them out and noticed something I had missed earlier. A few of the names on the tabs had a thin red slash mark through them. I had a suspicion that these were his failed recruits, the ones that he had deleted. The first one I opened was on a Mr. Cuffman. I scrolled down past a few paragraphs that looked to be his beginning progress, and flipped the page. At the bottom was an explanation for the red slash mark:

I feel that Mr. Cuffman isn't fit to continue training. He refuses hypnotherapy on occasion and has mentioned his old medications multiple times. My convincing data didn't alter his stubborn attitude. He will be removed from the program.

Below the note was the word DELETED, and a short note beside it:

Attempted to erase Mr. Cuffman's memory without success. He returned a few days later very irate and demanding answers to nonsensical questions. I couldn't take any chances. He could potentially damage all that I have built. I convinced him to try one more session of hypnotherapy. During the session, I ordered him to terminate himself.

There were four more files marked with a red slash, each of them ordered to self-terminate. Dr. Randal was ruthless in his endeavor, having his failed recruits commit suicide. His mission took priority over any morals that may have resided in him. The rest of the files, the ones representing recruits chosen to continue with the program, were even more disturbing. Family members, friends — basically anyone Dr. Randal decided was a minion of the Gamemakers — were chosen to be killed. The manner in which each was killed varied, depending on what I assumed to be Dr. Randal's dark fantasies.

Before setting the files aside and examining my mom's files, I noticed one of the last manila folders didn't have anything written on the tab. My question about whether Dr. Randal still planned to kill was answered the moment I opened the file. The title sentence read, "Contingency Plan in the event that I have been infiltrated or killed." It revealed that the war would continue. There weren't details, but basically he planted future dates into the recruits' heads so that they could follow through with the killings. All of his recruits were placed in motion once he realized he needed to harm his own wife and daughter, whom he believed were the Gamemakers' minions. With the length of time he has been in the asylum, the killings have probably been completed, but there was still the possibility that he was furthering his plan. What better place for him to recruit than from inside a mental hospital? Dr. Randal had to be put down, and my mom's memory had to be avenged. I needed a way to get him out of the asylum or me in, but how? Dr. Fortune was really my only answer. He would have to be persuaded to allow Dr. Randal a field trip. I had to think this through.

I picked up both of mom's files and began thoroughly examining them. I was pretty sure she didn't harm anyone, but after reading some of the atrocious acts Dr. Randal made others in the group perform, I was still a little nervous. As I began rereading the file with Dr. Randal's session notes, I couldn't help but wonder which parts were my mom's true words and which were based on his delusions. Comparing the journals and the files was difficult, and she's no longer here to reveal the answers.

After thoroughly examining her files, I didn't find any hidden orders for her to kill. I felt relieved, but with her death, I can never know definitively. But I *can* say one thing for certain: she never harmed her family.

I thought about one of my favorite entries from her journals:

They watch and wait their turn while we go blindly into the night, vulnerable and weak. So they think. These, these Gamemakers will not win. Never again will I let my guard down. Never!

The hairs on my neck stood, as bumps along my arms and neck took rise. I felt the exhilaration as strongly as I did when I first read the words. I wanted to stand beside her and yell into the heavens: We will not go silently into the darkness! We will fight until our last lung full of air is —.

The doorbell interrupted my silent speech.

I pushed open the bookshelf and stepped out into the library. I peeked around the corner toward the front door. It looked like the outline of Dave — a man his height and wearing a ballcap — but I wasn't expecting him. Dave always called first. I secured the bookshelf shut, repetitively touching the frame to a count of five. I didn't like unexpected guests, and my OCD knew it.

Chapter 21

Dave stood in my doorway, a solemn expression seeping from under the brim of his hat. In his right hand he held a midsize beige suitcase, and in his left was a case of his favorite cheap beer.

"Sorry, man, but everything happened so fast," he said. "And then my phone died on the way over here."

"I assume talking didn't work."

"No, and actually it went worse than even you suspected it would."

"How is that possible?"

"She actually went on the defensive, blaming me for opening her legs."

"What? Really?"

"She didn't put it like that, but you get the point."

"I caught your sarcasm."

"I just don't get it," Dave said. "I really don't."

I didn't have an answer for him. I had my own struggles at the moment. I led him to the spare bedroom — my little sister's old room. For years my parents left it exactly as it was. Eventually they began packing things away and storing them in a chest in the attic. The room has sat mostly bare for many years, with a few pictures scattered around. The one remnant I pulled from the attic was her teddy bear, which I rested against the middle pillow of the bed. It still bore a faint yellow stain on its right ear from when she spilled mustard on it at the fair. She had insisted that she could handle the corn dog on her own. We shared that stubbornness.

"Do I get to use the bear as a sleeping companion?" Dave asked playfully, heaving his suitcase on top of the bed.

"Sure, if my little sister will let you." He lowered his head and removed his hat. "I'm just joking," I said. "You got to relax a little, man."

"I know. Sorry, I just know how much your little sister meant to you —"

"Seriously, it's okay. Let's get a drink."

"Please."

I made myself a drink, but I didn't touch it. I only suggested drinks because he looked like he needed to get drunk and talk. And as much as I despised listening to self-pity rants, I made an exception for Dave this time. We sat in the living room, me in my dad's old recliner, him on the couch. He looked exhausted. Relationships tend to do that on occasion, some more than others, and Dave was one of those others. He'd been continuously pummeled by the opposite sex, but stubbornly, he keeps trudging forward to the next relationship.

"Earl, come here, boy," Dave said. "Come on, not you too." After hearing Dave's desperate plea, Earl reluctantly left his warm bed next to the fireplace and sat down beside him at the base of the couch. Dave scratched Earl behind his left ear and said, "Thanks. I don't think I could handle another rejection at the moment." Earl wagged his tail and offered up a dog's unflinching affection by licking Dave's hand.

"No decorations?" Dave said.

"Huh… oh, no, sorry. You mean Christmas, right?"

"Yeah, you do know it's in a week don't you?"

"I know. I just don't feel like it much. All the crap that's happened the last few years has taken away my energy to celebrate."

"Come on. I mean I get it, but we can't let life beat us down," Dave said. "Whatever doesn't kill us makes us stronger." He downed the rest of his beer.

"Or drunker," I said.

"That too." He pulled a fresh beer from the table next to him and opened it. "We've both had some crappy things happen to us. Heck mine is still happening. I don't get to see my daughter this year for Christmas, and I just found out my second cheating wife is having another man's baby."

I felt for the guy. I really did. He was way more cursed than I have been with relationships, but that was probably due to my avoidance of them for so long. Dave wasn't going to give up. He believed to his core that each of us is destined to have the perfect mate. I didn't quite share that optimism, having my own issues with women at the moment.

"Okay, you win," I said. "You get the pity award, for now." He didn't deny wanting to be pitied. He seemed to savor it, as I have come to expect from him.

"I know I just got here and all, and you were way more than gracious to allow me over, but can we at least put a tree up? I need something to bring me out of this hole I'm in."

"And decorations will do that for you?"

"I don't know, maybe. It couldn't hurt," he said, brooding over his own words.

"All right, all right. The decorations are in the attic, but don't expect me to help with them."

The idea seemed to bring him out from his temporary

slump. He even smiled and began preparing the layout for his Christmas display. My mom would have smiled along with him, humming carols and drinking wine. They may have actually been pretty good friends.

His excitement was short-lived, and he never got close to retrieving anything from the attic. When the day of disappointment and tattered relationships took their toll, he passed out on the couch, snuggling with his half-empty beer.

With Dave asleep, I headed out to my lab. It was the only suitable place to be alone with my thoughts now that my partner was staying with me. There was much I needed to process.

● ● ●

On the way to my lab, I remembered an old friend I hadn't visited in a long while. I missed his company.

Mr. Thompson was my neighbor when I lived in an apartment, back before my mom passed away. He had known my dad from way back when, and we quickly became friends. He liked telling me stories about my dad, and we both enjoyed aged Scotch. I had even done him a favor — unbeknownst to him — when I took care of the man who robbed and beat him in his home last year.

The last time I had seen Mr. Thompson was shortly after I helped him move into his new bottom-floor apartment. Failing eyesight, multiple hip surgeries, and the permanent attachment to an oxygen bottle were enough reasons to warrant a move from the top floor to the bottom.

I rang his doorbell, and seconds later I heard the familiar sound of an oxygen bottle thumping against the wall as he made his way toward the door.

"Tryke, I was wondering when you'd be stopping by again. How are you?" He sounded good, better than I expected.

"Good, good. And you?"

"Hanging in there." I followed him inside as he lumbered to the living room and sat down in his recliner. He had always appeared much older than he actually was — a few tours in Vietnam, an avid boxer in the Marines, and the loss of a lifelong spouse definitely takes its toll on the human body and mind, though in that area he hadn't dwindled much. He could more than keep up with me in a conversation.

"When did you get the cane?" I asked.

"It's the one I had back from when I had surgery," he grumbled. "Ever since they cut me, I can't seem to get back where I was. Not that I was much faster." He laughed and started a coughing fit. "Excuse me." He cleared his throat. "So, how's Lesley doing?"

"We're sort of... on the outs."

"For good? Or just a spat?"

"I'm not sure, but it's not looking good. We had a fight during Thanksgiving."

"You and half the country, I presume. Fights on a holiday among family and friends is tradition. It's okay to show a little passion. Only don't let it linger."

"This one wasn't just a simple argument. She thinks I'm seeing another woman."

"I'll be right back. This calls for another companion."

A few minutes later, he returned with two glasses, struggling without his cane. I got up and grabbed them from his hands, setting his drink onto the table beside his chair. "Thanks, but I had it. I ain't letting this cane stop me from being hospitable."

I knew better than to question his independence. His conviction on the matter was clear. He once told me that the day he lost the ability to take care of himself was the day he would die. "Is this what I think it is?" I brushed my nose along the rim of the glass and inhaled. "Laphroaig Scotch! What's the occasion?" Though I hadn't felt much like drinking earlier at my house, I couldn't turn down the offer of my favorite Scotch.

"Woman trouble," he said. "It's as good an excuse as any."

"All right. I'm not arguing."

"So, tell me about this other woman that has your Lesley all flustered."

"It's nothing really," I said, "a misunderstanding that got out of hand. A text message actually. This other woman, Kimberly, is a physician at Mercy and we had an interest in a patient I brought in."

"I'm gonna go out on a limb here and assume she's attractive."

"She's not bad looking. I mean, Lesley is much prettier."

"You don't have to convince me. Can I let you in on a little secret about the opposite sex?" I nodded and took a sip from my glass, eagerly awaiting an insight to the elusive female psyche. "They have this radar that can pick up subtle vibes we men ignore. We're not even aware that we're giving ourselves away at times. Back in my day, back before text messaging and cell phones, people had to face one another. We had to actually read one another's body language and facial expressions — a skill quickly dwindling away."

It was a skill I used quite often while searching for specimens. But for some reason, when it came to women I was attracted to, I seemed to forget I ever possessed it.

He continued. "If my memory serves me, my wife and I had an issue similar to you and Lesley, back when we were dating. A girl by the name of Carly Soren, red hair, long legs and a smile not easily forgotten. She had written her number down and a short message on the inside of my notebook. Needless to say, Susan found it. When she confronted me, I initially responded by denying any knowledge of it. Once she showed it to me by opening the notebook, I revealed that subtle vibe of guilt. We didn't talk for a week. I finally worked up the nerve to confront her between classes. What I said that day forever changed our lives."

He took a sip from his glass and stared over at the mantel, where the pictures of him and his deceased wife were displayed. He smiled, his lower eyelids moments from overflowing with tears. "I stood right in front of her, my back to the lockers, my face inches from hers. She had the most angry look, but still cute as hell. The halls were scrambling with students and teachers, but in that moment it was just her and me. 'Susan,' I said, 'will you marry me?' At first, I thought she was going to run, but her eyes swelled and she couldn't stop nodding yes."

"That's insane," I said.

"Yes, maybe, but something was pushing me toward her that day. I had an urgency to tell her how I felt. I was scared of losing her. My point, Tryke, is this: if you feel it's right, then it probably is. I'm not saying to get married, but I'm also not saying not to."

"Maybe I'll start out by just telling her the truth, and work our way to furthering our relationship later."

"Well, that's a start."

"I was curious about the note the redhead wrote you. What did it say, if you don't mind my asking?"

He smiled and wiped his face with a handkerchief he had just pulled from the pocket of his jeans. "She had written, 'I need your —' The rest was scratched out with her pen when she saw the teacher coming. 'Answers' was the word she had scratched out. She was referring to the math homework. No matter the innocence, she was pretty, and I let it show. I was caught off guard that day. I was tongue-tied, unable to explain it to Susan. Before we got married, she wanted to know the rest of the message that had been scratched out. We laughed about it for years."

"Context is important," I said, laughing now myself.

Chapter 22

After leaving Mr. Thompson's apartment, I couldn't quit thinking about Lesley. If I said nothing and let the event fester within her it would be damaging to us. But, was I ready to explain myself? Could I really afford to at the moment, especially considering how unstable Dr. Kimberly had been acting? If Lesley were to confront her, Dr. Kimberly might spill everything about the case, including the fact that we kept information from the police. I didn't know which path to take; both risked my fragile relationship with Lesley.

When I pulled into the back parking area to my lab, I noticed the back end of a white truck from around the far corner of the structure. I parked my truck close to the building, keeping it hidden until I figured out who was there and what they were doing.

I made my way toward the white vehicle. I lowered the brim of my hat and placed my hands inside my jacket pockets, giving the impression I was just a passerby taking a shortcut across the property to the nearby neighborhood.

When I reached the corner of the building, I stopped, slowly turned my head, and glanced toward the truck. The clear cab windows allowed me to see that there was no one inside. It appeared to be some sort of work-truck, though I didn't see a logo or business name along the door or rear window. I suppose someone could have parked it there, intending to pick it up later: lost, too drunk to drive, broke down and walked home. The possibilities were endless. But I had an eerie feeling this wasn't just some random, abandoned vehicle.

I stayed firmly against the wall of the building until I reached the front. I stopped at the edge, and before I had the chance to poke my head around, a man rounded the corner, coming the other way and nearly knocking me over.

"Sorry, I didn't see you there," the man said, stepping back to catch his breath. He was wearing an orange vest, the type a construction worker might wear; he also had on a white t-shirt, faded jeans, and boots.

"It was my fault," I said. "I should have been looking up instead of dodging the wind."

Still hunched over, he looked up at me and said, "Man, you scared the crap out of me."

"Are you okay?" He seemed to be having a hard time catching his breath, more than one should after simply being caught off guard.

"Yeah… I'll be… all right." He spit on the ground, his breathing finally slowing a little. "I get these damn dizzy spells, but they pass. I'll be fine."

"If you say so," I said. "I'll just be on my way, then." He waved me off, returning upright, and started walking back toward what I assumed was his truck.

"Sir," I said. He stopped and turned back around. "If you don't mind me asking, what's your business with the building?" He looked offended, like I had no right to question him. "I don't mean to be so frank, it's just, well, there weren't any markings on your truck and…"

"You must be one of the sons," he said. He sounded irritated. I didn't know how to respond. Sons? Of who? "My boss warned me that one of you Garrisons might be stalking the building."

"No, sir, I'm not one of them. My dad used to work here years ago, and the place has sentimental value to me, that's all."

He cocked his head, deciding if he should believe me. "So you're not related to the Garrisons in any way?"

"No, sir, I assure you I am not."

He looked relieved. "Well, I'm afraid you're not going to like me either. I work for Lester Development. We're in the process of purchasing the property from the bank. The owner defaulted."

"Sad to hear," I said. "I suppose in time it was bound to happen. What do they plan on putting here?" I was having a hard time suppressing the angst that was quickly forming inside me.

"Office buildings, I believe."

"Okay, thanks for the heads up."

"Take care," he said, and then he got into his truck and left.

I sighed and took a much needed gulp of air. It certainly put another twist into my life, as if there weren't already enough: Duncan Sims aka Elderly Slayer, Dr. Randal and his twisted plot, Dave living in my house, Lesley, and psycho Dr. Kimberly. And now my lab might be headed for the wrecking ball? I could hardly stop every game from playing out, but I knew I had to handle each of them one by one, in their own way and in their own time. It was the only way to get my life back on track.

Once the white truck was completely out of sight, I did a quick sweep inside the building, making sure no other strangers were lurking around. I then sat in my lab to think everything over. If someone were to take a glance around upstairs, I wasn't that worried. I covered my equipment with old sheets, which gave the impression that forgotten office furniture had been laid to rest underneath.

• • •

The next morning, Dave and I rode together to work. I had never shared a ride to work before. I had my routine, and he had his — to put it mildly. There was even conflict over what time we should depart for the station. Why couldn't we have just taken separate vehicles? That was my initial question, but Dave was still pitifully dragging me into his realm of despair. His constant pairing of loneliness and Christmas made me adhere to his requests, at least until the holidays were over.

The morning had been busy with routine calls: chest pains, seizures, minor MVAs. I was thankful to have the distraction, but it wasn't enough. On more than one occasion Dave asked if I was okay. My mind fumbled, my coolness faltered, every complaint from my patients slid off me like water on well-oiled skin. I couldn't hide the stress.

We pulled into Mercy to pick up a few of our backboards from that morning's vehicle wrecks.

"It's my turn," Dave said. "I'll grab the boards." Before opening the door, he paused with his hand on the door handle. He was about to ask me something personal. I knew it was only a matter of time, after all the signals I had been sending out all morning. "Anything you want to tell me? Come on, man, we're roomies now. Get it off your chest."

I frowned at him and said, "You aren't going to stop, are you, pestering me until I tell you something?"

He shook his head, smiling, and pointed his hand toward me in the shape of a makeshift gun. "Nope," he said, winking.

"I don't know why you have to be so insistent that I tell you about my stress. Does it make yours seem less threatening?"

"Misery loves company. Come on, it gets lonely down here in the dumpster. And it smells, too. Believe it or not, I can read you like a book."

"Oh, really?" I said. "I wasn't aware that you possessed that ability. What was I thinking… hmm let me see —"

"Don't use your sarcasm to avoid talking."

"What the hell, you sound like a woman."

"You're rerouting again," he said, scowling at me.

Okay, he caught me, but I still wasn't convinced of his powers to read me. "If you must know, it's Lesley. The holidays and all."

"I knew it! I freaking knew it!"

"Thanks for knowing. I don't see how that helps me."

"Sorry, I guess it doesn't. I was just happy for once that I got you to talk about something. I can never tell about you. You're one hard son of a bitch to read. Even Dr. Kimberly said —" He covered his mouth. "Crap, I didn't mean to—"

"No, go ahead, please."

"She… okay, all she said was that you were a hard man to get to know. I just agreed with her and that was it. That was all we discussed, I swear."

"Okay, but only because you swore," I said with a smirk.

"Ha ha. Anyway, back to a serious note. If you want, I can eat my pride and call Angie and ask her about Lesley."

"No! I mean, I can handle it. It's my problem. Besides, I wouldn't ask that of you."

"Seriously, I don't mind."

"Dave," I said, shaking my head.

"Look, I'll say one thing and then I'll shut up about it. I've never even come close to having what you and Lesley have. Do what you want, but don't forget about the rarity of the connection y'all share." I remained silent, staring forward through the windshield. Out of my peripheral, I could see him shrug. He opened the door and said, "I just thought you should know." He shut the door of the rig behind him and went inside to retrieve the backboards.

I mulled over his words. I wasn't quite as enthused as he was about the relationship at the moment. I'd avoided relationships for a long time before I met Lesley. In fact, she was my first long-term anything. Before, lust was my only reason to be with women. Some attempted to persuade me to further involvement, but none succeeded. Lesley was the first to infiltrate my defenses.

I looked down at my watch. Dave had been gone for ten minutes, way more than enough time to grab the backboards, even if he did have to hunt for a few in Radiology. Where the hell was he? I turned the rig off and grabbed the portable radio.

When I stepped through the double-door entrance, I sighed at the spectacle taking place next to the nurses' station. Now I knew what was keeping Dave from leaving. Dr. Kimberly was once again attempting to charm him, loudly laughing and nudging him with her elbow and hips. It was a disgusting display of deceit, meant for one purpose — retaliation toward me for rejecting her.

I didn't want to approach the situation, but I had to. The longer he spent with her, the deeper her stinger would penetrate his vulnerabilities.

I stood next to Dave, silently, until he turned toward me. The radio from my belt amplified, drawing his attention away from her tentacles.

"Tryke, guess who's having a Christmas party tomorrow night?" Dave said. The chipper tone in his voice was making me nauseous.

"I don't know Dave. Who?" I did the best I could to avoid eye contact with Dr. Kimberly. I imagined her attempting to squish my brain with her thoughts. I was hoping he would catch the lack of interest in my tone, but no such luck.

"Dr. Kimberly. She's invited us. And before you say anything, let me explain." I shut my eyes in frustration, but I didn't object. "We've been discussing things and she has decided to forget everything. Let bygones be bygones. We'll all start over and reacquaint ourselves at the party." What had she told him? More lies, I suspected, to draft him to her side.

I didn't feel like arguing, and anything I said at that moment other than agreeing would be seen as aggressive. That was the beauty of drawing first in a conversation of peace. "Fine, but as for the party —"

"Oh, and she even offered to be our designated driver. I told her I was staying with you for a few weeks." Even without looking at her, I could see Dr. Kimberly's wily grin.

"Great," I said with enhanced sarcasm. I didn't believe her, nor did I trust her noble offer to drive us. And now Dave had put me in a predicament, allowing her access to my house by letting her be his driver. I didn't know yet what she was up to, but it wasn't closing old wounds and starting over — that wasn't her style. Still, I had to be careful until I had the Elderly Slayer in my lab. "What time is the party?" I asked.

"Seven-thirty," said Dave. "So you'll go?"

"Maybe for a few hours, but not until later in the evening. I have some things I need to do." My pursuit of the Elderly Slayer was planned for that afternoon. This party might actually make a good alibi.

"You'll still be my designated driver, won't you?" Dave asked Dr. Kimberly, turning back toward her.

"Of course I will, Davy," she said, reaching down and squeezing his right butt cheek. It took every bit of restraint I could muster to hold my tongue. The last person I heard call him Davy was his first wife, Claire, the demon wife of the suburbs.

"All right, let's get out of here," I said to Dave. "Dr. Kimberly." I nodded, staring past her, and then I turned to leave. Dave stayed to say his goodbyes in private. He showed up a few minutes later wearing a boyish grin. He was falling into the arms of another deceitful woman, only to be dropped and left at the doorstep of the nearest foster home for shredded hearts. I tried to warn him, but he was already too far gone.

Chapter 23

After work, I dropped Dave off at my house and finally set out to track down Duncan Sims. My minimal hacking skills proved worthy once again. I retrieved his latest address, along with the make and model of his vehicle, after infiltrating the DMV's computer system.

Sitting in my truck, five houses down from Mr. Sims's address, I searched the internet on my phone for the number to the property development company. I needed to be sure they weren't planning demolition on my lab anytime soon. I knew eventually I would have to find a new place, although I didn't think it would be this soon. Unfortunately, I didn't have any prospects for another location at the moment.

"Lester Properties, how can I help you?" Her southern drawl was intense. Of course, having lived in Texas all my life, I had my own slight drawl, as Lesley often pointed out, but nowhere near as pronounced as this lady.

"Yes, ma'am, I was calling in regards to the property on Barksdale Avenue."

"Just a moment, sir. Let me see what we've got on that street."

"Thank you." She put me on hold. A soothing jazz mixture entertained my ears while I waited.

"Sir, the only address I'm showing on that street is pending."

"Meaning?"

"We haven't completed the process with the bank. I'm afraid if you're interested in that particular property, it isn't going to be available for sale. Is there another address you were interested in?"

"No, ma'am, thank you for your time." I hung up the phone, relieved to hear I still had some time before their process with the bank was complete. I didn't know exactly how long I had, but I felt confident it was enough to release Mr. Sims. I would just have to be more cautious, due to the turf battle that was taking place, according to the surveyor in the white truck.

Mr. Sims didn't appear to be home. His black 2005 SUV wasn't parked in the driveway. Work perhaps, or out doing what he does best, killing old people in their beds. I waited and watched thirty more minutes for continuity of the street — neighbors, traffic. I was glad he wasn't home. I needed to know the layout of the house, in case of unexpected complications, before I leaped in for a takedown. He was probably a cautious man, maybe even a bit paranoid.

A normal security system, one that contacted the local police, was not an option for a serial killer stalking the night. He needed a more private alerting device, perhaps hidden cameras, or infrared lasers surrounding the perimeter and feeding signals directly to his phone. Maybe even a dog. Of course, there was always the possibility of a brave and arrogant serial killer, one who thinks he is much too dangerous and elusive to be stalked or sought out personally.

The midmorning traffic was what I expected for a middle-class neighborhood on a Friday morning. But there was one creature, a lurking vigilant stalker, that seemed to never sleep. Always one eye open, waiting for the inevitable moment to pounce. They're usually on porches, sometimes hidden in the shadows of half-pulled curtains. This creature is known as the "neighborhood watch". As long as I kept my cool and looked like I belonged, I would be all right.

I slipped off my work uniform shirt, leaving on my white undershirt, and pulled on a sweatshirt I had in my truck's backseat. I didn't need to draw unneeded attention — which EMS personnel tended to do, lights or no lights.

The front of the house seemed normal: shutters open, blinds slightly bent forward, a few plants covered with sheets from the recent freeze. He cared more for his plants than he did for his fellow humans. The perimeter and backyard also appeared normal: no unnecessary high fence, a path of circular concrete steps leading to a covered patio complete with a grill and furniture. No cameras, no dog, no infrared lasers — not that I had yet discovered, anyway. If I wasn't hunting a serial killer, I might have thought I was visiting my grandmother's house.

I entered through the back door. No alarm. This was all too easy, I thought, as I glanced around the kitchen where the morning paper sat, folded after a reading. There were plants everywhere, hanging, potted, even a few in coffee cups along the edge of the kitchen window. When I entered the living room, I knew I had come across a sanctuary for plants. A botanist would be envious of the setup, wanting to spend hours exploring the variety of species. I was actually impressed with the knowledge and skill needed to care for such delicate life — I had trouble keeping a ficus tree alive. There were no decorations to be seen celebrating the holiday season, only foliage.

I made my way across the living room, through the jungle, and glanced around the few bedrooms — a quick sweep of the place to make sure no one was asleep or hiding, or bound to a bed. They were empty except for, of course, more plants. The first place I began my search was an obvious room, his study. A laptop sat open on the walnut-colored executive antique desk. No password. Come on, I thought, this is all a bit odd. Maybe he was an extreme narcissist, untouchable by us mere mortals.

I silently thanked him as I clicked through the files, searching for anything to clue me in to who this guy really was. I was getting nowhere on his computer. Most of the files were empty, his internet history cleared a day ago. There was no need for a password when you keep a clean slate. His bookshelf was also clean. There was just book after book about, you guessed it, plants. I wasn't buying this boring persona.

I knelt down and opened the top drawer of his two-drawer file cabinet. It was filled with instruction booklets and warranty information for appliances. The second drawer was full of empty green file folders. So it seemed, until I slammed it shut in frustration and heard a thump from the rear that sounded as if something heavy had fallen.

Reaching my hand behind the folders, I found a three-inch black binder, divided neatly in sections. The first section was full of newspaper clippings. Each article was about a victim suspected of being killed by the Elderly Slayer. Not unusual for these guys to have a record of their work. I flipped to the next section. Each page had two pictures of the same person beside one another, one in color, the other in black and white. I recognized some of the photos as obituary cutouts from the article section I had just flipped through. It took a minute for the information to process and then I realized what he was doing. This sick bastard snapped photos of his victims before he killed them. He compared their last moment of life next to the photo chosen by a loved one — a demented display of poetry from a sick mind.

I found the picture of the elderly lady Clyde and I made, the first one that I suspected he poisoned. I remembered his demeanor that day when Clyde told him to move, how he stared at us as we wheeled his victim down the hall. I also recognized the flowered blouse in the photo as the one she had on that day. He must have snapped the picture moments before we arrived.

The next, and last, section in the binder, at first glance seemed to be a tribute of some sort to one particular elderly woman; photo after photo of this same woman, some in groups with other elderly at a function, some with a small child, others alone. The ones where she was alone were in black and white. I found handwritten notes, and they all began with: Dear Duncan. The content of the notes was everyday jargon: I'm doing this, I went here, how are you. It wasn't until I flipped the pictures over that I found the connection. The woman was his grandmother, and the child in the photos was him. After flipping past the last letter, I found a stapled pile of papers, thick enough to be a small book. On top of this pile was a cutout of his grandmother's obituary. Behind the cutout was a copy of the same article, scanned over and over again. The contents of the article brought context to his operation.

Beverly Walker was found dead New Year's Eve in her room at Brook-friar Nursing Home. She had a single GSW to the head according to police. Two elderly suspects, also residents of Brook-friar, were taken into custody for questioning.

Maybe that was the reason he ended his reign on New Year's Eve.

The rest of the article went on to say how much the incident had shocked the community and the residents of the nursing home. One of the residents, a friend of his grandmother, stated, "Beverly didn't harm a soul her entire life."

Now her grandson kills the innocent. And for what?

Retaliation for his grandmother's death? Maybe the two suspects were let go and no one was brought to justice for the murder. But that didn't justify killing the innocent with no ties to her killer. I didn't have all of the details. Maybe we'd need to have a short conversation before the release, for curiosity purposes only — the real reason was a darkness deep within, aching to be let go. And as far as the fascination, or obsession, with plants, I assumed they were some sort of connection to the grandmother, a desperate plea for anything tangible to remind him of her.

• • •

Before leaving his house, I covered my tracks, wiping away any evidence that I had been there. The place seemed relatively normal, except for the whole plant thing. If he was alone, and the evening proved quiet, I wouldn't have a problem making a surprise visit.

I was going to watch the neighborhood and the house for a few hours, just in case he returned. I didn't have anything planned for the afternoon, other than needing some sleep, but that wasn't happening while my life was in disarray. However, I needed to make a showing at the Christmas party sometime, briefly for my alibi, and then I would return around ten o'clock. If he was home at that time, then I could have everything completed by morning and be on my way to the next complication on my list.

The last thing I remember was flipping through a magazine. The candy bar and energy drink didn't do what they were supposed to do. I drifted off, only to be awakened by a bright light being shone through my side window directly into my eyes. I wasn't sure how long I'd slept. It was a few hours, I suspected, seeing that it was now just past twilight.

I immediately assumed someone had called the police, reporting my truck as a suspicious vehicle. I rolled down my window, shielding my eyes with my right hand, and said,

"Sorry, officer. I fell asleep after a long shift at work. If you wouldn't mind removing the light from my face, I'll get my ID for you."

When I turned and reached over to the console, I felt a sudden rush of immense pain in the back of my head.

Chapter 24

When I opened my eyes, the room was dark. A faint light shone from under the door a few feet away. I tried sitting up, only to find my hands and feet were bound, and there was an intense throbbing on the left side of my head. I instinctively tried to reach out and feel the wound, but it was no use.

I was bound to a bed. The restraints were tied together under the bed, so when I tried stretching one arm or leg, it pulled on the other. From the shadows I could make out, I appeared to be in a small bedroom: nightstand, lamp, dresser. A bedroom setting ruled out police involvement. The situation finally dawned on me. I was in Duncan Sims's house; the organic smell of potted soil was unmistakable. How could I have been so careless and fallen asleep? But that wasn't the real question here. How did he know I was stalking him? For all he knew I was a friend of one of his neighbors. Unless he had become suspicious lately, spending his spare time watching his house from afar. He could have seen me break in.

I could speculate later. For now, I had to find a way out
before he returned to the room to interrogate me. First, I
had to determine what type of material I was bound with. I
felt around with my fingertips, and identified smooth
leather and a small metal buckle. Was it simply a belt? Or
was it a heavier material specifically made to bind human
hands, like the hospital restraints I used? Whatever it was, I
wasn't about to break it, or even loosen it, with brute force.
But I *did* have one advantage an amateur easily overlooks. I
always searched for this one trait before placing restraints
on my specimens. When compared to my wrists, my hands
are slightly disproportionate. The variation is minimal, and
easily missed by the untrained eye. After a short struggle, I
was able to free my left hand from the thin leather
restraints.

I flipped on the small lamp on the bedside table.
Curious, I examined the restraints and noticed black
writing on the underside of the leather: Property of
Magnolia Bend Nursing Home. I checked the side of my
head where it was still throbbing and felt a raised
hematoma; it was dry, no blood. I patted the rest of my
body down, checking for other injuries. My pockets were
empty, meaning he had my wallet, keys, and phone, which
also meant he had my address. He could be there right
now, searching my things. I wasn't too worried. There was
nothing to find, unless he figured out how to enter my
hidden room.

I quickly looked around for anything I could use as a
weapon. All I found were a few scattered books in the
bedside drawer and the small lamp. I would have to rely on
my fists, and tactics.

He didn't take my watch, the one Lesley gave me last
year as a birthday gift. She had somehow managed to find
the same watch my dad had given me as a high school
graduation gift. My mom found it for him on their
honeymoon in a small shop in Rome. When I lost it in

paramedic school, I didn't forgive myself for a long time. I looked down at the watch. It was 7:45. I had only been knocked out a few hours. I switched off the lamp and listened for a couple of minutes with my ear pressed against the door, all the while watching the light from below for moving shadows. I turned the knob on the door, cringing from the few subtle clicks it made. I slowly poked my head out into the short hallway. Empty. So far so good. If my memory was correct, the front door was just around the corner, past the study, one room over from where I was currently standing.

I inched along the hallway wall, narrowly avoiding head contact with a cluster of hanging plants suspended from the ceiling. When I reached the doorway to the study, I peered into the room. His laptop was open, as it had been earlier, but this time the LCD display was glowing. Either he had just been there or the screensaver was stuck. I remembered powering it back down, and I'm not that careless. I was about to continue toward the front door when I noticed the top of my black phone on the other side of the computer.

Quickly, I gathered my phone, wallet, and keys. My curiosity got the better of me and I glanced over at the computer screen and hit the refresh button. There was a map displayed on the screen. Closer observation revealed my address typed into the line at the top. I searched his history and found that my name was in every search. I didn't know what he was hoping to find, but I tended to keep a low profile. The only reason he found my address was that he had my driver's license. If he was out doing research on me, that would at least allow me a clear path out of his house.

From the entryway, I scanned the living room. It was empty as far as I could tell, but the massive amount of foliage could have camouflaged a family of four. A quick glance out of the side glass near the front door let me see that his vehicle wasn't in the driveway. I exited the house and casually walked down the walkway, unopposed. I glanced over my shoulders, failing at any attempt to keep my cool. I could see my truck a hundred yards away, still parked in the same spot.

Only a little bit farther, I told myself.

I circled my truck. The tires looked intact, and nothing else seemed out of place. The inside was untouched. I even found the binder I had stolen from him, still in the back seat under my work-shirt. He could have easily sabotaged my truck, or at least taken my keys and wallet with him. This guy really wasn't one for thinking things through. But then, preying on frail elderly nursing home patrons didn't call for much vigilance.

• • •

I circled around my neighborhood once, avoiding my street. I parked the truck one street over and walked the rest of the way. I had to be sure Mr. Sims wasn't there, and if he was, I needed a plan. Luckily I had a pre-filled syringe in a hidden compartment in my truck for occasions such as these. Unlike my green-thumbed friend, I had plans in place. But, he *did* manage to capture me, and I had to give him credit for that. I quickly retracted the praise once I escaped so easily.

The only vehicle in my driveway was Dave's, which may have scared Sims off. Maybe it wasn't a totally asinine idea for Dr. Kimberly to be his designated driver for the night. In fact, it may have saved his life in more ways than one. But if Mr. Sims wasn't here, then where was he? Watching the house from a distance? Waiting for the owner of the vehicle in the driveway to leave?

If I could make it inside to my hidden room, I would be fine for the night. I could set up surveillance in the house, and most importantly, use the time to think out a plan.

After a half-hour of watching, I became frustrated. Why was I hiding from this guy? He wasn't going to the police.

I wanted him to come to me.

I went back to my truck and pulled into the driveway as if mindlessly returning home after work. If he was watching from the shadows, I wanted him to witness my hubris and come after me. Syringe in hand, I entered my house. From the entryway, everything appeared normal. That is, until I entered the living room. I was baffled, unsure of what to think about the display in front of me. Then it dawned on me when I remembered my conversation with Dave. I was standing at the entrance to a winter freaking wonderland. It looked like a snow globe of Christmas cheer had exploded, raining debris of every piece of decoration my mom had collected over the years: Frosty, Santa, Rudolph, a variety of elves, lights strung in every crevice of the room, and a tree, an actual live Christmas tree, way too tall, bending at the top and pressing a shiny golden star into the ceiling.

The spectacle was enough to make me drop my guard. Finally, I snapped out of the childhood trance and checked the rest of the house. Not that it told me much, but Earl was resting quietly in his usual spot by the fireplace. A slippery rug would have given an intruder more of a struggle.

The rest of the house was surprisingly secure. I set up a few of my extra cameras, one at each entrance, and fed them into a spare monitor next to the others in my hidden room. I also brought Earl into the room with me and locked the door. We had a long night of surveillance ahead of us.

As I sat watching the monitors, I wondered why I was still alive. I shouldn't be. There was no way a guy who had gotten away with killing for so many years would make so many rookie mistakes. He captured me, but left my truck and keys. My house was secure. Something didn't add up.

When I couldn't come up with a reason to explain why he hadn't killed me, I started thinking about the next morning. What was I going to do if Mr. Sims never came to finish the job? I couldn't stay in this room forever. If he didn't show tonight, I didn't know if he was ever going to show. He might even run, especially after losing me. Wouldn't he think I would report my abduction?

I'd wait for Dave to get home and we'd go to work together in the morning. I'd treat it like any other day. Sims wouldn't mess with me at the station. This was our last shift and then we were off for a few days. I could talk Dave into staying somewhere else until I took care of Mr. Sims. I couldn't have a serial killer with my address and a vendetta against me on the loose. I might have gone too far on this one. I was even considering the idea of turning him into the police myself, anonymously of course. But, the thought was short-lived. I wasn't sure what he knew about me.

• • •

Having fallen asleep with my head tilted to the side and facing the surveillance monitors, I woke up with a crick in my neck. I stretched my eyes and checked the screens. The doors appeared to still be intact and secure. I hadn't heard Dave come in last night, which either meant that he never came back or that Mr. Sims got him on the way in. I wasn't too worried about the latter; I would have heard something. Knowing Dr. Kimberly, she took advantage of Dave's vulnerability last night and he was sound asleep somewhere in her dungeon.

I put on a pot of coffee and set out a clean set of work clothes. Before getting into the shower, I did a quick check of the perimeter of the house, inside and out. This entire circumstance was new to me, being chased — or stalked, rather — by a specimen. The uncomfortable adrenaline flowing freely in my bowels felt odd. I wasn't sure if it was refreshing or terrifying, but I was leaning more toward the former. It was the thrill of the hunt, right? A rogue prey on the loose, stalking the predator in the tall brush. Wait, which was I again?

After pouring myself a cup of coffee, I waited for Dave to return. I would feel better if we had gone to work together. At least that way, I would know he was away from the house. As I finished the last of my coffee, I realized Dave wasn't showing up.

I needed an excuse to give him so he wouldn't come back to the house until the next day. Easy enough, I thought. I'll tell him I forgot about an appointment I made last month to have the house fumigated. I would have just called him, but I didn't feel like answering questions. And then there was the inevitable awkwardness that would ensue if he was indeed beside Dr. Kimberly in bed. Worse yet, if he was in the shower, she would answer out of spite, seeing my name displayed on his phone. I was definitely not in the mood for that confrontation. This was one time the impersonal act of texting came in handy.

There were a few items I didn't want Mr. Sims to find, including Earl, so I placed them inside the hidden room, and then texted Dave the brief message. He was to call me before going into the house, and I brought him a fresh uniform, meaning he could come straight to work. I put the word FUMIGATING in all caps. I hoped the message was clear enough that he would at least call me if he did decide to go there before work.

When I arrived at the station, I noticed that the supervisor's Suburban was parked in the driveway. Great, what the hell was this about? I didn't remember doing anything of interest lately to warrant such a visit. Not at work anyway. Something might have gone down on the other shift, and they were in the process of getting chewed out before leaving — always a nice experience before going home to sleep.

The two medics Dave and I were relieving, along with our supervisor Jerry, were all seated at the kitchen table when I entered through the back door. From their jolly gestures and lively greetings when I entered, the conversation didn't seem to be hostile or disciplinary in nature.

"What's the occasion?" I asked.

"I'll be filling in until your partner gets here," Jerry said.

"Okay…" I said.

He noticed my bewildered expression and said, "I know this isn't normally something I would do, but these guys have to take their kids to school. And I was coming over here for the drug sheets for the month, anyway." The drug sheet was a strict log where the narcotics were accounted for at the beginning and end of every shift — a date, time and signature process. I never liked the responsibility of carrying the narcotics all shift. There have been a few occasions when I left with zippered pouch in my pocket after an exhausting shift, only to have to turn around and take them back after arriving home.

"All right, how long did Dave say he'd be?" I asked.

"Oh, he's not coming in this shift. I have a replacement for him on the way," Jerry said.

"Huh. He's not coming in?" I said. "All right then." I checked my phone. He hadn't responded to my text.

I exchanged the narcotics with the off-going medic and went to put my bag in the bedroom across the truck bay.

When I returned to the kitchen, Jerry was still sitting at the table, now absorbed by the daily crossword puzzle. I poured myself a cup of coffee and sat down across from him.

"What's essential for all animals and most plants?" Jerry asked me, not looking up from the newspaper.

"Huh?"

"Crossword puzzle," he said shaking the paper in his hands.

"Oh… water," I said.

"Two letters, second one an 'A'."

"N-A. Sodium," I said. He looked puzzled. "The element from the periodic table."

"Ahhhhh. I wasn't so good at chemistry. Thanks." He filled in the answer with his pencil. "You know your partner called into dispatch this morning to call in sick."

"He did? That's odd."

"Yeah, I thought so too. He doesn't call in sick often. Maybe he didn't remember protocol, or no one answered this morning at central." He shrugged and went back to his crossword puzzle.

"Maybe." Dave, more than anyone, knew the rules. I pulled out my phone and checked again to see if he had sent a response to my message. Nothing. I shook my head, and smirked. That snake was lying up in Dr. Kimberly's bed, nursing a hangover. He was probably too scared to call in himself, and got her to do it for him, hence using dispatch instead of calling Jerry. He could have texted me this morning, or at least responded to mine.

"So, who's my partner this shift?" I asked.

Before he could answer, the backdoor swung open. Clyde barged in, wielding a wry grin and said, "Damn, Tryke, what did you do to Dave? Did you ram —" He stopped when he noticed Jerry sitting across from me. Jerry turned around with a frown and stared at him from under his glasses. "Sorry, sir."

Jerry turned back toward me, shaking his head and said, "I apologize in advance, Tryke, but he's all I had to put with you this shift."

"It'll be all right," I said. "He's okay, just a little off, is all. He can't help it." I knew Clyde wanted to respond, but with Jerry a few feet away, he couldn't come up with anything that didn't involve crude gestures or an expletive. On his way through the kitchen, he struck me in the back of the head with the bag that was slung over his shoulder, apologizing sarcastically.

Chapter 25

After Jerry left, Clyde was eager to get out of the station. He didn't care where, just out in the open. He explained how the last few days had been a living hell, having to entertain his sister and grandparents who were visiting from San Antonio for the holidays.

We set out on the road with no particular destination. We wouldn't have been sitting around long anyway, being this close to Christmas. Loneliness, depression, and family disputes were just a few of the ailments plaguing our citizens around the holidays. Add to the mix a serial killer who hunts the elderly and you get a nice recipe for 911.

"I'd pay for a damn hotel if I thought it would help," Clyde said.

"How would it not?"

"They're insistent on being together, one big, damn hemorrhoid, bulging and ready to burst," he said, propping his boot on the dash.

I laughed. "Come on. It can't be that bad."

"Well, let's see. My sister is neurotic at best, constantly

pissed off at society for inventing the word *love*. She actually thinks Cupid has waged war on her soul. And then there's my grandmother. Holy shit, where to begin with her. Let's just say a straitjacket don't have shit on her. Bless her old ass heart." He shook his head. "Man, you're lucky most of your family is dead." I knew he was only venting, and that his mouth lacked a filter. I had too much on my mind at the moment to be pissed off. He took my silence as anger. "Sorry, man, that was wrong of me to say. Especially around the holidays."

"I'm good," I said, but didn't elaborate or make a sly comment, as I normally would have.

"So, uh, where's Dave? Is he really sick?" he asked, attempting to break the awkward tension.

"Yeah, hangover sick."

"What? That square drinks?"

"Beer, mostly. Supposedly he went to a Christmas party last night."

"Wait, what party? I didn't know about a party last night," Clyde said, removing his boot from the dash and slamming his foot on the round metal button located on the passenger floorboard — the secondary air horn. I forget it's there sometimes. I'd never had to use it before, trusting Dave to handle the driving. Clyde waved over toward a compact car beside us with two young blondes in the front. The blaring air horn nearly made the minivan in front of us swerve off the road.

"It was some party one of the docs from Mercy was having," I said. "I didn't go."

"Wait, are you talking about your nerdy doc friend?" I didn't respond, which he took to mean yes. He smiled deviously. "Misty was talking about her last week, but she didn't say anything about a party. I see… it was a party for two. Damn, you let Dave take your woman?"

"It's not like that. I was invited, too."

"A threesome. I get it. Doctor Nerd is trying to get her

super-freak on."

"I wish it were that simple. She may be a freak, I don't know, but I *can* attest to her insanity."

"The crazies are the best ones in bed," he said.

"Maybe, if you like being tortured."

"Tie me up, baby!"

"Medic 15, this is dispatch," the male dispatcher said over the radio.

Clyde removed the mic from the metal clip and said, "Go ahead dispatch, medic 15."

"What's your location?"

Clyde glanced out his side window and said, "We're coming up on the four hundred block of Lake Street."

"I need you to respond to Haven Tree Nursing Home for a male, unconscious, not breathing."

"Place us en route, dispatch," Clyde said. The MDT in front of him beeped, displaying the information on the screen.

Was Sims killing again? Could he be that bold?

Clyde scrolled down the page on the screen and said, "That's odd. It says unknown age, possibly thirties."

"It's probably Dan, one of our regulars. He was in a motorcycle wreck when he was eighteen and has been paralyzed ever since — a quadriplegic. He's also an epileptic, which is the reason we're called most of the time. It's been a while though. I guess he finally had enough and let go."

• • •

I pulled the rig into the half-circle driveway of the nursing home and parked. While Clyde and I piled our equipment onto the stretcher, I noticed two police units pull in with their lights on, no siren.

"What the hell are they doing here?" Clyde asked. "Was there a brawl in the bingo room?" "I don't know," I said, pushing the stretcher toward the glass doors. I had a feeling it had something to do with Sims. A mistake, maybe? Mistakes are made when your invisibility potion wears off and you haven't yet realized it, or are too narcissistic to notice. We didn't wait for the officers. For all we knew, they were actually there for a bingo brawl.

Inside, the place looked deserted. There were no random elderly residents hovering in the corners. Not even the normal group of window watchers in their wheelchairs near the array of front glass. It was daytime. What the heck was going on? I was used to being ignored, but this was a little ridiculous.

We rounded the first corner and entered the hallway where our room number was located. The room was easy enough to find, especially with the commotion taking place just outside the door. I looked back and saw the two officers rounding the corner toward us. It became obvious they were here for the same patient as we were. But why?

"Could some of you rubberneckers move the hell out of our way so we can do our job!?" Clyde said to the crowd that was spilling into the hallway.

As we moved through the cluster of distraught faces, we reached the inner circle — the ones actually working. I could see the top of a female nurse's head bouncing as she continuously compressed the chest of our patient. Clyde pushed his way through and moved onto the other side of the bed. I grabbed the monitor from our stretcher, prepping it in order to attach the fast pads from their monitor to ours.

"Tryke," Clyde said. His voice sounded shaken, rattled even. "Tryke!"

"I'm right here, man, what?" Monitor in hand, I moved around to the side of the bed next to Clyde. One of the nurses beside him moved so I could see. When I looked down at the patient, I froze. I couldn't move. I was instantly taken back to my sister's death, and the heavy sense of helplessness that had strangled me, smothering my existence and dragging me to the depths of wretched gloom.

Dave's pale, lifeless face stared up at me, pleading for help. His uniform shirt was cut open, his bare chest exposed and pounded on by a fierce female nurse.

"Tryke, come on, man, snap out of it," Clyde said. "I can't do this alone."

I took a deep breath and briefly closed my eyes. I had to get hold of myself and quick. There was no time to count my breathing. These were valuable seconds my friend didn't have. When I opened my eyes, I went to work. Oddly, the room was tranquil, with Clyde and the nurses moving fluidly. The symphony was in full force, and I took over as director.

"I'm all right," I said. I grabbed the intubation equipment. My hands danced seductively with the tone of the room, sliding the tube down Dave's airless passage. I attached the BVM and flowed life back into his desperate, aching lungs. I looked over at the nurse doing compressions — she was young, twenty-two maybe — and I asked her to stop. The monitor, sitting next to Dave's legs, displayed a scribbling line known as Ventricular Fibrillation. It is the deadliest of heart rhythms.

"Clear!" Clyde yelled. Everyone stepped back. When he pressed the shock button on the monitor, Dave's body flinched. The lethal rhythm continued on its destructive path, not releasing its deadly grip. "Clear!" Again, his body flinched. I had shocked countless patients, watched as their limp bodies jerked when the electricity entered, but seeing Dave lying helpless as we went through our routine sparked a madness in me. After Clyde shocked him one more time, I snapped.

I switched with the young nurse who had been doing compressions. I didn't count, I didn't position, I only pushed and pushed and pushed, until I heard Clyde yell, "It's time for another shock." I didn't want to stop. "Tryke, we need to shock him again." Reluctantly, I stopped and stood to the side. As I tried to catch my breath, time seemed to stand still for the few seconds Clyde took to press the shock button over and over. I stared into Dave's eyes, wondering if he was coming back. Was it his choice? Would he want to?

"Asystole," Clyde said, pulling me from my temporary trance. I went back to my rigorous up and down pushing, quickly finding my rhythm again. The young nurse beside me, pushing air into his lungs, looked over at me with kind, sad eyes. I must have been giving off hints of desperation, but considering her sorrowful look, it was much more than hints. It was more like a broken spout, pouring out of me, matching the sweat.

I don't know how many rounds of drugs or the number of shocks we were up to by the time I heard Clyde key up the portable radio, but it wasn't enough to warrant what he was about to do.

"What are you doing?!" I said to Clyde through pursed lips, keeping my stride.

"Calling Mercy," he said, as if I should have known.

"For what?!" The look on his face said, 'come on, you know how this works.' I knew very well how it worked. Hell, I'd be the first to stop a code if things weren't improving. But this was Dave. I wasn't going to let him leave. Not yet. Not without at least explaining himself. Why had he ignored my warning to stay away from the house? "If you think we're fucking stopping," I yelled, "you can hang that shit up now!"

He quickly lowered the radio, and hooked it back onto his belt. "Okay, man. Let's at least get on the road then," Clyde said.

"Fine," I said. I took a deep breath. With a calm voice, I looked at the young nurse who was squeezing air into Dave's lungs.

"What's your name?"

"Charlee," she said.

"Charlee, I need you to ride with me in the back of our rig to the hospital. Are you okay with that?"

She hesitated and looked across at an older man in white scrubs, holding a clipboard. He nodded and said, "Go ahead. It'll be a learning experience for you."

"Okay, I'll go," she said. Her facial expression didn't match the confidence of her words. We picked Dave up and loaded him onto the stretcher. With Clyde at the foot watching the heart monitor, I continued compressions from the side, all the way down the long labyrinth of halls. Charlee meticulously handled the airway, counting between breaths.

Once we were in the back of the rig, I yelled through the small opening to Clyde in the driver's seat.

"Go!"

"We're seven minutes out," he said, putting the rig in gear. "Do you want me to call Mercy and give them the report?"

"I got it," I said. "Just get us there."

Seven minutes, damn. I sighed out loud and started calculating the times of the call, from the time we were dispatched, to our arrival, to now. I couldn't concentrate. The numbers failed to make sense, forming a cluster of randomness. Hope was deteriorating quickly. The temporary adrenaline was held by a selfish strand of self-pity. Death had surrounded my life. From a very young age, it had followed closely behind, kicking the bottom of my heels with each step I took.

I looked over at Charlee. She was completely focused on Dave's airway, diligently delivering him oxygen down the ET tube. The odds of Dave returning were slim. If he were in my spot, Dave the righteous one would be at the brink of letting me go. His words, "Let God have me," amplified in my ears. Who was I to argue with another's wishes? What was I doing? How could I be such a damn hypocrite, not allowing the dead to rest peacefully, away from the incessant, selfish pleas of the living?

I stopped compressions and sat back on the bench seat.

"We've done all we —"

A beep from the monitor interrupted my speech of failure.

Chapter 26

I didn't immediately perk up from the beep. I leaned up casually and turned the monitor so it directly faced me. It was most likely a ghost bump, the heart's farewell wave to the living world.

Once I realized what I was seeing, an organized rhythm, I nearly knocked the BVM out of Charlee's hands as I reached for Dave's neck to check for a carotid pulse. I didn't feel anything, at first, but once I repositioned my fingers — "Son of a bitch, he's got a pulse."

"What?! He does?" Charlee said.

"Weak, but it's there."

"A decent rhythm too," she said. "Slightly bradycardic, but still sinus. What's the BP?"

I pumped up the BP cuff and palpated a blood pressure.

"Seventy-palp," I said, spiking a premixed bag of Dopamine (an inotropic drug used to increase blood pressure, among other things). How far along in nursing school are you?" I sparked conversation to keep my mind on track.

"I have another month before I can take the NCLEX exam," she said proudly.

"Where are you going to work?"

"Mercy ER, hopefully. But they don't usually take nurses fresh out of school."

"Ah, so you like punishment? It's the right place to break you in. Who knows, maybe they'll make an exception for you."

"That would be cool. It's not punishment if you like it, right?"

"I guess."

"Is he a friend of yours, this guy?"

"Yeah, he was supposed to work with me today."

The blood instantly drained from her face. "He's a paramedic?"

"You didn't notice his uniform shirt?"

"When they called the code, I was dragged from another room by my supervisor. I just ran in there and started bagging the airway. Tunnel vision, you know."

"Yeah, we all get it now and then." I had a temporary bout of it at the moment myself, watching Dave's rhythm intently on the monitor.

"How did he —"

"I don't know," I said, shaking my head. But I did know, and it was my fault. Sims was taking his vengeance out on me by trying to kill Dave. I picked up the mic and asked dispatch for a med channel for Mercy ER.

"Mercy ER, this is medic 15," I said.

Dr. Hudson answered, "Tryke, what do you have for us?"

I took a deep breath and said, "Thirty-one-year-old male found in cardiac arrest at nursing home. CPR in progress when we arrived." I lowered the mic, trying to remember how many rounds of drugs we had pushed. My thoughts were scattered, my emotions taking over yet again.

Charlee interjected. "Here." She motioned toward her

pocket in her scrub top. I pulled the piece of paper out and unfolded it. It was the list that the man in white scrubs at the NH had been jotting down. Every process and medication was listed in neat chronological order.

"Thanks," I said. I skimmed over the list and relayed the information to Dr. Hudson. "Can you meet us at the back door in ..." I peered out the side window of the rig, "thirty seconds."

I knew that my pause in radio contact and hurried voice would be enough to pique his interest. I needed to see him first and explain the situation before the mob closed in.

Three police units were already parked beside the ER entrance, along with a growing crowd of onlookers in a variety of scrub colors.

"Jerry and a few other supervisors are here too, Tryke," Clyde yelled back to me, placing the rig in park and pulling the air-brake.

Dr. Hudson opened the back door of the rig. His face was hardened, his eyes focused on Dave. "Your supervisors told me after I got off the radio with you," he said in a solemn, but serious tone. "Is his blood pressure holding?"

"Yeah, one-hundred over sixty." I placed all of our equipment beside Dave and jumped down to assist Clyde with the stretcher.

"Let's put him in code room two," Dr. Hudson said, leading the way.

We wheeled Dave down the hall he and I had traveled so many times. I had that familiar feeling that onlookers were patting me on the back, comforting me with their eyes, just as I did when I took the walk after my mom died. Dave lay on the stretcher, still unconscious, a tube shoved down his trachea, monitor wires hanging, and plastic tubing inserted into both his arms. Though we got a pulse back and a blood pressure, he was far from okay. I knew the odds of him returning to normal were very low. How long was his brain without oxygen?

Was this an act of the Gamemakers toying with me yet again, for getting close to a prized player of theirs? A cruel trick to allow Dave to live only to suffer? A reminder? A punishment for making mistakes, possibly? If I was to be a worthy opponent, I couldn't allow the enemy to discover my true identity. It would take away from the allure, the mystery behind me as the cloaked player.

After loading Dave onto the bed, Clyde grabbed the stretcher and placed it into the hallway. I waited in the room for Dr. Hudson's analysis of his condition, helping where I could. He ordered an array of tests and pulled me out into the hallway.

"Tryke, tell me what you know," Dr. Hudson said.

"Do you remember me telling you a while back about my suspicions of the poisoning of a nursing home patient we brought in? I asked if you would run a toxicology report." This was risky, especially if he dug around and discovered Dr. Kimberly's tampering with his orders. But he needed to know about the cyanide if Dave had any chance of survival.

"I think so, yeah. Wait… now that you mention it, I never received those results."

"I think Dave was poisoned," I said. "Cyanide, if I had to guess."

"Cyanide? How do you know?"

"You weren't living here at the time, but did you ever hear about the guy who murdered the elderly during the holiday season five or so years back? The Elderly Slayer was what they named him."

"Actually, yes. There was a nationwide alert sent to all ERs."

"I think he's back out of hiding, and Dave and I saved one of his victims. Obviously pissing him off," I said.

Dr. Hudson turned toward the nurses' station.

"Tracy, I need the Cyanokit, stat please." Appearing confused, Tracy lifted her hands and shrugged. "Cyanide antidote kit. Hurry, please." This time, she turned on her heels and shot off toward the medication room.

"What's his prognosis?" I asked.

"Since he's still alive, and if indeed the culprit was Cyanide, it had to have been a smaller dose. Or there's no way y'all would have been able to resuscitate him. He may pull through, but, well, you know as well as I the usual outcome of patients brought back."

Vegetative state, helpless, a defenseless soul held captive in a dying suit until death was ready.

"I know, but he doesn't deserve that cruelty," I said.

"Who does? It's a horrible existence."

I knew one who deserved such a fate. What a perfect payback, to be placed in a NH, beside the ones he preyed on. But he also didn't deserve to be treated with dignity, and be cared for by hard-working nurses. Taxpayers would not bear the burden of keeping Sims alive.

• • •

Outside, in the ER driveway, I described in detail the entire call to my supervisors and two police officers. It was less formal out there — breathable air — and I didn't have to sit and stare as if under interrogation. They all seemed legitimately concerned, which didn't surprise me, considering Dave's respect for authority figures, even if it was forced at times. He never failed to embrace an opportunity to greet a higher ranking officer on the job. I made fun of him quite often for it, but he normally just shrugged it off.

Once my interpretation was thoroughly explained, and after I endured a few exaggerated pats on the back, I stood around and pretended to give a shit about Jerry's failing marriage and his son's tee ball dilemma. Thankfully, my phone vibrated in my pocket and saved me from having to strain my neck further with another nod.

"Tryke, I just heard the news." It was my Uncle Frank.

"Did you know the paramedic?" "Unfortunately, yes. It was Dave."

"Dave? Your partner Dave?"

"Yes, sir."

"Tryke, I'm sorry. Did he …"

"Die? No, not yet. We were able to resuscitate him. But we're not sure how long he was down, how much brain damage he sustained."

"Let's hope none. At least he's alive."

"I guess." Being alive didn't constitute celebration, not without knowing the quality of life remaining.

"Listen, I know there are officers on scene there, and you've probably already given them a statement about the scene, but I need to ask you something."

"Okay." I wasn't sure where this was heading.

"Did you find anything that would make you suspect that Dave was poisoned?"

"Poisoned? No, I don't think so. Why?" Though I had told Dr. Hudson, I needed to know what my uncle knew before I ran my mouth on the subject.

"This may come as a shock to hear, especially with this hitting so close to home for you, but there is significant evidence that points to a serial killer coming out of retirement the last few months."

He had no idea how close this was to me. "You think Dave was targeted by a serial killer? Wait, you said last few months. So, y'all have known that this guy was out there? I hadn't read anything in the papers."

"It's been kept quiet, mainly due to the media. The guy we suspected back then, Duncan Sims, was clean. We didn't find one shred of evidence. I didn't like the guy, there was something about his demeanor that spooked me. Anyway, he threatened all kinds of lawsuits and crap, so we had to back off. If anyone was pissed, it was me. I worked that damn case night and day."

"Do you still think this Duncan guy is the killer?"

"If not the killer, I think he has something to do with it. But we can't go near his house without some sort of evidence." I guess that made me damn lucky, or unlucky, depending on how one looked at the situation.

"Look, we're going to keep a few officers up there with Dave. I'll even have one outside your house if you'd like."

"No. I mean... I'm fine, seriously," I said. "Besides, I have Earl."

He laughed. "Earl? That rug you call a dog? Tryke, at least come stay with me until we catch this guy."

"Uncle Frank, I'll be fine."

"Stubborn, just like your old man was. All right, but I'm driving by your house a few times a day, whether you like it or not."

"I'm okay with that." But I wasn't. I had planning to do, and searching. "So is there anything you can tell me about this psycho? Why Dave?" A little more information about the guy couldn't hurt, and it just might have led me to him. I didn't think he was going to be hanging around his house after our little exchange.

"They named him the Elderly Slayer, killing residents in nursing homes, primarily during the holiday season. That's why this incident with Dave is so odd, but I think I know what happened. I'm thinking you two might have thwarted one of his attacks or saved one of his victims sometime recently. This guy has been known to deviate, not often, but when someone interferes with his plans, he doesn't like it. There have been a few nurses killed along the way."

"I'll keep an eye out on calls at nursing homes," I said, "and I'll lock up the house and call you if anything weird happens."

"One more thing. Tell the docs up there to search Dave for traces of cyanide. That's what the killer used. And Tryke, this doesn't go further than me and you, got it?"

"Okay."

"He'll be ending his spree on New Year's Eve," Frank

said. "Point being, we don't have long before he quits for the season, and then we may never catch this guy. Keeping the media out of the loop is key to finding him. Bagging this SOB will be a great retirement gift to myself."

"I hope you do." But sorry, Uncle Frank. This guy is mine.

After hanging up the phone, I met up with Dr. Hudson at the nurses' station, and advised him about Charlee's ambition to work in the ER at Mercy after graduation. After telling him how perceptive and keen she was on the call, he seemed delighted to offer her a position on the staff.

"Welcome aboard," he told her. "Once you obtain your license, of course."

"Don't thank me," I said to her on the way back to the NH. She had asked to ride in the front with me. I was more than happy to put Clyde in the back, if only to watch him sulk. "You made an impression when it counted, under extreme circumstances. And more importantly, you helped me out in a tough spot. Thanks again."

She blushed, but smoothly transitioned: "I don't see a ring. Are you married?"

I smiled back at her. "Not yet, but I have a complicated... let's just call it a situation, with a beautiful woman who happens to be quite angry with me lately. Why do you ask?"

She shifted her head and flung her long brunette hair across her right shoulder, revealing a frown. "No reason," she said. "Just curious."

Yet again, the opposite sex had baffled me with vague requests and comments, and a tendency to avoid explaining their true intentions.

Chapter 27

I spent most of the night lying awake, thinking about Dave and the entire situation. To say the least, I was physically drained and mentally exhausted. The anxiety that nearly ended me last spring was inching nearer, testing me. It had already sneaked up on me and slapped me awake in the storage unit. I knew there was no way to control it entirely, but keeping my thoughts in some sort of order would help to keep it at bay. I couldn't let information, or the lack of it, overwhelm me.

When I got home, I poured myself a stiff drink and did some more research on Mr. Sims. I needed a former address, a relative, even an ex-girlfriend, anything to help me figure out where he might be hiding. He had proven his point that he wasn't screwing around. I couldn't take any chances with this crazy bastard.

After perusing the internet for hours, I wasn't able to find any more than the few articles I had already skimmed over when I first started my research. He was a ghost after the initial harassment from the police, and even more so before. I couldn't find so much as a parent or a sibling. With today's social media, along with his history of activity, I found it hard to believe there wasn't more — despite lawyers threatening on his behalf. I suspected *Sims* was an alias. He'd probably had more than one over the years, but since the media involvement, he'd been forced to stick with Duncan Sims.

Mr. Sims wasn't finished killing. I was almost sure of that. He was waiting, hoping time would erase suspicion so he could complete a full season. But his patience wore thin. He couldn't help himself but push the limits. He had already proven his ability to outsmart the police and the media. Once he had finally redeemed himself and fulfilled the unfinished season, I suspected he'd leave for good. But there was one more loose end, another incomplete process lingering — me — and that's what I was counting on.

With my drink half empty and my forehead lying on the left side of my keyboard, I woke to my cell phone ringing loudly and vibrating on the wooden desk. I lifted my head and glanced over at the name displayed. I immediately perked up and answered.

"Lesley," I said.

"Hey, I didn't wake you did I? Sorry if I did."

"No, no, I was just reading." I looked down at my watch. It was a few minutes before noon.

"I just heard about Dave... Tryke, I'm sorry. How is he doing?"

"Not good. I mean, he's alive, but he's in ICU on a vent."

"I couldn't imagine having to work on a friend of mine. That must have been horrible."

"It was... wait, how did you find out that I was on the call? I haven't told anyone yet." Then I remembered Angie, Dave's soon to be ex-wife. She must still be his emergency contact.

"That's another thing I wanted to talk to you about,"

Lesley said. "That Dr. Kimberly woman called me."

"What, really? How did she get your number? And how the hell did *she* know about it?"

"She left a message on my phone early this morning from the hospital."

"Huh, that's kinda strange." Not really, considering what I knew about her. Now that dirty woman was using Dave's attempted murder to harass Lesley and me.

"Tryke, be honest. Who is this woman?"

"The truth?"

"Yes. And before you explain, know that I am ready to move on if I need to."

"We had a mutual interest about a particular patient. I gave her my number — for conversing about the patient only. Apparently she got the wrong idea, and eventually began texting me about more than just the patient. When I attempted to put an end to it, she became angry, obviously not handling rejection very well. I had no idea she had your number, or how she got it."

"It's not that I don't believe you. I do, but…I don't know. That really bothered me at Thanksgiving. And now we haven't talked for weeks. I went back to school to take my finals. My head was a mess. You were just going to let me go and never speak to me again?"

"No, I was going to call you. I really wanted to, but seeing you react the way you did that day, I was afraid you wouldn't believe me. I know, I know, it was a bad choice on my part and I'm sorry. I shouldn't have let you leave without saying something. It was my fault."

"So, that's it? You told her to leave you alone?"

"Yes, I promise."

The phone was silent for about ten seconds. "Fine," she said, "but I'd like to talk about it, face to face."

"Things are kind of complicated at the moment. With Dave being in the hospital and the killer on the —"

"Tryke, stop making excuses. You owe me. How about I

meet you at the hospital? I can see Dave, and then we can go have a drink somewhere."

I hesitated, but not long enough to draw a remark. "All right," I said.

"Three o'clock okay?"

"I'll see you then. And Lesley... I'm glad you called."

"Me too."

I pressed End and put the phone down. I was surprised Lesley was even around, especially after our incident at Thanksgiving. Initially, she was supposed to spend Christmas back at school in order to get a head start on the spring semester. This was a good thing, I hoped.

• • •

Because it was Christmas Eve, and knowing Dave's love of holiday decorations, I selected one of the many small trees that he had displayed in the living room and brought it with me to the hospital. I knew Lesley well enough to know she would confront Dr. Kimberly if given the chance, especially now that she had my take on the situation. I arrived a few minutes early and suggested that we enter Mercy through the front entrance, avoiding the ER, just in case Dr. Kimberly was working.

"What's with the tree?" Lesley asked. "Oh, wait, is that for Dave's room?"

"Yeah, you know he's staying with me right?"

"Yes. I'm sorry about the Angie situation. I had no idea she would do such a thing to him. As long as I've known her, she never seemed like the type. If it matters, I haven't spoken with her since she told me." I kept quiet, knowing my comments about Angie would likely escalate matters. "I think it's cool of you to bring the tree for him. It's a nice gesture."

"If you saw the living room, you'd know why," I said. "He took every decoration that my mom had in the attic and vomited them everywhere."

We both laughed, stepping into the elevators. "Yeah, he's always been a little cheesy and over the top, but he's also always had a good heart," Lesley said.

I agreed and pressed the button to the second floor. When the doors closed, she slid her hand into my free one. I missed her soft, small hands, the gentle squeeze of our future endeavors — a closeness never experienced until I met her. I abruptly let go of her hand when the elevator doors opened so she could exit first. She sighed, once again expecting me to interpret the meaning. I wasn't up for it at the moment.

Before we entered through the double doors leading into the intensive care unit, I said, "I don't expect Angie to be here, nor should she, but I hope at least one of his parents is here."

"Me too," Lesley said, looking at me oddly. She was probably wondering why I would suggest such a thing. Dave hardly spoke about his parents. From what I knew, he didn't see them often, and I got the impression it was more their choice than his.

The nurse led us to his corner room. When I slid the glass door open and pulled the curtains back, I was immediately brought back to my mom's room, and that moment the physician relayed the news to me that she had passed away. The cold room made me shiver. Dave, alone, lay quietly in his bed, a tube shoved down his throat, air being pumped into his lungs, wires and IV lines hanging like poorly placed tinsel on a tree. If he were to survive, there wouldn't be much of a life left for him. He would need constant care, and years of rehabilitation, at the very least.

Two cheating wives, a young daughter, and parents who hardly come around — even now as he lay in a coma, they weren't there. They could have at least brought his daughter up to see him. It might have been her last chance to see him alive. This was a new hell he was in, and I was the one to blame. I should have let him go. Life had already been cruel enough to him. I was being selfish for bringing him back, letting self-pity override my common sense. Listen to me, I sound like one of those self righteous medics believing I actually had a hand in him being alive — I knew better. That thought process only leads to a permanent fog of the real world.

Lesley stood next to the bed, crying softly into a tissue that she had grabbed from beside the sink. I set the tree next to the window, a direct view from his bed if he were to wake up. On the wall below the TV, facing his bed, was a dry-erase board with the date and the name of his nurse. His uniform, the one he was wearing in the NH when I found him, was wadded up in a clear bag in the chair by the window.

I wanted to stand next to Lesley and comfort her, place my arm around her and let her cry softly on my chest. I was never good at those situations, even when things were going great with us. My choice of words usually seemed to make things worse. Also, I was unable to read her body language, so my interpretation was almost always wrong. I had thought I was getting better over the summer, but then the Thanksgiving incident happened. The hand-holding in the elevator only made matters more confusing.

Dropping down into the chair, I leaned over and placed my hand to my head. As I sat there watching the vent pump air, Lesley sniffling, and the heart monitor beeping to a steady rhythm, I thought about yesterday morning. It wasn't that odd, Dave being in his uniform. Knowing him, he probably brought it with him to the party, in case the night turned out lucky for him. Sims could have waited in Dave's vehicle and drugged him in the driveway after Dr. Kimberly dropped him off. But I still didn't buy it.

I needed answers, at least a timeline, and the one person who could help me was also the one I had been trying to avoid. I suspected the conversation with Dr. Kimberly would be easier with her at work, with other people around — less chance of a spectacle. I *could* have simply called her, but I knew she wouldn't answer. She liked playing games.

So how could I get out of my committed talk with Lesley? I mean without her saying to hell with me? I stared down at the floor for answers.

A few minutes later I lifted my head and noticed Lesley was standing next to me, silently, letting me finish with my thoughts. She sat on the arm of the chair, leaning her head on my left shoulder. I had an idea, not a terribly clever one, but it was all I could come up with. For this to work, I had to escalate my fury as I spoke.

"I have to find out what happened to him," I said. "I need answers."

"Give them a little time," Lesley said. "This just happened. I know you're hurting, but they'll find whoever did this."

"He was my responsibility. He was staying at my house. I let this happen to him!"

"Tryke, you can't be serious." She lifted her head off my shoulder. "This isn't your fault. You can't take responsibility for the crazy people in the world."

"I'm not! This is just too damn —. Look, I'm sorry, but I can't just sit here and watch him die like this. Until they find this guy, I have to do what I can to figure out what exactly happened."

"Let the police —"

"I have to go." I gently brushed my hand over the top of hers, letting her know I was still in control, furious, but still in control. I said goodbye from the door. I knew it wasn't the right way to handle our fragile relationship, but I needed Lesley away from me until this was over. I needed time to find this guy, and being anywhere near me would put her in danger. If I warned her, she would want an explanation, and then she would refuse to leave my side. Things were better this way.

In the ER, I found one of the nurses, and asked if Dr. Kimberly was working. She told me that she wasn't scheduled to come in that day. According to Lesley, Dr. Kimberly had called her from the hospital when she left the message about Dave. I didn't inquire whether Lesley learned that information from her caller ID or the message itself, but I had a feeling Dr. Kimberly was lying to make her story sound believable.

• • •

Duncan Sims had a fetish: voyeurism. It was his calling card. He liked watching from nearby as his victims suffered and ultimately took their last breath. The trophy binder I obtained from his house was proof. He kept candid photos of his victims' last moments. Did he snap a picture of Dave? Was he watching Clyde and me from a safe distance while we worked him? The thought infuriated me. Sims could have been inches away, witnessing the terror as it unfolded on our faces. At the time, this idea had never crossed my mind. Once I realized it was Dave, I became completely absorbed in the moment.

By administering a smaller dose, Sims must have been counting on Dave living, or at least the possibility. But for what purpose? To watch me suffer as I attempted to revive him? A distraction maybe, so he could finish his work? I wouldn't know until I had him face to face.

Something I hadn't quite figured out was his obsession with plants. I had my initial suspicion, given the manner in which he killed his victims, as well as the past toxicology reports. I didn't search his entire house, but just from the sheer number of species that I observed — and I'm far from a botanist — he wasn't your average green thumb granny. But something I did know a little about was chemistry and medicine, specifically the makeup of pharmaceutical grade medications. Throughout human history, plants have been used for medicinal purposes.

I wasn't quite sure about Cyanide, his choice of poison. Despite there being many plants that contain cyanide in nature, obtaining the concentration that he needed to kill would have probably required some form of synthesizing. As for sedation, or other combinations that his sick mind formed, these could be obtained from particular plant species more readily. Maybe he had a homemade pharmacy of toxic herbs to torture his elderly victims.

I wasn't looking forward to this confrontation with Dr. Kimberly. As pissed off as I was that she had used Dave's near-death as an excuse to call Lesley and harass her, I had to keep my cool. An argument would only fuel her misdirected anger.

When I turned onto Dr. Kimberly's street, I noticed another vehicle parked in the driveway behind her yellow Jeep. I immediately pulled my truck to the curb and removed my sunglasses to get a better look. I had to take a second glance just to be sure I was seeing what I thought I was seeing — a black SUV.

Chapter 28

What the hell was going on? Sims's SUV in her driveway?
He must have followed Dr. Kimberly and Dave the
previous morning, intending to return once he was done
playing with Dave. This was his new hideout until his
season of killing was complete. That meant Dr. Kimberly
was lying murdered somewhere in her house. As angry as I
was at her, I didn't want her dead, just far away.

I wanted to wait for nightfall, or at least twilight, which
was still an hour away. But with the police now searching
for Sims, I couldn't wait. I didn't have time for a plan. He
had one-upped me again. It was time for this back-and-
forth to finally come to an end.

I sneaked up to the house and into the backyard. There
were no blinds on the kitchen windows, only sheer fabric
curtains permanently tied in the open position. From the
vantage point of the window I was peering through, I could
see all the way to the orange stained living room. The
kitchen light was on, but I hadn't seen Sims or Dr.
Kimberly. If she was still alive he probably had her tied up

in one of the bedrooms, out of sight. And if she was dead, well, she was probably in the same place.

I saw a shadow approaching the kitchen from the hallway on the left. Lowering my head, I positioned myself just far enough behind the cover of the curtain so I could still see. I was shocked when I saw Dr. Kimberly stagger into the kitchen, looking as if she had just woken up. She filled the tea kettle with water and placed it onto the stove. She was wearing a short silk nightgown and no shoes or socks. The second I saw her alone, I wanted to knock on the window and tell her to make a run for the back door, which was only steps away from her. But something told me not to. She was acting strange, and her gait was definitely off. She moved sluggishly, like a zombie, toward the refrigerator. After retrieving the milk and plopping it down onto the counter, she pulled two coffee mugs from the cabinet, dropping one in the process and shattering it on the floor. Without so much as a flinch, she reached up and grabbed another.

"What was that?!" It was a man's voice. I inched my head back completely out of view, but from where I stood, I could still see the reflection from the window above the sink. The man entered the kitchen, and it was definitely Sims. His frail build and thin grey mustache were easy to spot, even in a window reflection. His voice was raspy, like that of a smoker. "Can't you do anything right?!" he yelled. "Shit, I may have given you a little too much." She waved a hand aimlessly in the air. "I don't need you injured right now. You have a lot of work that still needs doing."

What work was he having her do? Perverse sexual favors? This was all too weird. It wasn't going to be easy getting her out of there, but I had to try. Not even a deviant like Dr. Kimberly deserved to be a sex slave to a perverted serial killer. Maybe after I helped her escape, she'd finally leave me alone.

I needed to find a way in, ideally once he was asleep.

With her being drugged, I didn't know how cooperative she would be. And unaware of her actions, she could possibly give my presence away. It might be easier to knock her out. I had enough extra in my syringe. She wouldn't need much, considering her current state.

Searching the windows around the back of the house, I noticed that all were locked, except one, which happened to be shattered — probably from Sims when he broke in. Once I lifted the blinds out of my way and cleared the jagged pieces of residual glass, I managed to make my way into the small slit of a window. The room was dark, the door cracked open and letting a faint beam of light enter from the hallway. But it wasn't enough to keep me from bumping into a desk and revving the computer awake. If someone had been in the hallway, they would have heard the fans come to life and seen the glow from the screen.

I slipped behind the door and waited. After a few minutes of silence, I felt it was safe enough to continue. Before turning off the computer monitor, I scanned over the web page displayed and noticed a list of hotels in New Orleans. Was he planning a vacation after he was done? Or was he finally relocating? Mardi Gras was a perfect place to get lost, with thousands of people in the streets twenty-four hours a day. Not a bad idea, actually. He'd have a new batch of victims in New Orleans, too. And if he kept heading east, he would reach the mother load in Florida. He could retire, saturated in a pool of the elderly. Maybe *that* was his ultimate plan.

Sticking my head out cautiously from the room and into the hallway, I heard Sims's voice. It was muffled and sounded like it was coming from inside a room at the end of the short hallway. There was a room adjacent to where I was, and the door was open. Once I heard him speak again, I stepped across the carpet smoothly, in four long strides, to the entrance. I quickly glanced inside. It was an empty guest bedroom.

Now that I was closer, I could hear Sims more clearly. But, he was no longer the one speaking. Dr. Kimberly was talking, and she sounded coherent.

"I still don't understand why we have to kill him," she said.

• • •

The next words out of Dr. Kimberly's mouth were the ones that turned this entire endeavor into a muddled nightmare.

"We don't need them both," she said. "Just take the girl. That's enough insurance until we leave."

"You got too close to him. I warned you what would happen," Sims said.

"No, it wasn't like that. I promise. You know about him. He would be a perfect addition. For that reason only."

"Loose ends, Kimberly. Despite my like for the guy, I don't have time to trust him. And I can't be competing with another man."

"It wouldn't be like that and you know —"

"I know what I saw. Don't worry, this will all be over soon. It's better this way. I trust you can handle them both." There was a long pause. "I'm serious, tell me you can handle this without my having to worry about it."

"Yes," she said, "tomorrow morning."

"When we get to New Orleans, we'll forget all about this place," Sims said. "Finally, after all these years, a new start."

Dr. Kimberly sighed loudly and said, "You promised we would have a normal life, with no more killings. I'm tired of it all."

"And I intend to keep that promise."

They were a team, a husband and wife, or boyfriend and girlfriend, or whatever. I didn't want to think about it. And to think I was vaguely attracted to her for a brief moment. I should have known all along — stakeouts, strategically placed texts, tampering with lab work. How could I have been so naive? I was blinded by lust, smoke-screened by a professional seductress. They intended to kill Lesley and me, and finish the season they began five years ago.

I slid back into the shadows when I heard Dr. Kimberly's voice moving around the room. She said, "I'm going to bed, since I have to be up so damn early to do something I don't want to do." It sounded like she was leaning against the door.

"Come on, stay in here tonight," Sims pleaded. "I'll keep the TV volume low."

I heard her twisting the knob of the door, likely mulling over his request. She said, "Fine, but only if you promise to keep the volume low. Let me go grab my glasses."

I heard the television turn on and the door close. I quickly left the shadows and followed her down the hallway toward the kitchen. She never heard me come up behind her. I slid her limp body back down the hall and placed her on the bed in the guest room, then searched the dark room for anything I could use as a distraction. There was a glass figurine on the nightstand. I tossed it down the hall into the kitchen, shattering it on the floor.

I slipped back into the guest room.

"Another one? Damn woman. Are you all right?!" Sims yelled from the room. When she didn't answer, he came to the door and opened it, mumbling to himself, "Shit, this is getting fucking ridiculous. Kim!" He marched down the hall. I followed.

He must have heard me or seen my reflection in one of the picture frames lined along the hallway. When I was just a foot away from his neck, he swung his elbow around, knocking the syringe from my right hand. "You son of a bitch!" He yelled, jabbing his bony right fist into my ribs. He may have been frail, but he was agile. Without hesitation he lunged toward me, wrapping both of his arms around my waist, attempting to push me backwards. Outweighing him by at least fifty pounds, I stopped his momentum and slung him off me into the wall. He tumbled to the floor, but got up quickly.

Sims stared at me from a few feet away, a rabid look in his eyes and heaving for air. Past him, I could see my syringe lying on the carpet. He tried to taunt me, between breaths.

"Is that all you got?"

When I smirked at his remark, he charged me like a feral prey attacking his predator. Once he closed in, I sidestepped and ducked, wrapping my left arm around his waist and my right around his neck. As he struggled to breathe, I could feel warm spittle running down my arm. I dragged him backwards down the hall, his feet flailing, curses struggling to exit with the spit. Once I was able to reach the syringe, his writhing was in full gear.

"Mr. Sims," I said, "it's over." Seconds later he went limp, lost in slumber. I pushed him away and sighed in relief. With no time to linger and reflect on the screwed-up situation, I got to my feet and began the prep work. I was able to find his stash of cyanide salts and some of the narcotic blend Dr. Kimberly had been using for personal use. Now they would get a taste of the terror they had inflicted on their victims.

After wiping down the house, I backed my truck to the side fence and loaded them both into the cab.

Chapter 29

On the drive to the lab, I considered the next plan of action, now that my goal had been achieved. My lab would soon be demolished and turned into a cluster of mundane office buildings. Unless I was able to find a way to keep them from destroying the place, it would be the end of an era. I would have to move. Dr. Randal and I would have to have our lengthy conversation in a different location. I still hadn't planned out how I am going to get him out of the asylum. I knew Dr. Fortune would have to play a part, either willingly or not. And that was the problem, having to potentially harm an innocent to get to my specimen.

The hidden room in my house had never, and would never, be an option as a site to perform releases. The potential for interruptions and getting caught was too great, not to mention the possibility of the released deciding to hang around. I didn't like the idea of unexpected reunions. I could search for another abandoned building, though none would have the same meaning for me, or provide a feeling of closeness to my dad. There was also Lesley to consider. Our relationship, though rocky at the moment, had been progressing rapidly since I met her. According to Lesley, it wasn't fast, but in my realm of avoiding romantic entanglements, it was moving quickly. I still wasn't sure where we stood, but her willingness to talk about things was an indication to me that it wasn't over.

Future endeavors with her scared the hell out of me: moving in together, marriage, children, all of which would mean an end to my current lifestyle, or at the very least, a stealthier and more cautious operation. Dave had moved in for a few days, and look where he was now. I didn't know if I could handle it if something happened to Lesley, especially if I were the cause.

After lugging Sims and Dr. Kimberly up the stairs and switching the machines on, I sat and waited until the medication wore off. This was my first twofer, releasing two at the same time. I found another table from below, though not completely intact, and connected it to the original. I had their IV tubes conjoined in the center — one dose for them both. I had one of their own concoctions prepped in a syringe, which I'd slipped into the pocket of my overalls. With only one heart monitor, I decided to attach it to Mr. Sims, for intimidation only, just in case he decided not to talk. A few hundred joules of electricity can be very convincing. It was important that we have a short discussion on the events that led to this moment. I needed some answers, if only so I didn't repeat my mistakes in the future.

The image of them resting beside one another reminded me of Romeo and Juliet, in a demented sort of way, as if the story wasn't twisted enough. I watched them — their heads tilted toward one another, both lightly snoring — and wondered if they knew they were mere moments away from releasing. Would I want to know? Would I want to pass over alone, or with Lesley? I had never really considered life that far ahead. From a young age, I'd never pictured myself growing old, dwindling down to nothing on the front porch until the rocking chair suddenly stopped. My dreams certainly never allowed me to relax in a placid meadow of bliss. They plunged me into oblivion, leaving me hanging helpless in empty space. To me this was the farthest reaches of a hell I could imagine, a place I didn't even wish my specimens would have to endure.

Dr. Kimberly was now shuffling around on the table, attempting to process her environment. When she realized her movements were limited she started to panic, thrashing her bare feet and slinging her head from side to side. When she saw her lover beside her, also bound, she immediately attempted to wake him with indiscernible noises through the gag in her mouth. She managed to wake him, and his reaction was much more subdued than hers had been. His expression seemed to say, "I know what's about to happen to us."

Not that either of them deserved an explanation, but they had been my most worthy opponents up until that time. They showed ingenuity, using a woman's sensual allure to draw me in and cloud my senses. And they played on my interests to gain my trust, and stalked me before I even knew their identity. But why? Why me? I wanted answers even more than I wanted the satisfaction of releasing these two. If they cooperated, I would offer them an explanation of why they were there, and in that predicament.

When Dr. Kimberly saw me silently sitting in the chair a few feet away, her eyes went from frustrated confusion to inflamed rage, attempting to spit out the gag. I stood, letting them see me remove the syringe from my pocket and place it on the table. Then I disrobed, revealing my work uniform. Neither of them seemed surprised. It was as if I took off my jacket and set it on the chair. Though it wasn't entirely intended that way, my attire served as a tribute to Dave. Sims would be reminded of his last victim during his release.

"Before we begin," I said, "I want to remind both of you that we are in a secure location, meaning no one can hear you. Let's keep this civilized and it will go much quicker. Also, Mr. Sims, you'll notice you have a pair of fast pads connected to your chest that will deliver a painful jolt of electricity whenever I desire. Answering truthfully is in your best interest." He nodded, nonchalantly. He looked worn and ready to get this over with. Dr. Kimberly, however, was still defiant, staring at the ceiling and ignoring my words.

I removed their gags and picked up the black binder that I had found in Sims's house, opening it to the article about his grandmother's death. After I read the short article aloud, neither of them seemed fazed by the words.

"Dr. Kimberly, were you aware that your lover possessed this binder of death? Does the name Beverly Walker mean anything to you?"

She had a look of disgust on her face. "Lover?! He's my father. How have you not figured that out yet? Maybe I *was* wrong about you."

"Your father? Is that true?" I looked over at Sims. He nodded yes.

"Yes!" she said. "Why would I lie about that?!" She rolled her eyes.

"That explains your hospital name tag only having Dr. Kimberly on it," I said.

"That's the only precaution she took," Sims scoffed. She huffed and turned her head away from him.

"I did my research," I said to Sims, "and I never found anything on you. No family, no daughter. Why is that?"

He smiled and said, "I threaten to sue and suddenly my past disappears. It's funny how that happens."

"Hilarious," I said, switching my attention to Dr. Kimberly. "So, you knew about the binder? The pictures? And your great-grandmother being killed?"

"Of course I did," she snapped. "I took some of the pictures of those old shits. They deserved what they got. I watched the misery of being old slide off their faces when they died."

"Charming. I get it. You hate innocent old people."

"Innocent?!" she yelled. "They weren't innocent! They killed my grandmother!"

"Every elderly person in a Dallas nursing home was involved in the murder of your grandmother? Is that your rationale?" She continued to huff and turned her gaze toward her feet. "I see we're getting nowhere with this ridiculous argument. Let's talk about how you two found me. And why the hell me? Why try and kill Dave? Which, by the way, you failed at doing. He's alive and well." I didn't want them to have the satisfaction of knowing he was in a coma, and that he might not make it.

"I can't say I'm that surprised to hear he's still alive. I gave him a small dose," Sims said.

"Why? To watch him suffer longer?"

"Actually, no. I waited until the last possible minute, just before you arrived. I knew you would be able to revive him. You're quite a talented medic, among other things." I didn't ask what he meant by "other" things.

"How did you know I wouldn't be on another call?"

"Hello!" Dr. Kimberly interjected. "My scanner?"

"Right," I said. "You never answered my question, Sims. Why Dave?"

"Truth be told, I didn't choose your friend. That was Kim," Sims said.

She sneered over at her father and then glared up at me.

"Blame yourself, Tryke. Your sniveling idiot partner actually thought he had a chance with me. All he did was whine about how cursed he was with women. Pathetic, really. You should think about choosing a better class of person to acquaint yourself with."

"Oh, like yourself? And your upstanding father next to you? No thanks. I'll take my chances with Dave." I looked over at Sims. "So, why me? Why did I attract the attention of the infamous Elderly Slayer of Dallas?"

"Her again," Sims said. "I had no interest in you, even after she explained your aura."

"Aura? What are you talking about?"

"Let her tell you. She's the damn reason we're here."

"Thanks, father. Another cynical remark from my loving parent."

"You never listen to me," Sims retorted.

"Enough," I said, interrupting the family dispute. "Back to this so-called aura."

Dr. Kimberly lowered her voice and stared at me menacingly. Gritting her teeth, she said, "I saw what you are."

"And that would be?"

She forced a laugh. "You really are narcissistic, and not just for fun. You don't even have to try anymore do you?" She turned away from me. "I'm not going to boost your ego."

"Fine," I said. "Sims?"

"I was never as convinced about you as she was, but I left you alone," Sims said. "You do your thing, we do ours. That was until she began getting too close to you. I didn't know how stupid she had gotten until I looked into it — toxicology reports, stake-outs, inviting you over — she was playing with our lives."

Dr. Kimberly turned toward her father, scowling at him and said, "That's what you think I was doing? Playing with our lives? I needed someone. Someone I could trust to be with us. Someone I could talk to other than my damn father!"

"It was supposed to be a family endeavor," Sims said.

"Family, hah. Like mom was supposed to be with us too, right? And then you had to kill her. When was it my turn to die?" Dr. Kimberly said.

"Kim, baby, I would never harm you," Sims said.

"Touching, really," I said, interrupting again. "But you two have had enough fun in this world."

"You think what we did was for fun?!" Dr. Kimberly said, diverting her anger from her father to me.

"Actually, I do think it was fun for your father on occasion. And I think *you* were doing it for the age-old reason all little girls do things: for daddy's attention and approval. You just weren't good enough, no matter what you did. You weren't sent by them. You are a byproduct. Maybe that was their intention, players creating new players. Clever."

"What? What are you talking about?" Dr. Kimberly asked. "What players?"

"Soon enough," I said. "Now tell me, how did you find me?"

"You were easy to spot if one knows what they're looking for," Dr. Kimberly said. "You think you're better than us, using your conscience as a guide. You think you're a righteous bringer of death. What a pitiful excuse for our kind. And to think I wanted you inside me. Now my insides cringe at your weakness. And as for your little girlfriend, I would have had fun playing with her, slowly draining her life, listening to her beautiful screams for her valiant knight, Tryke, to sweep in and save her."

My anger was building with her comments about Lesley. Desperation was seeping out of her, grasping for anything to allow her pride one last moment of stardom. But I couldn't allow her to get inside my head. Why was I even letting her continue to speak? I shoved the bandage back into her mouth.

I shut my eyes briefly, and managed to gain control of my temper. I took a deep breath and said, "You want to know why I do what I do? Why you two scum are in the predicament you're in?" I moved behind them and lowered my head between the two of theirs. "Because in just a few minutes you will shed your organic suits, and for the first time you will see your true selves. In that moment you will no longer attempt to compare yourselves to others. There is only you, and you alone." I stepped back and walked around the room. They were both silent, mulling over my words. "You see, I'm not afraid of myself. I know who I am. I know what I was meant to do." I walked over to Sims and stood next to him. "Now, as for you. Tell me about grandma."

I didn't know why I was so curious about his story. Maybe it was because he was on a mission of retaliation for his family. My entire family had been taken from me and retaliation played its part in my venture, but never on the innocent. My specimens were foul creatures sent here for one purpose — to wreak havoc and instill fear in their victims.

"They killed her and I took vengeance," Sims said. "What do you want to know? How I thought about the hole in her head before each old person I killed?" He clenched both of his hands into a fist. "I will never stop until they are all dead. Every! Single! One!" He began breathing deeply through his nose, jaw clenched. And then he abruptly stopped. When he spoke again, his voice was soft and childlike. "Grandma was the only one who ever listened to me." He started mumbling words to himself.

"You took your vengeance too far," I said. "You killed innocent people."

He snapped out of the trance and looked over at me with desperate eyes. His voice was back to normal. "I couldn't stop the rage inside. It flowed like a river inside of me. You have it too, Tryke. Kim's right, you're one of us. The aching, pulling inside of you, it's part of who we are."

"No!" I said, and shoved the wadded bandage back into his mouth. "There is no *we*. There is only you two psychos, and then there is me. I'm on the other end of the board, sent to send your kind back from where you came. Sure, there will be another to take your place once you release, but that's the game. I can only hope there are more out there like me, enough to tip the scales back to an even zero. Though I know the playing field will never be completely fair, at least not in this dimension, I can still dream of that place."

I smiled at the thought, briefly drifting away, but was quickly brought back to the disgusting sight in front of me — a demented father and his corrupted only child. "The story of you two is a tragic one. A daughter tainted by one of the few people we are told we can trust in our lives. Unfortunately, this deceit is not a terribly new story. Sims, you really are the worst kind of dirty soul in the world. Go now, and use what you regretted here on the other side, to set things right. If they allow you. I'm not sure what they do with your kind once they're finished playing with you, once your pathetic mission is complete."

The substance slowly made its way around the bend in the tubes and into the bifurcating section, distributing itself to them both. I switched the monitor connected to Sims off and sat in my chair and waited until it was over. I watched, but only briefly, for a glimpse of the darkness. When they released, both close to the same time, the room cooled, but not for long. The shadows along the wall could have been either of them. I didn't think Sims would hang around, considering his initial demeanor when he realized his fate. He would bow out and move on. But I figured she would linger, if only for a second, and then swiftly leave, realizing what she had become.

As I sat in the dim light of my lab, a haze brushed over me, draining my energy. For some reason I wasn't feeling the same satisfaction I usually had after releasing a specimen. Was it because there were two of them? Did the darkness of two evil specimens fill the room with too much foul stench, and now it was penetrating me and shrouding my purpose?

As they both lay there, motionless, I thought about Sims' last words. Was I one of them? Could I actually be one of the bad guys? My mission was to keep balance, give the innocent a fighting chance so the evil didn't overrun the world. It made no sense for me to be like them. If that were the case, then I would be a double agent, working from the inside to gain the trust of the ones I was meant to release. I liked that idea much better than being one of the scum I despised.

I wasn't buying the false feelings. I knew better than to let them take over. First the blurs and partial images, then the fully formed apparition revealed to me in the graveyard, and now the tampering with my endocrine system, messing with my neurochemical balance. I needed perspective to pull myself out of their quickly deepening rut. Sims's black binder was lying beside me, and I opened it.

I had seen plenty of faces of death since the beginning of my career, but never had I looked upon photographs taken of their last moments. Were they simply trophies, or was he hoping to catch a glimpse of something? He didn't seem like the type to be curious about the afterlife. He was too saturated in hatred, unable to find his way out and see the world for what it was. He wanted to witness the suffering, and to see it on their faces. The two of them weren't fighting for anything other than themselves. How many families did they wreck and torment with misery by senselessly taking a loved one? How many people suffered in fear at the hands of these two during their years of holiday terror? There had to be a balance of good and evil in the world, and that came from the middle. A willing force that was able to see both sides and choose. My free will was used for the good. I dirtied my hands so others didn't have to. It was my burden to bear.

I closed the binder. I felt better now that I had gotten another glimpse of the destruction my enemies had caused, and been reminded of my own purpose. I realized something after shutting the binder. What about the picture of Dave? If Sims's pictures were his trophies, then he would have had a camera on Dave at all times. I pulled his phone from the plastic bag I had placed it in earlier. Opening the picture files and scrolling through them, I saw all of the victims he had in the binder, and more. There was picture after picture of dying elderly. I imagined him sitting alone in his house, clicking on them, talking to his dead grandmother and showing her how he had avenged her death. Afterwards, he would fall asleep mumbling to himself, enjoying dreams of false revenge.

When I got to Dave's picture, I clicked on the small image, bringing it to full screen. He looked peaceful lying in the nursing home bed, his uniform neatly buttoned to the top. It was as if I were looking down into his casket. As I stared at the picture, I saw my own face replace his. I suddenly felt weak, and sweat started beading down my face. My breathing became labored. I threw down the phone and looked around the room, attempting to focus on anything but my thoughts. I couldn't fight the loneliness, the closing of casket walls pressing against my lungs and sealing me in.

Three, six, nine, twelve, I began counting aloud to myself. I counted in increments of three, changing up my normal repetition of single digits, hoping it would distract my mind enough to find my way back to reality. I couldn't stop the influx of thoughts that rapidly took over my mind. Dreams from childhood tore through my head and left remnants of more loneliness. Next came my sister's death, followed by my dad, and then my mom. I saw each of them in their own dark casket, time rapidly eating away to their bones. "Stop!" I yelled aloud. I leaned over the table and closed my eyes, squeezing them as tight as I possibly could. I used my thumb and pointer finger to hold them shut. It seemed to be helping. I lowered myself to the cold floor.

After a few minutes, I slowly opened my eyes. Once the blurriness subsided, my breathing finally slowed and I could no longer hear my heart pounding in my ears. I gradually got to my feet and shook off the feeling that had ensnared me moments before. I grabbed a towel from the chair and wiped the sweat from my face. I had known it was coming. The attack had been waiting at arms' length with sticky fingers, teasing me with short bursts and near misses. The brief one I experienced in the storage unit was a mere tremor, warning that another was to come if I didn't get things under control in my life. Hopefully, if I was lucky, they would leave me alone now that I had taken care of two issues at once.

I slipped my overalls back on and began packing up loose items around the lab. As I was placing Sims's phone in a bag, I saw something out of the corner of my eye. At first, I thought they weren't done playing tricks, but then I heard its movement. The soft drumming of my heartbeat started picking up pace in my ears once more, my insides twisting with trepidation.

When I turned my head toward the ceiling, the camera moved again. There was only one place from which to control those cameras, and that was the hidden room inside my house. As I stood there in fear, staring up at the camera, my phone vibrated inside my pocket.

Chapter 30

My stomach plummeted. My chest tightened. The walls of the small room began closing in like a trash compactor, slowly squeezing the air out of my lungs and smothering me. I immediately controlled my breaths and regained my composure. Losing control again wasn't an option. This was my fight and I had to face the coming wrath.

When I saw the camera move, my instinct was to run as fast as I could down the stairs to my truck and drive until I ran out of gas. But that was only a thought. This moment had been inevitable, right from the beginning.

I pulled my phone from my pocket and looked down at the display. After the fourth vibration, I reluctantly pressed answer and placed it on speaker, waiting for the one on the other end to speak first.

"I know you're listening. I can see you. So let me start out by saying I'm not really surprised by all of this. Disappointed, but not surprised." I pictured him sitting there in my hidden room, his cowboy hat perched beside him on my desk. How long had he been there, watching?

Was he alone?

"So, what do we do now, Uncle Frank?" I was surprisingly calm. I didn't know if it was because I was worn out from my recent attack, or because I was thankful that it wasn't Lesley on the other side of the camera.

"It seems to me there are two choices," he said. "One, you can run. Or two, I can come get you and we'll talk about all of this."

I knew what he meant by *talk*. He would talk to me while I sat, handcuffed, in the back seat of his brown police issue vehicle.

"What's there to talk about? You obviously know what I've been doing." I was trying to figure out my options. Did he have police units surrounding the building? Did he know where I was, or did he just stumble upon the room and flip on the monitors?

"I know a little, but we have a lot to discuss. First, the two on the table. Who are they, and are they still alive?"

"You don't recognize the man you've been trying to catch?" I asked.

The camera moved and turned toward the table. "Duncan Sims! How the hell did you find him?"

"He found me. Actually, his daughter did. They tried to kill me and were planning on killing Lesley, too. And you already know about Dave."

"As bad as I wanted the guy stopped, I didn't want it done this way. I wish I could say I was proud, but... Tryke." He sighed. "You can't go around and kill like a damn vigilante. It doesn't matter if they're bad guys or not. We have laws, son."

With all due respect, how many more died while y'all were playing by the rules and trying to figure things out? That's what I wanted to say, but I also didn't want to anger him. I still wasn't sure where all of this was heading.

"What do you want me to tell you?" I asked "That I'm sorry for killing them before they killed me?"

"I want you to tell me you're going to turn yourself in to me. We'll talk first, just you and me, I promise. And then we'll take it one step at a time down at the police station. You're my nephew, and they'll treat you decent. I'll make sure of it."

"You know I can't do that," I said. "Bars and tight spaces aren't really my thing."

"Look, I know I've failed, too. I'm your only family left and I should've been around more. I would have seen the changes in you, the same ones your dad had that I missed." I wanted to tell him that his brother wasn't the one who was sick, but he would find out soon enough. "I'll testify on your behalf," he said, "and we'll get you off on an insanity plea. Tryke, what other options do you have?"

Dr. Randal's roommate? No thanks. I could picture him trying to recruit me during group sessions, attempting to persuade me to take over where my mom left off. I would eventually end him and avenge my mom's memory. But to do that, I had to survive the situation I was currently in. I thought about asking my uncle to simply walk away and pretend none of this ever happened. But I knew better than to even suggest such a thing to a man who called his police issue vehicle his "horse" and had pictures of famous lawmen from history plastered on the walls of his garage.

"Thanks for the gesture," I said, "but I don't think so. I don't belong there either."

"Tryke, I'm pleading with you. I can't hold off the hounds for very long. They'll hunt you down and kill you. Tell me where you are and let's end this peacefully."

He didn't recognize the space. He hadn't spent near the amount of time that I did in my dad's office growing up. I began planning my escape route. I remembered Sims's computer and the list of hotels on the screen. New Orleans didn't sound like a bad idea. The crowds on Bourbon Street would hide me for a few weeks. But what about Lesley? I didn't know. I would have to figure it out on the way.

I looked up at the camera and said, "Take care of Earl for me, will you?"

"Tryke, don't do this. I'm begging you."

I hung up the phone and yanked down the wires from the cameras perched in the corners, and then the cameras themselves. I smashed all of them and placed them into a bag. He tried calling back several times, but I didn't answer. He left a voicemail after each call, likely pleading with me to turn myself in. I didn't have time to check them.

While gathering the items I was planning to take with me, I heard a sound coming from outside. A car door. No damn way he got over here that quick. Did he call it in? I peered through the small hole in the blacked-out glass, searching the empty space below, sweeping from one end to the other and looking for men in black wielding flashlights and assault rifles. I had already destroyed the power to the cameras, which included the one I had placed on the back of the building. The feed to my phone wouldn't show anything but a black screen.

I sat against the door and waited, anxiously tapping my boot on the floor. I wasn't sure what was coming next, but I wasn't going peacefully. They would have to kill me.

The next few minutes seemed like hours. After the sound of a car door shutting, I hadn't heard anything else. I imagined them all lined up outside, surrounding the building in full tactical gear, waiting for my uncle to arrive so he could attempt to talk me into surrendering peacefully. I would be deemed a threat to society, and treated like an ordinary thug. And why? Because people weren't ready to accept the truth about the world. They would rather rehabilitate the child molesters, the rapists, the murderers of the innocent, just so they could lie down at night with a clear conscience. I knew the truth, that these dirty souls could never and would never change. They had to be released from this place. I had waited long enough. It was time to either face my end or run. I opened the door and started down the stairwell to see which way fate would take me. Two steps down, I heard the door creak open from the bottom of the stairwell. I leaned against the wall in the dark, hiding in the shadows. It was too late to slip back into the room.

A few seconds later, I heard someone yell up the stairwell. I had been expecting a harsh voice saying something like, "You're surrounded. Come out with your hands up." But this voice was soft and familiar, and was riddled with uncertainty and fright.

Chapter 31

"Tryke… are you up there?"

It couldn't be happening. Though my adrenaline was nearly drained after dealing with the last few events, I still had enough residual to cause another near attack. This was it. This was the moment I had been dreading. Forget jail, forget the electric chair, and forget a loose serial killer with my address. This was much worse.

Lesley.

How did she find me? There was no avoiding this now. I could hear her shallow steps treading cautiously up the stairs.

"Tryke, it's Lesley. I saw your truck parked outside."

The door shut behind her, bringing full darkness back to the stairwell. My options were limited at that point. Now that it was pitch black, I could sneak back into my lab and bolt the door shut and wait until she left. Just because my truck was outside didn't necessarily mean I was there. I could have parked it and then left with someone else. From the uncertainty in her voice, she wasn't completely convinced she'd found me.

My eyes were adjusting to the dark. I could see the faint outline of her body. She was past the halfway point and almost to the top. I shoved opened the door, acting as though I had no idea she was there. She screamed, and I heard the jingle of her rings as she fumbled to find the railing with her hands.

"Tryke! Is that you? Please tell me it's you." She was slowly backing down the stairs, waiting for me to answer.

"Lesley?" I said.

She took a deep breath and let out an exasperated sigh. "Yeah, it's me. I can't see you. Is there a light in here somewhere?"

"One second," I said. I pulled out a small flashlight from my pocket and aimed it at the wall. She looked me up and down, studying my navy-colored overalls. "How did you find me here?"

"I was worried when you left the hospital so angry. I had this weird feeling that you were going to do something stupid. So I followed you and saw you turn onto Dr. Kimberly's street. Yes, I did a little investigating of my own and found her address. Anyway, I waited at the end of the street until you left and that's when I followed you here. I've been parked in the front of the building, too afraid to confront you. I've been going over and over in my head what to say."

"I don't know what to say, either." I was stalling as much as I could, not knowing how to proceed. She was thinking that I brought Dr. Kimberly there, for what? Some sort of secret meeting place?

"As mad as I was at Thanksgiving, I didn't want to believe it. I left hoping you would call me and tell me… I don't know… something other than that I just misunderstood. I wanted you to chase me, tell me you loved me. Fight for me, dammit! Is that so much to ask for?"

"No," I said. And it wasn't too much to ask. In fact,

going after her had been my first instinct when she left that day, but the circumstances didn't allow for it.

"That's all you have to say? No? Tryke, I need you to talk to me. What is going on with you and her?" She lowered her head in frustration. "And what the hell are you doing in this abandoned building? Wait, don't tell me. This is your lair, where y'all play out fantasy roles." I couldn't tell if she was joking or if it was rhetorical.

When I didn't say anything in response she took it as a yes. "You can't be serious. Really? She's in there, isn't she? Just be honest with me. I can handle honesty better than a dragged out lie. If you tell me you love her, I'll turn around and leave."

She was giving me a way out. Was it really going to be that easy? If I said yes, then I'd lose the only woman I had ever truly loved. I hadn't even had the chance to tell her I loved her. Not once had she heard me utter the words. But if I told her the truth about everything, it could have been worse than simply losing her. She might despise me, unable or unwilling to understand my reasons. I didn't think I could handle her hatred. Her unknown reaction or interpretation of my actions was what scared me the most.

Though only my dying flashlight illuminated the stairwell, I could still see how beautiful she was. I know I'm biased, but I have always thought she was the most gorgeous woman I would ever meet. Even there in the poor lighting, a dank cold setting, she made the area glow with warmth. I wanted to reach out and touch her straight black hair where it rested along the contours of her delicate face. I wanted to wipe the tears sliding out from her captivating blue eyes and down her perfectly sculpted cheekbones. I wanted to hold her small soft hand.

I decided, in that instant, what I was going to do.

"Lesley, before I let you into the room, there are some things I need to explain. I'm not exactly who you think I am."

• • •

She glared at me and crossed her arms. Her shadow even appeared furious. She was waiting for me to tell her that Dr. Kimberly was behind the door and had been listening the entire time, and that this was our hideout of love. Part of me wished that were true. It would have been easier to explain.

"First, you need to know who Dr. Kimberly is," I said, "and the infamous person she is related to."

As I relayed the story about Sims and Dr. Kimberly and their streak of terror on the elderly, Lesley's defensive pose switched to that of shock and disbelief. And when I told her how Sims poisoned Dave, the anger rose back inside of her. Though I had her riled up and ready to release Dr. Kimberly and Sims herself, I still didn't think she was ready to see what was behind the door.

"Before I let you in, just know that whatever you decide or however you feel, I will accept it. If you decide it's too much —"

"Tryke, open the door already. I'll be fine."

I pushed the door open and moved to the side, letting her slide by me. I stood against the wall and waited anxiously for her response. I found myself picking at my nails while I waited, something I hardly ever did. She quietly walked around the room, examining the equipment, seemingly avoiding the two empty suits on the table. She wasn't one to be disgusted by, or fearful of, the dead. In fact, she had told me that she was quite comfortable around death. She raved about her gross anatomy class, infatuated with the complexity of the human body and its inner workings. Being comfortable around the dead was imperative to her career goal, not just as a physician, but a medical examiner. But this was different. How different, well, that was for her to decide.

After a few minutes she finally spoke, standing against the wall across from me. "So, this is how you've been spending your time while I've been away at school?"

I nodded, "Some of it, yes." I placed my hands in my pockets to stop myself from picking at my nails.

"How many have seen this room?"

"You're the first."

"No, how many of them?" she said, pointing to the tables.

"I'm not sure. I'll have to check my journals."

"You keep track of them, and write about them?" She closed her eyes. "Please don't tell me that it's some sort of souvenir book."

"The short answer, no. My journals have evolved over time and now serve as a reminder. What I do, I do it for a reason, not as a hobby. Lesley, everyone who's been in here has deserved it, I promise you. These dirty souls torment the innocent and prey on the weak: children, elderly, the disabled. They seek out and kill them for pleasure. They're the ones looking for prizes. I couldn't sit by and watch the stuff happen. I've made too many calls and had to watch the pieces of shit smirk at me while I carried their victims away in the rig. I'm playing the game and doing everything I know to keep the scales from tipping over in their favor."

"I'm not going to argue that bad people don't deserve what's coming to them, but Tryke, you have to know this isn't the way. There is justice in this life, if not here on earth, then whatever is next. I know you believe that. You convinced me. Remember all of our long philosophical talks —"

"Of course I remember," I said. "I still believe in that justice, but I also believe we each have a purpose. And this is mine." I removed my hands from my pockets and walked over to her. I noticed her stiffness as I approached, so I stopped a few feet away. The short conversation had already taken its toll on the makeup around her eyes. "Do you remember when we agreed that if one of us ever discovered the existence of the human soul, we would share that knowledge with the other?"

"Yes…" she said, shifting uncomfortably in place.

"I've seen it a few times, even felt its presence. In this very room. Don't you know what that means?"

"It means we have souls, but… Tryke, I thought deep down inside, we both knew we possessed souls. We talked about some goofy things while we were drinking, but we never discussed anything like… This is going too far."

"It wasn't as if I planned this back then," I said. "It just sort of happened."

"This doesn't just sort of happen. I don't know what you expect me to do. I mean, you've put me in a tough position here."

I was expecting more shock, more tears and pushing me away. Maybe even a few punches to my chest, and threats. She was calm, coherent, keeping a cool head and asking me legitimate questions.

"I didn't plan that far ahead. To be honest I wasn't expecting you to sneak in here and catch me. I thought about telling you many times, of course, but I couldn't plan out your reaction and my response."

"Well, I wasn't expecting this either. I was expecting a girlfriend conflict. I had the entire argument rehearsed in my car. I was going to tell you both off and go back to school and be miserable for a semester. I'd get over it, in time, but this… this changes things. I'm lost entirely." She walked past me and stood next to the door. Was she about to run? I wouldn't have stopped her. In fact, part of me wished she would just leave and forget that she ever knew me. She'd be better off. Her survival rate would dramatically increase.

"Not that it would make a difference or make it easier for you to accept," I said, "but I *would* like to tell you everything from the beginning one day. If I'm still alive."

"You're not getting out of this that easy. I want to know what your plans were. I mean, were you really ever going to tell me? Where did I fit into your future? Or did I at all?"

"Of course you did. But after the incident at Thanksgiving, I didn't know if you even wanted to be with me anymore. I've always wanted to tell you, but I never knew how." I looked down and noticed the bag of smashed camera parts next to my boot and remembered that my uncle was in the process of hunting me. I glanced at my watch. "I'm sort of in a hurry, so let me tell you something I've been holding in for a while. I don't expect anything from you after I tell you this. If you want to run away and never see me again, I'll understand. All I ask of you is to let me get a head start before you call the police."

"Tryke, I'm not —"

"Here goes. I have never met anyone in my life who makes me feel right, calm, and good about myself on a constant basis. I'm near you and I immediately feel better. You are the most beautiful woman I have ever seen. Flawlessly gorgeous, and I mean it. You make me smile, you make me no longer yearn for rain. What I'm trying to say is that you're the first woman I have ever thought about loving. I think… I know, I love you." There, I had finally said it. I didn't know which was harder to tell her, that I released souls or that I loved her.

She was trembling. I wasn't sure if it was residual fear, or delight. She flung her hair out from in front of her face, revealing a brief half-smile. She said, "I have loved you for a long time, Tryke Harper."

"So, we're okay? I mean, I know we're not good, but you'll at least give me a head start before calling the police, right?"

"I'm not calling the police."

"You're not?"

"No, how could I? How could I turn in someone I care about? Someone I love?"

"Thank you," I said, stunned by her loyalty. "I'm sorry to tell you that I love you right before I have to leave, but…

I really have to go. I'm sort of being chased at the moment."

She stiffened. "By who?!"

"You remember my Uncle Frank? The homicide detective?"

"Yeah."

"Well, he knows about me, too. He found my room and... you know what, it doesn't matter. The point is, he knows. The good news is, he doesn't know where this place is yet. But he's probably closing in, so you need to go. I don't want you to be caught up in this."

"Where will you go?" she asked. "Are you planning to run forever?"

"What choice do I have?"

She stood in front of me, staring into my eyes, blocking my path to the stairs. I don't know exactly how long we stood there, but it felt like minutes instead of seconds. Lesley appeared to be contemplating something. A goodbye speech, perhaps, but I didn't have time to listen. I planned to call her from the road. Just as I was about to break the silence, she spoke.

"They'll be looking for your truck. We can take my car."

"We? You're not going with me. I can't be responsible for —" Her resolve was palpable, stopping my words. Her mind was made up.

"You just told me that you loved me. Now you're going to walk out and leave?"

I wanted her safe, and there was no way that was happening while she was by my side. I wanted to put an end to this madness and demand she get away while she could. I wanted to shun her, lie to her and tell her how miserable she made me. How when I told her I loved her, it was out of desperation, so she wouldn't turn me in. I would see her cry and then I would walk away coldly, as if her tears didn't faze me, as if they didn't sear my heart. But I couldn't. I felt ashamed, but a good shame. For the first time in my life, I believed in the elusive, fantasized feeling of romantic *love*.

Chapter 32

I told Lesley to go ahead of me and fill her tank up with gas. While dropping off the empty suits back at Dr. Kimberly's house, I thought about Dave. I didn't want to leave him behind, alone, but I didn't have a choice.

I met up with Lesley at the airport and parked my truck in the long-term lot. I was still a bit surprised when I saw her there waiting for me, bravely leaning against her car, as if no one could touch us. A part of me wished she had come to her senses, and had raced back to school to get away from this insanity. But there she was.

We stopped at the bank and withdrew all of the money we had, then headed east on I-20.

"How far is New Orleans from here?" Lesley asked from the passenger seat. She was calm and appeared content, despite our predicament.

"Depending on traffic, between eight and nine hours." Plenty of time to reconsider her choice. I wanted to reassure her that she could change her mind, and that I would be okay. But I thought it would upset her. She would think I didn't want her there.

"Just in time for breakfast," she said. "I can almost taste the beignets."

"When have you had a beignet?"

"I haven't, but come on, who doesn't love fried dough and powdered sugar?"

"Good point. What's the name of that famous cafe…?"

"Cafe du Monde," she said, attempting to simulate a French accent.

"That sounded more like an Australian accent," I said, stifling a laugh.

"Whatever." She nudged my shoulder and smirked.

"Mardi Gras is in a couple of weeks. It'll be a good cover. We can get lost in the crowds until we make our plans." When she didn't respond, I looked over at her. She was facing her window, staring out into the night.

"Hey," I said softly, "are you okay?"

She pulled her hair up and turned toward me with a smile. "I'm glad I came with you," she said, sliding her fingers through my hair. "I love you."

"I love you, too." I didn't hesitate. I just blurted the words out. It still didn't feel completely natural, but it felt good to say it without reluctance.

I was elated that she was beside me. Still, there was some degree of unease. I was now responsible for involving her in this mess. We were both fugitives. She would be hunted the same as me, and they would put her away just as fast. No mercy for the girlfriend sidekick. I pictured her romanticizing the entire endeavor, filling her head with long walks along the river and smooth jazz music, morning beignets and after-breakfast French Quarter tours. But how long would the outlaw romance last?

She leaned her seat back and lay on her side facing me, her left hand curled under her head like a make-shift pillow. She grabbed my hand as it rested on the gear shift, intertwining her fingers with mine. "Did you really see it?"

she asked. "The soul?"

I grinned and looked over at her, lowering the brim of my hat.

"What do you think?"

A note from C.S. McMillian

Thank you for reading Grey Matter. I am currently in the process of writing the third book in the Dark of the Mind trilogy. Please, don't hesitate to connect with me on Facebook: www.facebook.com/darkofthemind

www.ingramcontent.com/pod-product-compliance
Lightning Source LLC
Chambersburg PA
CBHW031702170626
46808CB00005B/1566

* 9 7 8 0 9 9 1 2 9 8 9 3 8 *